ATTACK OF THE STAR DEMONS

J'erik dared to look up when they crossed the side of the ridge. Their speed was so great that the noise had to run to catch it. Never did he dream of anything so magnificent. The cacaphony racing after the Demons shook the ground and rattled the iron tree. Amilglibs rained from the branches.

Wave after wave of noise, each more formidable than the previous, deluged the land of Cassilee. J'erik clapped his hands over his ears and held them with his knees. He felt the land tremble. It was a frightful sensation. J'erik wondered if the ground would open up and swallow him.

Other Avon books by
Susan Coon

RAHNE   75044 $1.95

CASSILEE

SUSAN COON

◢ **AVON**
PUBLISHERS OF BARD, CAMELOT AND DISCUS BOOKS

CASSILEE is an original publication of Avon Books. This work has never before appeared in book form.

AVON BOOKS
A division of
The Hearst Corporation
959 Eighth Avenue
New York, New York 10019

First Avon Printing, August, 1980

AVON TRADEMARK REG. U.S. PAT. OFF. AND IN
OTHER COUNTRIES, MARCA REGISTRADA, HECHO EN
U.S.A.

Printed in the U.S.A.

For my sons, J. Michael and Steven Jeffry.
Glad you're not twins.

Abandoned by the intelligent races she had nurtured out of the primordial slime, Cassilee endured the ravages of their wars. She preserved what remained and stored it for a time when the scattered remnants would mend their differences. Through the bleak and countless millennia, the differences became vaster and the land harsher. The descendants of her children who had fled to the stars in the face of her doom returned, only to assault her again.

Chapter 1

J'ERIK WATCHED THE HORIZON. EVERY NERVE in his body quivered with anxiety. Uli, the flaming sun overhead, parched the land. The fear which confined others to the Stronghold during Uli's time in the sky had never touched him upon the surface. Watching, he wondered if their fears should have been shared.

Stars twinkled over the horizon. The growing intensity of one made it a miniature sun.

"Star Demons," he whispered, looking desperately across the expanse to the caves two kilometers west.

Twice in recent history they had unleashed a fury upon Cassilee unrivaled by temperamental Uli. Star Demons did not dance at night. No dark-red skies heralded their arrival. Fiery orbs which gouged craters on the land neither preceded nor followed the Demons.

In ancient times, Star Demons came and fought. When they departed, cooled lava and shiny fragments inundated the surface. Their offerings to the calantani had been great. Legend said the beasts fed for weeks upon the carnage. The Demons were enormous and held together by bones no larger than those of a man. But so many had been needed under the metal skin decaying on the far side of the valley.

J'erik crawled around the massive gray trunk of an iron tree shading him with thick, rubbery-textured round leaves which were larger than the spread of both of his

1

hands. A hollow, used as shelter many times, received his body. Wide-eyed from the terror seeded in the legends, he continued to watch. The compulsion to witness what no other in the Ah-te Stronghold had seen tempered his fear.

More stars that were not stars brightened over the tan-colored ridges, which once were mountains high enough to snag the clouds and coax a blanket of white powdered water upon themselves. The closer the Demons came, the farther his head retreated into the hollow.

He dared to look up when they crossed his side of the ridge. Their speed was so great that the noise had to run to catch it. Never had he dreamed of anything so magnificent. The cacophony racing after the Demons shook the ground and rattled the iron tree. Amilglibs rained from the branches. J'erik pulled his feet closer and pointed his toes at each other. The fruit struck his feet and shins. The needles protruding from thick oval husks punctured his skin. Drops of blood collected between his toes. Numbness set in below both knees. Uli would journey one sixth of the sky before the anesthetic would wear off enough for him to walk.

Wave after wave of noise, each more formidable than the previous, deluged the land of Cassilee. J'erik clapped his hands over his ears and held them with his knees. Beyond the hollow, amilglibs ceased to fall. Still, they rolled and skittered along the ground as though alive. The small daggers impaled leaves. The added weight failed to hinder their motion.

J'erik too felt the land tremble. It was a frightful sensation. He worried that the ground might open up and swallow him where no caverns existed.

The tremble gradually lost its force and dissipated completely. The roar lingered in J'erik's ears and made him reluctant to move his hands more than a few centimeters. He was afraid the Demons would scream again.

He straightened, wondering if the pain above the curve in his jaw would bring deafness as a reward for the jaunt which brought him onto the surface. He clapped his hands. The sound was that of one far away whose echo managed to tweak his attention before it died. But the silence manufactured a ringing similar to the one experienced during adolescence when he fought for his sister's right not to Choose T'lar. The very thought of the man was distasteful. Though T'lar had lost, he exacted a price and never forgot who bested him in the Square. T'lar's hands had slammed full force over J'erik's ears and left him hard of hearing and in a groggy state for several days after the battle.

"Listen with your mind," Fir'ah had said to him at the time. Now, he tried to do just that, though he was unsure what he should be listening to.

What he was sure of was that he was alone on the surface. Who else but a Betweener dared upon Cassilee in the light of Uli when it was not an absolute necessity? Small wonder. The Great Catastrophe (last time the Demons swarmed) had opened volcanoes in the middle of ancient Holds. The Ah-te shook for days. When the Leaders returned from a Meet a hundred revolutions later, they had related the Demons' extermination of over half the known Holds.

He checked the sky. It seemed Uli dawdled when he waited, but raced to the stars when he explored the wonders of Cassilee. Feeling returned to his calves and feet slowly. The tiny holes were scabbed over. Blood was caked on his sandals and the soles of his feet.

Carefully, he reached for an amilglib and savored the ripeness when the needles fell off. After locating the place where the stem once held it to a branch, J'erik slipped the tip of his knife in and turned. The husk split in half. Juice spilled across his knees and down his legs. He hurried to drink what remained in the center of the semi-hollow fruit.

Uli felt hotter as the day wore on, hotter than usual. Perspiration rolled down his ribs. He cracked more amilglibs for the liquid.

When the anesthetic wore off, he used a sandal to move the spiny fruits out of the way, crept out and stood.

It felt good to stretch. His arms were still in the air when he spied the Star Demons making a return. He checked the opposite horizon.

More Demons, these closer than the first, rushed to meet them head on. Awe gave way to panic. J'erik ran for the caves. If the Demons wanted to eat him, they would have to catch him in the old river gully first. Perhaps they would not bother with one so insignificant. The legends were not specific on whether they ate people. They did detail the fact that they killed, sometimes without a mark.

His lungs filled and emptied with the rhythm of a distance runner. The pack on his back flopped in set bounces. Puffs of dust, hills pulverized into nothingness by the severe mood changes of Cassilee and Uli, formed instant clouds under his feet as the long strides took him closer to the caves. He stayed in the bed where once he had seen a trickle of water and thought it strange he should remember it now.

He covered half the distance and was beyond the protection of the iron trees when Cassilee erupted into a ball of fire that matched Uli.

The light grew brighter and brighter, bleaching the tan-colored land white. The brilliance hurt his eyes deep inside of his head. He closed them and kept running, relying upon memory. Even through his lids, the world was white.

Noise knocked him off his feet. For a moment, he could not determine which was left or right and thought he was walking on the sky. The caves changed shape. He closed his eyes again. The vertigo worsened. He compromised and peered through slits while the white light faded. Acrid dust filled his nostrils and set him coughing.

Finally, the land sloped up. Stumbling, groping for reliable holds, J'erik clambered up the talus. He found his rope and hauled himself up, hand over hand. He pushed wildly against loose rocks and solid boulders. Over and over he reiterated the ascent as a vertical direction. The light and noise made it seem anything but straight up once beyond the slope. Knots in the rope kept him from slipping when he faltered.

At the top, he dragged himself over the smooth lip and craved for the black silence of the inner chamber hidden by a dozen turns and channels. He did not run for it; instead, he pulled up the rope. Later it would be coiled. Later, he mused.

Coolness whispered through the passages. It promised to ease his burning skin and rest his eyes. The noise diminished. Still, the echo lived in his head, and the clumsy sounds of his sandals grating small rocks were inaudible.

Inside the chamber a single calidrium burned a low flame. The meager light sufficed. He dropped his pack and grabbed a bowl. Water dripped from between two rocks and into a drum, which brimmed with the precious liquid. J'erik shook, restrained to take sips and not gulp the entire bowl. The cold water sent a shiver through him from the inside out.

Gingerly, he removed his clothes and stood near the calidrium. Tiny blisters, red and growing, covered the skin exposed to the light and noise of the Star Demons. The nausea climbing his esophagus was induced by fear and illness. He thought himself immune to the surface light, and he had been, until now.

A childhood memory of an elder caught in the morning light popped into his mind. A few minutes' exposure and the white skin began to redden with blisters. They spawned more blisters, until the man was a swollen mass of puffy skin. Purulent drainage oozed within a quarter day. After half a revolution, the man was unburdened of his agonies and his life.

J'erik cringed.

No. Not Uli. Star Demons. That's what the man had screamed over and over in delirium of pain. Star Demons. The words rolled over his mind.

He moved the band on the calidrium to brighten it. The pain behind his eyes intensified. He examined his skin. "No, it is not the same," he said, reassuring himself. "The growths are small and only where my clothing does not cover." An angry pride changed the tone. "I am a Betweener! I am strong! The weak skin of the Dwellers is not my weakness. This must be something else. It must be . . ." His voice faded in uncertainty, then boomed again.

"I am not blinded by the whims of Uli, nor the Demons spitting light, as my father's people are. I am strong! I will conquer this land and dwell upon her surface."

The words fortified him. The voice tremor could not be distinguished from the thunder captured in his brain.

Using a bowl and his shirt, he bathed the blisters and tried to recall what herbs and leaves the delicate-skinned

5

people of the Ah-te used to alleviate their ailments. For a moment, he wished for Fir'ah, his twin, knowing she would take care of him and ease him through death's door if the time was at hand.

Thoughts of her bolstered his determination. If he appeared at the Ah-te in this condition they would both be cast out, most likely at night, during the time of the calantani. The beasts were not finicky when it came to an easy meal, and the consciences of the leaders would be cleared by a mass rationalization.

No. Better to remain in the cave and face the uncertainty alone, he decided. Going back would give Ulni-da enough leverage to banish Fir'ah or force her to Choose T'lar.

He ground up the leaves, herbs and tubers he remembered as part of a healing salve. It took as much effort as an all-day climb. He wiped the perspiration from his body and spread the concoction over the blisters. Exhausted, he lay upon scattered bedding set in the midst of the treasures collected from the surface during his explorations.

Staring at the ceiling, "Oh, Fir'ah, it is so difficult for me to be of both worlds. We can go anywhere, yet we belong nowhere. I cannot understand it. We are not wanted, and we aren't cast out without reason. But we are outcasts in our own home.

"Cassilee? Is there not one fertile valley on your surface where there is room and peace for Betweeners? Where we will belong and be welcomed?"

A fitful sleep claimed him with dreams of a place to stand tall upon Cassilee's skin, where the stars looked back at him without the horrible night creatures, and no metallic death sparkled over the horizon.

He woke, startled by visions of gray calantani ready to gobble him and Fir'ah.

The calidrium's dim light promised safety. The cool walls chilled his soaked body. He shook his head, flinging moisture in all directions. The ringing in his ears was out of beat with the throb behind his eyes. The blisters grew, forming a solid layer. An incredible thirst thickened his tongue and flayed his throat. The pain never lessened, only increased.

6

Again, after a long sipping process that did little to quench the thirst, he bathed his fiery skin. Each part he touched felt as though it had been thrust into the smelter at the Ah-te. Too agonized to sleep, afraid he would not wake up, he wandered through the passages out to the mouth of the cave overlooking the valley. It was a much longer walk than he remembered.

Night had settled, but the gray calantani were not out. Was this the same night, or a different night? The land had changed.

The gully he had run through no longer existed. Instead, the area melted into a oneness with the rest of the plateaus and stretched for kilometers, eating the places where rounded hills and dust-laden valleys once lent a difference to the land.

He held the rope and leaned out.

His high plateau face continued to stand, winding against the stars and the black sky. Whatever changed the land below had shied away from the massive chain of cliffs where his sanctuary hid. He wondered if the monsters from the stars would return to dine upon his mountain.

Vertigo made the earth begin to spin. Groping, clutching the rope, he slumped down to the solid floor and crawled away from the edge. He lay there half the night, then made a mark on the wall to indicate the passing of a day.

As long as he could drag himself through the passage, he would check the lowlands and look for calantani. When the beasts flew at night, the Demons would be gone. And for each mark at the mouth, a corresponding one would be made over his sleeping area. It would give a purpose to wakefulness. Should he return to the Ah-te and Fir'ah, he would need to account for the lost days. Only death could prevent that return.

He began to crawl away from the mouth. Bright stars appeared over the land. Below them, Cassilee glowed. Moving stars popped up all around the opposite mountain recently chopped off at the top.

He was unsure if they were moving slower than during the day or if his bounding heart made the time pass at a different rate. J'erik watched over his shoulder until the light became too bright and the noise caught up to the Demons and ran ahead to taunt him.

A rough wall helped him stand and supported him back to the chamber. The heat of his body formed a dripping river which left footprints wherever he walked. Another drink, and he collapsed onto the stone at the base of the water barrel.

Chapter 2

SEVENTEEN MARKS LINED UP BESIDE J'ERIK'S bed, five more than at the cave mouth. The calantani took possession of the night some time ago; when, he could not remember. The Demons were gone, but they would return. It bothered him that he knew they would, without knowing how he was so certain. It seemed that the time of isolation, coupled with the worry of being eaten alive, mountain and all, by the metal Demons, sparked an awareness.

Fir'ah spoke of strange abilities and knowledge, but she did not know how to make it work for her. J'erik began to understand what she meant. Listening and seeking with his mind, he experienced many strange things, not all of which could be attributed to the illness.

New skin grew where the blisters peeled away in sheets two layers thick. The fever had drained both his body and the water supply dangerously low. Time would restore the water. Effort was his only means of replenishing the dried-out food supply.

He fastened the rope to a narrow jut beside a ledge leading to the upper plateau. Caution marked his progress. A sharp awareness of the distance to the scree below steadied his weakened legs. The dawn's coolness lent a spiritual vigor to the journey. Climbing was one of his joys, excelled only by the thrill of adventure and the exploration of places no other dared to see.

More than the land had changed during his confinement. A thin mist clung to shadow-laden crevices and turned the rock dark. Its presence contradicted Cassilee's seasons, though it was rare even during the cooler periods.

At the top, he moved onto the flatland and looked up at the blue-black sky, where the last stars looked back. Gaping, he slumped to the ground, staring, forgetting to breath.

Things floated in the air. Uli reflected vibrant colors against them.

Nothing held them up.

They moved, changing color and shape.

They looked soft, but when they fell, perhaps they would smother him.

There were so many, stretched across the sky like a thong, disappearing into forever. And like a thong, they were narrow. He could see the beginning and end of the width.

Slowly, shock yielded to amazement.

These had to be what the ancient tales referred to as clouds. Since the time of the Strongholds began, no one had seen a cloud in the sky. They were truly a splendid wonder to behold.

The old books decreed that the return of the clouds led to the eventual habitability of the surface. Suddenly, the notion of living on the land was an ambiguous one, considering the calantani threat at night.

But, this day, it was a beautiful thing to be out in the open air. The top of his flat mountain faded into an irregular line dotted by vegetation. J'erik set a brisk pace toward the nearest iron tree, thinking that one day he would travel all the way across the plateau to see what was on the other side. He suspected it was similar, but that was of no consequence.

Several dozen amilglibs, the staple food when away from the Ah-te, lay scattered beneath the tree. He ate the ripest one, then used his knife to flick others into a heavy bag taken from his pack. As a precaution, he cut a few leaves from a low branch to update the medicine stock in the sanctuary.

Nearby, herbs and azaix tubers were gathered. The soil clung to the fat tubers as though reluctant to part with them.

Farther on, a tangle of gadid vines laid a carpet and

climbed a strangled iron tree. J'erik ate his fill of yellow berries and cut clusters of less-ripe ones to take back. The reddish-blue leaves veined with green hung on small twigs in groups of six. Their fragile appearance belied Cassilee's harsh days. He chose the most-veiny leaves for the collection. When the twigs were cut, their strong aroma filled the morning air. The strength of it purged his sinuses and lungs, heightening the rush of oxygen conversion and making him light-headed.

As he collected the yellow sponge leaves of the olca plant, a shadow walked the land. Quickly, he searched the sky.

More clouds in a line moved against the rich blue, white and fleecy. He wondered if these were the same ones, before deciding that they could not run around Cassilee that fast.

His packs were near full. The kaloer bush he sought for leaves and bark which could be pounded into cloth and paper was deep in the growth patch.

A low moan rifled the natural silence.

J'erik froze in midstride.

An agonized whine followed.

He glanced around at the red-blue walls trying to climb up to Uli. Suddenly they seemed very high. He could not look over them or see through them. Without moving his feet, he checked behind him for the most expedient path of retreat.

A deep groan came from all directions. There was a finality in it which sent a tingling up J'erik's backbone and raised the hair on his neck.

Cautiously, he moved toward the closest iron tree, holding tendrils of gadid silent and stepping lightly.

He slipped out of his pack and set it on the amilglib bag, jumped and grabbed a low branch close to the trunk, hands on opposite sides. The slippery width was difficult to hold. His body swung as his hands worked to meet over the branch. He hooked his right foot into the crook where the branch met the tree and labored until he was seated upright.

There was nothing to be seen but the iron tree, gadid and the desolation of the valley in the eastern distance. The ravaged expanse between the vegetation and the end of the plateau had not seemed as large as it was during

11

his crossing. He glanced at Uli, surprised by how long he had been out.

On his belly, he moved along the branch, bending it with his weight, venturing out as far as he dared.

Deep, labored breathing rattled the wall twining below his perch.

J'erik scooted out another meter and parted the leaves.

In a bed of old gadid a female calantani stood guard over her mate. The male was prone. His enormous bulk hardly moved with his raspy breathing. Both sets of wings were folded around the male, the strange pink color of his back turned bright red under the scales as they patterned toward his front. Webbed, three-toed feet showed his talons rigid, while his mate's were retracted. His slender neck bent, angling his hairy round head toward his chest. A thick whitish tongue drooped from between sharp pointed teeth. J'erik knew the tongue should be pink and slender and wished that he could see more of the beast's face. Calantani like these had never visited this part of Cassilee. The colors of this new breed fascinated the adventurer in him.

The forelimbs were tucked under his wings, as though he used the wings to conceal as much as possible. Even his coiled lengthy tail tried to hide under the tip of his lower great wing.

Betweener? Will you understand me?

J'erik glanced around frantically. The words he heard were not with his ears, but inside his ears, inside his head. He thought he had been on the surface too long and Uli was playing games with him. Cruel games. He began a retreat. Better to take his chances running across the desolated strip and try for the sanctuary than to suffer delusions on the surface.

Betweener, I know you understand. Please. You will help if it is in your power to do so?

Repetitive swallowing did not clear the lump in his throat. He held the branch tighter, thinking his heartbeat was making it pulsate and it would attract the calantani female if he blinked. She was so large! And the male was even bigger.

There is nothing to fear. You are among friends if you will choose to be.

12

He put his head down and tried to speak to the delusion in his mind.

What do you want? Who calls me? he thought, bringing down the barriers he used in the presence of Ulni-da, the Seeress at the Ah-te.

I call you. I am Ladida, Mate of Chamblis, who is Great Lord of the Northernmost Plateau. I wish you no harm, Betweener. I desire your help, if you can give it. See into my soul and know I impart what is there.

A stab of realization paralyzed him. The calantani female was Ladida! How could this be? Why did she not attack and eat him if she knew where he was? And a soul? Which revealed the truth?

Soul?

Unseeing eyes stared at the branch while a war raged in his head. The years of Stronghold training beseeched him to flee. Yet, the spirit which made him proud to be a Betweener demeaned the fear with the promise of an adventure never before dreamed of or considered. She can smell me, he thought. If she is not sincere, why doesn't she attack? Why does she play with me like this? No. This is a delusion of the fever. But there is no fever now. If I leave, I will never know if it is real or an illusion.

He lifted his head. *I do not know how to soul-see, nor do I know what soul is.* Looking up into green eyes the size of his fists and veiled by the elastic iron leaves, *Tell me what it is.*

Ladida's head bowed to Chamblis as though she felt his life depended upon her answer. The white ringlets of hair flowing from her head and down her back jiggled in waves. Her forelimbs came together; the three long fingerlike protuberances flashed claws, then folded. *It is the heart, Betweener, the essence of what a being is inside his facades. It is what makes an individual like no other, whether Calantani, Betweener, Dweller or Techi.*

J'erik considered her answer for a fair amount of time. Ultimately, her words made sense and quelled more of his fears.

I assure you, I mean you no harm. I ask only help if you can give it.

Surprised, J'erik regarded her sharply. Ladida knew his thoughts. Was that "soul" too?

13

"Can you understand if I speak aloud, Ladida? I, too, have been ill. It tires me to speak without words." His head throbbed as the war shifted battlegrounds to another part of his mind.

Right forelimb raised, she nodded.

"It is unlikely that I could help you. I know nothing about calantani, except . . . " He cleared his throat. "What has happened to your mate?"

Two turns ago, before Uli threw warnings over the eastern land, the Demons came. They lit the night brighter than Uli has lit the day for all of time. Chamblis found shelter for our group. The cave was small. The light burned.

He is Great Lord. He spread his wings across the entrance to protect us.

Soon, he sickened. We were unable to travel farther than here. The hot sleep eats his life. I do not know what to do to rid him of this plague. Uli does not take back the heat in his body.

"Where is your group? Have they deserted you?"

Never! I am the Lady of Chamblis. It is my privilege to stand guard over him while he is ill. Even if I cannot help him.

The sorrow she conveyed touched him deeply. As long as he did not view her directly, he could perceive her as another Betweener. "He must be moved. Are your numbers sufficient to do that?"

We are many, but I do not know how we could move him to shelter.

Slowly, J'erik explained his recent illness. He was dubious about the value his self-treatments would have to the Lord. Empathy for what Chamblis was experiencing made his tender skin sore. Before he realized what he was doing, he offered the front of his cave as a place to treat the monster. The faint hope of companions on the surface blossomed. Perhaps he would live on the land yet.

Ladida took three steps and extended her forelimbs to J'erik. *I will fetch my Lord's subjects while you keep watch. The kodjelu nip at his flesh if there is no guard.*

Her light-pink limbs were centimeters away, her head well above and in easy striking position. J'erik looked up, beyond the extended snout and into the languid green eyes, afraid to hope. Yellow tears formed above the lower lids and crept onto her leathery white skin. Her breath was filled with a briny odor mellowed by a strong musk scent. Her serpent tongue flicked away the tears.

The test of trust is now, he told himself. But fear, nurtured in childhood, dampened his spirit for a moment. Putting himself into the arms of a calantani had to be certain death.

I will not harm you, Betweener. This I promise. You are my friend from this day on, even if you are powerless to save my Lord Chamblis.

The nonverbal communication made it impossible to continue viewing Ladida as a man-devouring beast, though that fact tried hard to crawl out of a black pocket. Desperation he understood. And a calantani would have to be desperate to turn to a Betweener. He reached for her arms and felt the coolness of her hide against his sweaty palms. Ladida helped by holding the upper branch in her teeth.

Once on the forelimbs, the branch snapped, shuddering with freedom.

You are big for a man, Betweener. Your bones say you should be heavier. I am glad you are not. Your new skin, it is light. Will it also turn bronze?

"Kodjelu at his head!" J'erik yelled, astonished by the striking speed of the armored creatures.

Ladida's tail snapped. The end, no larger than a thin rope, coiled around the scavenger's neck. She snapped the tail a second time. The cracking of small bones against the gray overlapped shells was the end of the kodjelu's existence. Ladida tossed it high into the air and away from Chamblis. The kodjelu's comrades would make short work of his carcass. In a continuous motion she set J'erik beside Chamblis and flexed her upper wings.

J'erik drew his knife, prepared to protect himself as well as Chamblis from the undiscriminating kodjelu.

"Ladida . . . you do not have to go far, do you? Should he wake . . ."

It is not far.

Wind, generated by her great wings, almost knocked him over. She flapped hard, climbing a circle and angling west. Her labor was detectable to his inexperienced eyes.

The gadid quieted and the lingering aroma settled. For a long period, one seventh of Uli's journey, only the calantani's breathing noises against the breeze were not sounds of J'erik's making. He cut long vine streamers and laid them atop Chamblis. Stretched, he figured the Lord at an easy fifteen meters to the tail tip. He cleared a zone around the calantani, attentive to stay upwind of the pungent odor until the breeze cleansed the area.

The rasp sounded less forced once the gadid scent reached Chamblis. Noting the effect upon the beast, J'erik split leaves and placed them near the flaring nostrils.

When he had done all he could to occupy the time and make the Lord comfortable, he walked a circle guard and watched for the kodjelu.

Scrapings and clunking noises under the thick vines came from the middle distance. Squinting, he saw nothing.

The noise increased with the boldness of the creatures.

J'erik scanned the heights, no longer enthralled by the cloud ribbons.

Pointed snouts and red eyes poked from under generous leaf clusters.

It was too late to run. They would attack en masse before he surmounted the barrier.

Ladida! You must hurry! Ladida? Do you hear?

No answer filled his head.

He tried to rouse Chamblis, pushing, tugging and prying at the wings. Desperate, he sought to speak without words and found only a smooth darkness in the beast's mind beset with slow-moving images.

The first kodjelu scouts ventured out from the red shadows. They approached the hulk, skirting the guard warily.

J'erik did not register the danger. An image in the calantani's mind imprisoned his attention.

A young Betweener stared out of the memory. Tears ran down her bruised face framed by tangled sandy hair. Her eyes, aqua in color, seemed to look straight through him. Torn rags hung on her body. Gouges ran through the bruises everywhere her bronze skin was ex-

16

posed. Her back was pressed against a massive iron tree. Gnarled ridges reached out to form iron constrictions. She grew nearer and nearer as Chamblis reached for her.

J'erik wanted to warn her, to protect her from the calantani's jaws, and he wanted to know her, another Betweener upon the land.

She covered her face with dirt-blackened hands and cried, seemingly resigned to her fate.

Sickened, powerless to help, J'erik gripped his knife tighter and considered yielding the heinous monster to the kodjelu.

The small predators did not give time for a decision. They gushed from under the leaves and swarmed. High-pitched squeaks became a continuous noise, drowning out the clatter of blunt claws and the clack of armor against armor as they tried to crawl over each other.

Their numbers were too many for his knife to be effective. He sheathed it and grabbed them two at a time, slammed them together and threw them aside.

He felt the pain of sharp little teeth penetrate his legs, arms and back. Still, his only alternative was to keep moving. The vermin might triumph, he thought, climbing up Chamblis, but not too easily.

Once, he glanced up.

The sky was empty.

Explorer First Class Fancher Bann read his orders, then reread them for the ninth time. Disbelief evolved into dread. Either this was the act of a thoroughly incompetent commander (which was unlikely), or he was suspected of a wrong and this was a contrived disciplinary tactic. He thought his record was spotless. Not a single infraction of rules or regulations came to mind.

Palama, he decided. It must be. They found out. The faces of his parents, his sister, Kreista, her husband, Alva, and their brood of seven, all looked in from the clear edge of memory to see what he would do.

He snorted. Strange how the dead never age.

Appealing the wisdom of the orders would be considered insubordination. Fancher felt trapped. He sat on his bunk, propped his elbows on his knees and read the orders again.

The cabin door retracted. A wiry blond man strode

17

through. "Hey, you on a diet that excludes eating? It wasn't bad—considering. Here." The intruder extended a napkin-covered ball. "It's a real piece of cake."

Shaking his head, Fancher stood. He required only a few minutes to collect his gear. "No thanks. I'm not hungry."

Mikel leaned against the top bunk and finger-combed his beard. "What are you doing? Resigning? You picked a lousy spot. That place down there isn't fit for any kind of life—yet." His grin faded as Fancher continued to shove his things into the opened duffle.

Fancher paused long enough to toss the beige copy over his shoulder in his friend's general direction. It floated through the recycled air before it was caught near the floor. Mikel read the orders. Color drained from his features before he finished. He glanced apprehensively at Fancher, then back at the serial number on the top. Other than the fifth and last digits, his ten were identical. Mikel checked the time on his wrist, folded the orders and said, "I'll walk you down."

Fancher hit the magnetic clasp on his duffle and slung it up to his shoulder. "I'm ready." He reached for the orders.

Mikel was hesitant to return the paper, but did so. He glanced around the clean white cabin, causing Fancher to do the same. "Ten days isn't so long."

"It is when you're on a planet that has never been properly surveyed in the first place." Fancher could no longer stifle the bitterness and contempt he felt for the terraforming company of New Life Enterprises. Palama would never allow him to forget what could happen.

There was no one else he wanted to say goodbye to, other than Mikel. And, other than Mik, he did not think anyone would miss him for more than a week or two.

They left the cabin and entered the busy main concourse. Fancher looked around and slowed. Head down, "Look, Mik, there's something going on here I don't understand. Oh, it's not just sending out *one* recon sampling ship, but this whole operation. I know it hits you close to home, but there's something wrong here."

He resumed a normal stride, head still bowed to the hall monitors like a marked man subjected to open defeat. "I don't know why this is happening to me. Not the real reason. I suspect it has something to do with the inquiries I made. Maybe I got too close without knowing it.

"But I've hit somebody's nerve. When I get back . . ." His voice faded. He cleared his throat and started again. "When I get back, I'm going to try to find out a few of the whys and a who or two."

They walked in gloomy silence, turned into a side corridor and matched strides. "Mik? If I don't happen to, ah, to make rendezvous, promise me . . ." Fancher shook his head and quickened his step.

"I promise you, Fancher," Mikel said under his breath. "I promise."

Fancher handed the duffle to his friend and palmed off the orders at the same time. They made the last turn down a short hall ending at the cargo elevators.

Six hours of processing would finish once he was inside a Star III Recon Prober.

After that, Cassilee waited.

Chapter 3

J'ERIK FELT LADIDA'S RETURN BEFORE THE
sonorous tornadoes generated by the calantani's great
wings reached him. The kodjelu reluctantly fled, tram-
pling the gadid to a pulp. Fragments of the red-blue
soared into the vortices of the beasts, hiding the sky.
J'erik fell on Chamblis and clutched the front wing edge.
The surge of gadid dilated his senses, making the air he
gulped suffice for the times he could not breath the dust-
laden air slamming at him from all sides as it tried to
suck him skyward.

The calantani settled around their Lord in a respectful
quiet. J'erik attempted to relax. The effects of the fuming
drug made him woozy. Awkwardly, he struggled to get
his feet under him.

The myriad of colored beasts watching seemed like a
dream which lacked the good sense to know fear. He
saw only their massive size and the colors ranging from
the pink and white of the Lord and Lady to the blues
and browns of those guarding the perimeter. The darker
ones were slightly smaller. Hair, corresponding to the
color of hides and scales, hung in the same perfect ringlets as those of the lighter colors. A bright-orange one
behind a green female at Ladida's side appeared to be as
large as Chamblis.

I am in your service, Betweener. Tell me, how do we

move my Lord to the place where you will try to help him? Ladida bowed low.

J'erik rubbed his eyes, trying to clear his head and join the surrounding reality. The idea he had earlier disintegrated whenever he thought of Chamblis and the Betweener girl. The barriers he fortified around Ulni-da rose stalwartly to hide the thoughts from Ladida. It helped to gaze only at her and ignore the gargantuan he used as a crutch.

"The gadid vines. Use them. Work them into a net." The words came hard. He stumbled down the side of Chamblis and let go, weaving when he stood clear. "You must get me upwind. I cannot think here."

Ladida spoke to the orange one in sounds unmistakably a language, but not one remotely familiar to J'erik. The tone inflections were musical, each series like a stanza of the songs sung in the Ah-te. The orange one responded in deeper tones, slower and hinting a dirge comparable to one from the ancient times when Cassilee had flourished with life of many kinds.

When the orange one approached, J'erik backed away into a snarl of vines. Seeing only the huge calantani near, and feeling the ingrained fear explode into his brain, he struggled, tangling himself deeper into the mesh. The teeth wounds from the kodjelu seeped red onto the tight jungle.

Betweener. I have given my word that no harm will befall you. Do you not accept this? Diearka is bound to me. Do you fear harm from him?

Openmouthed, J'erik lifted his eyes to see her. The sun behind her head made the white ringlets glow in a translucent aura. Her soft presence and the influx of gadid mesmerized him into submission. He felt another body, certainly not his, lifted by the orange one. The smooth reptilian skin eased the panic accelerating his blood through open gashes. The strength in the forelimbs denied his weight. When Diearka flapped his wings and lifted into the air, awe and terror combined to leave J'erik immobile.

He clung to the calantani's left forelimb, lest he should fall to the ground below. They cleared the iron tree, Diearka's tail whipping a kodjelu on a limb as they rose.

Warm air, free of gadid, filled J'erik's lungs. Gradually, the fuzziness besieging his senses washed away.

He noticed changes. The pores in the thick orange hide took on more details. The tiny hills and valleys formed a pattern which made no sense and vanished when he blinked. He could smell the parched land in the air and the musk odor of the orange one after a night of calantani rituals.

Looking up, he could not see Diearka's face. The long neck and the lower jaw stretched into the wind.

The hypersensitivity ebbed, leaving only the calantani and him flying over the plateau, climbing higher and higher toward a lone white puff lost in the royal-blue sky. The air rushed at him in jaded whispers.

As though Diearka embraced the same reverence for the clouds as J'erik, he extended his great wings to their limit and soared along warm air currents the Betweener never imagined existed. After he was confident the calantani would neither crush nor drop him, he ignored the questions in his mind and reveled in the spellbinding adventure.

The calantani toiling below were splashes of alien color on the bland plateau and miniaturized by distance. A slow smile grew on J'erik's bearded face. He was touching the sky and still alive. Were he to die this day, he felt that Cassilee had smiled favorably upon him.

Diearka swooped low over the flat valley, tilting almost vertically up the scree. A half-circle climb brought them to the upper plateau. He settled beside the iron tree and put his passenger down. The gadid aroma lingered. J'erik retrieved his belongings and moved away from the vines.

Soon Ladida joined him. They spoke in their peculiar manner as she broke her nonverbal side to issue orders in melodious notes. The sounds fascinated J'erik. He expanded on the details of how to make the net strong enough to support the calantani, listening to her relay. The workers performed their tasks in close quarters, never infringing upon the space of the next one.

J'erik watched, cleaning his wounds and pondering how all of this had happened. It seemed an unreality to that part of him forged in Stronghold training, and a delicious dream to the adventurer. Fir'ah would regret not seeing the colorful beasts and riding in the clouds. Fir'ah.

23

I should be at the Ah-te, he reflected. This time, I have been gone too long.

The spell broke. Hordes of questions tempted him to interrupt Ladida.

For the present, they needed him. Or thought they did. Prudence dictated a silence which, in turn, fertilized a growing curiosity peppered by anxiety. Fir'ah was shuffled into the back of his thoughts and temporarily forgotten.

A truth flowered. Neither the calantani nor the surface were as the Hold Leaders described. Perhaps the legends had warped over the years of reiteration throughout the generations. Or perhaps they were misleading intentionally, or maybe they were true at the time and Cassilee had changed over the countless millennia J'erik's people had spent in hiding.

He did not doubt that the calantani would kill him under different circumstances. The Ah-te had lost too many hunters to them in his lifetime for a doubt to exist there. Should he fail to save Chamblis, only Ladida's promise stood between him and that fate. It was an uncomfortable feeling.

The workers hurried when J'erik informed the Lady of Uli's strength-sapping abilities. It was light and heat. Too much light was the cause of his illness. Ladida's wings spread out to shield Chamblis, but the heat remained.

Uli was well beyond the high point when the mesh was completed. The calantani spread it on an open space just beyond the gadid boundary. They clustered around Chamblis, preventing J'erik from seeing how they managed to hoist him. The lower great wing drooped beneath the flapping wall of color. The dead weight ripped through the gadid as though it was composed of frail, young seedlings and easily damaged.

Once Chamblis was loaded in the net, the ends were secured in forelimbs and Diearka came for J'erik. He bent his head low to the ground and placed the Betweener in the crook where his upper wings spread from his back. When the mass of orange lifted, J'erik could see his mount's eyes. Leaning forward onto the ringlets, he pointed to the valley.

Airborne, J'erik wondered if Cassilee had eyes, for she surely would enjoy the sight of him atop the orange one,

24

leading the Lady and Lord's subjects, carrying their royal cargo through the afternoon. His private exultation was greater than it had been on the first day he survived upon Cassilee's skin.

Diearka set him down at the cave entrance. J'erik communicated steadily with Ladida, instructing maneuvers and relaying the need for a support under the net during the transfer.

Ladida responded immediately.

Diearka circled beneath the mass, working his front wings while bringing his great wings along the length of the sag. The strength of the orange one stunned J'erik. Chamblis's weight rested upon the wingspread. The front sections of the net dropped away as the Lord's head and neck settled on the protruding cave lip.

Diearka spoke a dozen notes.

Those who had carried the front swooped over Chamblis and maneuvered him across Diearka's great wings and into the shelter. The grating of wings and talons against the rock step screamed over the flapping wings. Bits of grit pelted the workers as it shot through the air.

No sooner was Chamblis secure on the ledge than two blues and a brown worried the net free and away from Diearka.

J'erik walked around the Lord. The exposure to Uli and the strange light shone by the Demon's eyes upon the Lord bothered him.

Ladida sensed his unease. Lord Chamblis was as far into the cavern as possible. J'erik alone could fit between the head and the wall where a passage led to the inner chamber.

He shed his packs and hoisted the rope. Carefully, he explained to Ladida how the rope could be woven into the net and the net fixed to the higher rocks. It would function as a door to be raised and lowered when needed.

While the calantani worked, J'erik moistened a spongy olca leaf in the chamber and carried it out to Chamblis. He dripped water onto the Lord's thick tongue. It absorbed the expanded leaf, which was as long as J'erik's forearm and three times as wide. Dismayed, J'erik knew the water would be gone before Uli slept.

Again, he confided the problem to Ladida. A green and two yellows flew away.

J'erik ground amilglib husk, needles and all, with dried azaix tubers and iron leaves, and threw in a measure of gadid. Water, in small quantities, blended with it until the lumpy paste became a creamy soup. There was enough to coat the calantani's head and wing joints.

The net hung over the cave with the rope dangling around and through it. J'erik pulled. The curtain went up hard.

Inside his living area he rummaged for several hewn ironwood blocks and more rope.

Ladida, we are all tired, but the work has just begun. We must lace the net with young leaves from the iron trees. They will fold when the net is up and keep the light and heat out when it is down.

I must have greater quantities of the mixture I used upon myself. Chamblis is so much larger. . . . Still, I cannot promise anything.

It is enough, Betweener. We did not know to shield him from Uli, though it makes sense to me now. There is much we can learn from one another. Cassilee changes. All who will survive must change with her or perish.

Diearka hovered at the cave mouth.

He is strong, and partial to you, Betweener. Diearka is partial to few. He will take you to gather what you need. Can three others carry enough to last through tomorrow's day?

J'erik nodded and climbed over Diearka's face to the perch above the wings.

Betweener? Have you a Hold name? Or are you an outcast?

I am J'erik.

J'erik. Erik, son of . . .

J'osh-uah, the Techi leader.

As Diearka took to the air it struck J'erik odd that Ladida had become very quiet after the small burst of curiosity. How could she know about the naming of Dwellers, which branded Fir'ah more than himself? The Holds were secured inside mountains and below the ground. Strange.

The last time a Meet brought them onto the surface during the twilight hours, he and Fir'ah had been on the

26

other side of puberty. The year that followed was scarred by ugly memories. Never would he understand why Ulni-da killed her daughter and the baby her daughter had borne by a Techi.

The tiny Betweener babe would not have had it so difficult. There was Fir'ah, and he. And how they cried when old Kali-te brought the news. The three of them had cried all day, holding each other for comfort and safety.

J'erik shook the memory loose.

Long shadows darkened the land. In the distance, a herd of panavers sauntered across the plateau. Uli's reddish light blazed on the open spaces soon to become part of the long night shadows.

On the ground, gnarled iron trees took on a grotesqueness, twisting branches into ghouls against the fiery sunset. J'erik set to work showing the calantani what he wanted. Night was not his favorite time. Off to the north, the local calantani cried in the wind.

Suddenly, there was a great deal he wanted to know about Lord Chamblis and Lady Ladida.

One Star III Recon Prober fell away from the mother ship. Fancher Bann wondered how many of the two hundred and forty-eight, a quarter of the *Minaho's* capacity, knew of his departure. He accelerated slowly, taking his time to clear the spearhead of the *Minaho*. The tactic dared the mother ship to issue a caution.

The *Minaho* stayed silent.

His anger subsided in the face of a hard-won optimism. Mikel's jovial nature, which complemented his own personality, had aided him in the battle with himself. But then Mikel had never known a truly difficult day in his life. It was easier to be optimistic when a knowledge of exactly how bad life could get had not touched home.

Fancher had known hunger, cold and thirst and became acquainted with life's harsher realities long before his baby teeth loosened. Death was no stranger.

A smile pushed his cheeks into the helmet. What an incongruous friendship—Mikel, only child of the chairman of the board at New Life Enterprises, and the struggling colonist from backwater Palama trying to make good. It did not seem to gel in the light from Cassilee growing ahead.

He chuckled, remembering the promise he had evoked from his friend.

The sound died. Looking back, Mikel had shown a chink in his positive armor. Fancher wished he had paid more attention to his friend's reactions. Mikel attended the processing session with him, then inspected each bit of gear loaded onto the Star III Recon Prober. It seemed now that Mik scrutinized everything as though he were taking mental notes.

Fancher shrugged the anomaly away.

Mikel was serving a hitch before going on to bigger and better things. That's all. He was concerned, Fancher mused. In a few years, he'll be gleaning the wealth from crowded planets willing to pay a premium to be rid of part of their population—generally the undesirable part. It was the duty of the rich to "help" the poor along— and out—with the dregs of society.

But that was not to be Cassilee's fate. None of the undesirables would touch her surface.

He keyed the program, leaned back and watched the planet form a pandemic across the first three circular viewplates. "No question about where we're going to land, baby. Just how. Hard? Or soft?"

Fancher chuckled. "I'm getting paranoid already, talking to a ship."

Cassilee took on more colors. The predominant ocher cast a hundred shades before the entry window swallowed them with speed.

By the fourth day of sample gathering and analysis, Fancher had almost convinced himself of the folly, possibly genuine paranoia, in his speculations that the mission had been created for his end. Reports were beamed back to programmed locations at the computer's discretion.

The one and only survey team sent to the planet five years earlier had reported no signs of life. After seeing a kodjelu and monitoring the electrical impulses from a roving horde, he concluded that the survey had been taken from an out-system vantage point. Critters like the armored beasties did not sprout up overnight.

More bothered him.

They should be covering the land, knee deep, at the rate they multiplied, if the gaggles of young traveling in the center of the hordes were an example. A natural enemy, or enemies, could account for the discrepancy. But if there were such things, they stayed well hidden, day and night. Neither his eyes nor the sensors picked up a sign.

It was dawn. He flew through morning fog, measuring the moisture content and watching the instruments. The Star III rose and dipped with the land contour.

A yellow square on the side control board winked slowly and matched a faint sound emitted by the panel speaker.

Fancher ordered the guidance system to approach and track.

In seconds, the yellow light flashed so rapidly that it looked continuous. Fancher aborted the sound. Hard copy began piling out of the data bank.

"Give it verbal and simple."

"New life form. No previous log. Large. More than three. A fourth weaker emission is present. Readings show a second species. Sixteen-point-oh-five kilometers south there is another weak reading."

Fancher ordered brain scans, electrical and magnetic prints and size, weight, height and spectrogram analysis. The first series made no sense to him at all. The second was familiar.

He inhaled, hoping he was wrong. "Computer. Those readouts are human life. Aren't they?"

"Mission complete. Transmission sent and ended. Disengage."

"You pregnant-mother rapers!" Fancher pulled at the controls, fighting the overrides from the *Minaho*.

The Star III Recon Prober climbed a vertical kilometer before the override succeeded. Fancher plummeted toward the ground, spinning odd circles as he fought to compensate with the damaged manuals.

First contact, nose up, was a glancing blow. The prober shot into the air, hit the branches of an old iron tree and sent them flying in all directions.

The second contact flipped the ship end over end. Tons of earth and snared vines mounded into a backstop. Another iron giant tried to put a halt to the metal screaming against the land.

Inside, the viewports shattered along the front. The side ones cracked and buckled under the impacts. Metal beams shrieked, then folded and snapped. The control board disintegrated. Plastic, metal and piriglass flew around the crumbling interior, careening off the mangled bulkheads.

An iron branch caught on an extender arm snapped and shot through the front viewport as the ship came to a halt and teetered. The point reached through Fancher and pierced the com chair before the last forward momentum died.

Chapter 4

SEVEN NIGHTS AND SIX DAYS MARCHED through the skies beyond the cavern. J'erik spent long hours dripping water into the calantani's mouth. Balm preparation and administration was an endless process. It required three calantani and a tremendous effort to turn Lord Chamblis. Scales littered the floor. Their sharp edges were something else to be wary of in the dark. Long sheets of wrinkled skin peeled from the beast's head, forelimbs and belly. The skin area down his back and along the tail peeled in layers, as many as four in places.

J'erik braided the streamers of hair Chamblis had lost into a rope. Within the escarpment on the other side of the plateau, the calantani fashioned nets for gathering whatever J'erik required.

Time and need exacted a toll from the plateau. Parts of it were stripped down to the kodjelu holes in the rock. The herds of panavers which usually roamed the highlands moved on to more plentiful territory.

Diearka led groups to places where the foliage differed. The new booty excited and worried J'erik. The smell was the same. He tried each compound upon a patch of his skin before spreading it in quantities over the calantani.

Several times he caught himself laughing at his attitudes and actions. The beast was an enemy, yet he

31

could no longer look at him and say, "You are my enemy." He was also Ladida's mate, and the Lady stood watch day and night through the hours of chaos and quiet.

By the seventh day, new skin and stubby scales emerged in odd-looking patches. His bulk had shrunk. Skin lay in folds along his belly. At midday Chamblis moaned, unsettling the watchers.

He stirred and let out another painful sound.

Holding his head before it vibrated off his shoulders, J'erik hoped this was not the beginning of a series.

Louder noises rattled the sanctuary.

Ladida and Diearka were holding a frenzied discussion which covered the entire range of audible sounds, many at the same time.

In the Ah-te he had never required a mediator. He had watched the two designated ones work their magic to calm arguments many times. A scanty working knowledge brought him far with the calantani, but not far enough to intrude. It disturbed him to hear the two he liked most engaged in a discord of so great a magnitude.

Raise the barrier! snapped Ladida.

Jolted, J'erik scrambled for the rope. He pulled rapidly and lifted the curtain.

It was less than halfway up when both Diearka and Ladida pushed inside. They pressed close to Lord Chamblis.

Daytime stars approached the valley. For a frozen piece of time, J'erik was fascinated by them. He did not try to count their numbers. Numbers imparted no understanding. Distance made them glittering points of awful death. The sky turned white behind the first wave. Still, he could see them.

Shaken, he released the rope. It snaked upward. The curtain fell and shuddered. The heavy mesh, lined and worked in dual patterns, now seemed flimsy protection against the Star Demons.

J'erik crawled over Chamblis's tail, shoved the tip toward Diearka and checked the bottom of the curtain. He stepped on webbed feet and talons during the security check. The edge was turned inward, as were the sides as far up as he could reach. The heights were left to Ladida and Diearka.

The first wave of noise sent J'erik over Chamblis to his work area. He tossed out supplies with both hands until he found two squares of iron leaves stuffed in the folded center with olca. These he set on Chamblis.

Next, he searched for the hair rope, again throwing the once-sorted contents over his shoulder before finding it beside his foot. He tied the rope around his head from the base of his skull to above his eyes. It flattened his shoulder-length brown hair and indented his skin. When he tried to shove the pads against his ears, they did not fit.

He tried it again, leaving slack to accommodate the earmuffs.

The third time it worked well. The noise had ceased. Knowing it would come again, he found the bundle of ear protectors fashioned for Chamblis and placed the first one over the beast's exposed hearing orifice. The underside, lodged against the rock, was impossible. Instead of rope, J'erik used the calantani's hair to secure it.

Diearka waved his forelimbs.

J'erik glanced up.

He had forgotten that he was not alone.

He grabbed for three experimental protectors and crawled over Chamblis to Ladida.

Suspended by her tail, J'erik tied them on while she held them in place with her thick fingers. Done, he hurried to Diearka, threw up the last one and scurried back to fashion another before the next wave of noise inundated them.

The last was not neat, but effective, and it stayed in place with a second knotting of hair.

He sat on Chamblis's great wing and felt a physical sag as adrenalin stopped surging through his body.

The noise returned. Cassilee trembled in fear.

Grit, followed by loose rock fragments and more grit, rained from the ceiling. J'erik thought about the buttes which no longer existed. The noise was loud, but not so loud that it rattled his brain and changed all his reference points. He had no desire to feel the strange sky-walking sensation. Better to fly with Diearka in the sky than to walk upside down upon the land.

Light.

The curtain became a translucent wall. The veiny skeletons quivered.

Your eyes! Cover your eyes!

J'erik did not wait to see if Ladida heeded his warning, nor if she managed to communicate it to the orange one before the intensity touched his skin in warning. He cowered from the light, eyes pressed shut, and groped the rest of the way over Chamblis, until the calantani provided a shield. Panting, he waited.

He did not understand the inconsistency of light and noise. The Demons sought to keep them guessing. And succeeded.

A new phenomenon gave him more to consider.

His left shin began to rise, unsettling him and throwing him onto Chamblis. The floor kept rising. J'erik banged his knee and ankle against a fleet of jumping work pots seeking the lowest spot. He straightened the leg and swung it into the cramped niche shared with the calantani.

The light stopped. The noise faded. The land settled slowly, as though wary of a return. Heat inside the cavern turned the fine grit sifting down from the heights into mud balls on J'erik's skin.

He relaxed the muscles around his eyes. His eyelids felt welded together. A sigh escaped when he could not see through them. The heat stabilized.

Friendly noises eased his mind. It could not have been more than twitching muscles relaxing that let him know the two calantani at the mouth were alive. The fall of tiny rocks from the enormous beasts was music to his ears.

J'erik opened his eyes. The hair-rope ends parted on both sides of his nose. He glanced over to the Lady. Nerves and relief brought a laugh at the ridiculous calantani with protruding gray-green leaves for ears and the knots of white and orange hair sticking straight out.

Ladida informed him of his own peculiar mien, droopy horns growing from the middle of his forehead. Several minutes of bantering took the edge off the seriousness of their situation.

As a precaution, J'erik mixed and dispatched buckets of the salve he used on Chamblis for Ladida and Diearka. They coated each other with an extra thickness where they had faced the curtain. J'erik lavishly painted his skin and worked the mix into his beard and hair. Before he rested, not a bare spot existed on the calantani Lord.

The next assault was prepared for by grinding leaves and pulverizing tubers.

Noise and light continued throughout the day and into the night. Before the Star Demons abandoned the area, J'erik had pulverized every scrap of leaf, tuber, bark and berry the calantani had stored. The only empty container was his water dish.

The rest of the night he slept with the rope tied around his head and his body packed with cracking gray balm. Sometime during the respite he heard Ladida and Diearka conversing, but paid no attention. His exhaustion was too great.

Around midday, movement from the calantani Lord woke him. He sat, groggy and dry-mouthed.

Chamblis flexed his front wing, knocking J'erik against the wall. The calantani's head moved slowly against the floor. Old flesh and flaking balm piled mounds at both sides of the arc. Black lips moved over the sharp teeth. Jaws opened and closed.

J'erik inched back, trying to watch the head and wings simultaneously.

Ladida snapped her tail in the air, then brought it to dangle over J'erik. Desperate, he grabbed it. She lifted him above Chamblis and placed him between her haunches.

Where is Diearka?

He is checking the others and telling how you taught us to protect our hearing from the loudness. I would like to send you away for a time, J'erik Betweener. It would sadden me greatly if my Lord Chamblis were to injure you while he strives to come among the living again. Is there a place you may go and be safe?

Yes. I should return to the Ah-te. I am afraid I have been gone too long. Fir'ah will be worried. He pulled off the ear protectors and wore the rope around his neck like a medal.

She is your mate?

J'erik smiled. *She is my sister, born with me. We are the only Betweeners to survive in the Ah-te.*

35

I am concerned, J'erik. Will they give you shelter? You may stay with the group on the other side of the plateau if you wish.

If I am not permitted to stay, I will take Fir'ah with me. They cannot deny that. He shrugged. *At worst, I would have to fight T'lar for her again. Ladida, sometimes it is very hard to be a Betweener and belong nowhere. But here on Cassilee's surface, my skin is strong and my eyes do not go blind. So here, there is a freedom and a place for Betweeners. The calantani rule the night.* A sharp glance upward took in her nod of comprehension. *Star Demons rule everything. Yet they can be guarded against. I think.*

Chamblis lifted his hind wing and scraped loose shards from the ceiling.

We will leave as soon as he is able to travel. You will return to us in three days, J'erik?

Head tilted to the side, the significance of a three-day wait eluded him.

We are in your service, Betweener. We would take you with us to the north, if you wish to go. Never would we force you. Never.

J'erik became excited at the prospect of exploring Cassilee with the giant calantani. Days ago they lost any ugliness he had thought they possessed before knowing Ladida. He smiled, remembering how he had planned to cross the plateau to see the other side, knowing it was like this one, only facing the opposite way. To see beyond the valley and the plateau . . .

The smile faded. *I must speak with Fir'ah before I am free to answer. I cannot abandon her, especially to T'lar. She fears him, but does not know why.*

Diearka swooped from high above the valley and glided along the escarpment before settling on the lip.

You may communicate with him as you do with me, J'erik. We have debated long and hard about this and it is what he wants. He will wait for three days after we leave, in case you return with Fir'ah to go to the north.

"Ladida . . . is the goodness and tenderness I feel inside of you a soul?" He felt the warmth of a smile he could not see.

There is one better qualified to explain that than I, J'erik. You are a seeker and perhaps that is part of your quest. She wrapped her tail around him, lifted, and placed him on Diearka. *Your greatest journey has only begun. You have scratched the surface of what you are and what Cassilee will make of you. She has decided, as we knew she would.* A yellow tear moistened the gray balm caked below her eyes. *You must find yourself, then find out for yourself.*

Diearka turned away instantly. J'erik lunged for the orange ringlets and grabbed on before losing complete balance.

"Ladida? Explain. Please? Ladida?"

He knew she heard, though she did not answer. The sadness he felt was not entirely his.

Diearka circled high over the plateau, flying so fast it was hard for J'erik to breathe and meditate upon Ladida's words at the same time.

For a moment he forgot Ladida and the sadness. He opened his hand and reached for a fluff of cloud. It slithered through his fingers like the oracular statements of the calantani Lady. The white fleece moistened his face and gleaned away the worries.

Diearka took him from cloud to cloud, playing with the wind. J'erik lost all sense of direction and time, content to revel in the wonders of the present and the marvels blessing Cassilee's blue sky.

J'erik would have stayed in the air all day if Diearka had not asked where the Ah-te was located. He pointed, dismayed. Coming in empty-handed would not make him a welcome sight to any, save Fir'ah.

Diearka, how is it that those with Lord Chamblis are different from the other calantani?

How is it that you, Lord J'erik, are different from others under the rocks?

I am a crossbreed of two warring peoples. Is that what changed you, also?

You are different beyond the physical traits of eyes and skin. Can any of your people speak with the mind as you do? Can they swallow fear to make room for compassion to an enemy who asks for help?

J'erik slid down Diearka's back. The hot ground was covered by odd little seeds similar to those inside ripe olca fruit. He had not noticed them previously. Crouch-

37

ing, he ran his hand through them. Absently, he deposited a few in the shirt tucks at the side.

Patting Diearka's scaled haunch, *You answer my questions with questions.* He walked around to the mouth of the caverns and stopped. *Why did we not communicate before?*

It was not permitted, Lord J'erik. More, I cannot say. The great wings stretched, flapped once and lifted the orange to the sky.

J'erik watched, eyes squinted against the flying dust. After the calantani disappeared, he started through the black maze to the Ah-te.

Crumbling stalactites and columns lost more phosphorescence after each journey. The echo of dripping water building limestone was louder than he had remembered. And the dismal black shadows depressed him, as they did each time he left Uli behind. Only the coolness stayed unchanged and friendly.

It was difficult to switch mental gears and reconcile himself to the confines of subterranean existence. Momentarily, he felt ashamed of the Dwellers. Was it imagination, or were they digressing from the social structures of his childhood? The lack of children was not imagination. It was hard to remember what a baby sounded like. One day he would actually be allowed to touch one.

"One day, I will have my own," he said to the cavern, then listened to his words bounce among the stalagmites, pleased with the sound.

"You have nothing of your own, Betweener."

J'erik stopped. The voice was T'lar's.

Chapter 5

J'ERIK LEFT THE PATH IMMEDIATELY.

If T'lar sought an advantage in the wide caverns, he did not know his prey. As children, Fir'ah and J'erik had played in the lime forest and at the maw where none of the Hold members would look for them.

Ears straining, he heard T'lar move. He was close.

J'erik sneered. It was an old trick, turning around to speak in the caverns. Sound and direction confused the listener. How many times had he and Fir'ah played that game? Hundreds? Thousands?

Stealthily, he moved away, skirting massive columns glowing with a live slime bacteria, keeping to the blackest shadows. T'lar's night vision was better, but neither could see where the absence of light was supreme.

More than one trick was in the offing.

Were he to confront T'lar anywhere except in the Square, he would become an outcast and forfeit the few rights to which a Betweener was entitled. But one of the things to be taken was his family. Life without Fir'ah was nothing. Worse was the thought of T'lar being forced upon her as a Chosen.

No. That would not last. Fir'ah would run away or kill herself with T'lar as a mate. Had the Hold already acted? Had he been gone too long this time? A flash of panic shot through his body.

"Show yourself, you ugly Betweener with skin the color of poison dirt. Or has the light sapped your courage?"

J'erik worked a circle around T'lar and slipped into the chamber leading down to the Stronghold tunnel. He shrugged away the bleak speculations and hurried. The soles of his feet touched the wear-smoothed floor lightly.

The zigzag path angled down for six hundred paces. Curving steps of irregular lengths and widths, each memorized over the years, were last before the straight hall that ended with a right turn into the Common.

Halfway down the stairs, the smell of cooking kodjelu and dried panaver assaulted him. Roasted, baked, boiled, fried; it always tasted the same. Once Fir'ah had managed to slip a few leaves from an herb bush into the main pot. It was the best meal they had in the Stronghold—and the last for the Betweeners for two days. In secret, they ate well from a private stash subsidized by Kali-te, the old woman who cared for them through the rough years. Outwardly, they perfected martyrdom and expressed contrition for their transgression.

J'erik smiled.

If Stronghold life was difficult for him, he knew he had been less than an easy child to tolerate, and Fir'ah had not been easier.

Ulni-da stirred the Hold caldron, perspiring with the rising steam. Her tangled gray-black hair hid her dark eyes, though J'erik knew she saw him. As Seeress, Ulni-da saw everything, mostly before it happened. When she did not launch a tirade, his suspicions and concerns grew. He mumbled a greeting and strode toward the Hall of Rooms.

The Ah-te was unusually quiet for a time before the main meal. This, too, was an ill sign.

The faint sound of crying leaked into the Hall.

Listening, he walked faster.

It did not sound like Fir'ah.

He ran.

The sound was coming from their room.

Heart thudding in his temples, he stopped short of the door. The sobs were regular and bordered hysteria.

Fists tight at his sides, body as rigid as the rock molding the walls, he dreaded seeing what was on the other

40

side of the door, yet felt frantic to get to Fir'ah. He gathered his forces, feeling a worried rage creep over him and set his nerves on fire.

While he was still flat-footed in the hall, the door banged open in front of him, crashed against the wall and stayed without a backswing. He willed himself to enter, unconcerned about the force which cleared the door out of the way.

The sobs choked into silence. Three of the Ah-te women wore black mantillas and sat upon his bed. Two of them regarded him in open horror. The third, Kali-te, stroked Fir'ah's cheek and spoke. "You left her too long this time, J'erik. It is good you are back."

He staggered forward, shoved the two women lurching for the opened door aside and saw only the bruises upon Fir'ah's left arm and face.

"F-Fir'ah."

She did not move.

He licked the back of his hand and held it under her nose.

"She is alive, J'erik, but I don't think she wishes to be among the living. Yet she has not gone." Kali-te touched his arm and guided him to the floor. "Fir'ah is where she cannot be hurt. Do you understand?"

The void consuming his insides showed on his face when he gazed upon the old woman. "The more I learn, the less I understand. Where is this place? How can I get her to come back?" He turned to Fir'ah, lifted the coverlet, a little at first, then flung it back to reveal her nakedness. His scream shook the walls and rattled down to the smelting area.

Kali-te did not try to calm him. She watched like a mother who knew her son.

His heavy breathing swelled and caved his chest again and again. The second scream, mixed with fury and pain, was that of an animal in the throes of agony.

Fir'ah's bronze skin screamed a pain of its own in the numbers of multicolored bruises. The sides of her breasts were bound with a light cloth holding healing poultices in place.

Through clenched teeth, the name "T'lar!" seethed into the room with a hatred Kali-te cringed at hearing.

The old woman covered Fir'ah and tucked in the

41

edges. When she stood, her wiry frame ended below J'erik's armpits. She took hold of his arms and shoved him onto his bed, went to the door and slammed it.

"Yes. T'lar. No! You have to walk through me, Betweener. I have cared for you two since long before your mother died. I will have my say!

"T'lar raped and beat her. That is true."

J'erik lifted his head to see the old woman. Bile crept up his throat and filled his mouth. He would kill T'lar a little at a time. He could see T'lar staked in an open cavern where he would not get the full impact of Uli. Blisters would fill with body liquid. T'lar would swell and scream. He would coat T'lar with the same balm used on Lord Chamblis and keep him alive for days, while he carved at the body and slowly, painfully, whittled away T'lar's manhood. Yes, he would make him suffer and beg for death many, many times before oblivion claimed him.

The illusion faded slowly.

Kali-te was still blocking the door and speaking.

Unhearing, he looked at Fir'ah. An iron blanket put a damper on his hate and his plans for T'lar. Kali-te's words shaved a fuzzy patch from his brain.

"I have kept her warm and fed her broth. The bruises cannot be severe enough to cause this, this nonliving. There is nothing else I know to do, J'erik." Callused feet shuffled against the stone floor as she came to sit beside J'erik.

"The marks are not all of one color. Some look older." He picked up Fir'ah's hand and looked to Kali-te, mistrusting his own judgment. "Is that true?"

Her voice was a whisper. "Yes. She was gone five days. T'lar was gone only the last three. He brought her into the Common when he could not revive her. In his fear, he admitted more than he wanted us to know. She went out to look for you on the surface."

"For me?" His back teeth dammed the surge of bile when Kali-te nodded.

"Time will heal her body." Kali-te pressed her palms together and twisted. "Cassilee knows no justice when she would deny our Hold children so many times. It would be her greatest unkindness to thrust one upon Fir'ah after such an abomination."

"It is her mind I worry for, Kali-te." Elbows on knees and holding the limp hand straight out, J'erik bowed his head and thought. Recriminations and vengeance were temporarily shelved. They would neither undo the wrong nor help Fir'ah now.

After several minutes, he looked around his arm to Kali-te and asked, "Would you care for her a while longer? Do not feed her or give her anything to drink. I will be back soon."

The old woman's face wrinkled in a faint smile. Black eyes twinkled when she lifted the mantilla of mourning from her head and placed it around her shoulders in a show of faith. J'erik took her face in both hands and kissed her forehead.

Silence in the Common became absolute when J'erik exited the Hall of Rooms. Twenty-nine pairs of eyes watched him pass the circle of tables and approach Ulni-da at the caldron. The bulky folds of the Seeress's flesh matched those in the garb roped in the center below her pendulous breasts. Through his own agony, J'erik saw that the woman had also suffered from the atrocity perpetuated within the Hold. As Seeress, she should have known it was happening and dispatched help.

"Ulni-da, I leave for a short time. When I return, I will require hot broth. You will save a small caldron so I may prepare it as I wish?"

She nodded, clutching the long stirring paddle resting in the bottom of the pot. "I will send someone to relieve Kali-te and tend Fir'ah."

"No! Fir'ah will not be fed until I return. Kali-te has been mother to us when no other would give us even the back of her hand. She will stay. It is her choice and my decision.

"Know that I claim T'lar's life for what he has done to my sister. Stronghold Law. He is in the cavern entrance."

Again, she nodded, as did the adults in the room.

"I do not go for him now, but later. He is dead to this Hold." J'erik turned abruptly, feeling the rage fight at the prison containing it. For a second, he stared at the entrance to the caverns and saw himself wandering through the lime forest. He could feel the coolness, heavy with moisture. The paths were empty and dark. He became a stalking calantani, listening, watching, waiting for his prey to make the slightest disturbance. Then cut him to kodjelu fodder! But nothing moved, except the hunter. The prey had fled in terror.

He jerked his head as the vision blinked out. He crossed the rest of the Common and rolled back a stone which led to an escape tunnel.

A small girl, Star-ii, ran through the room, oblivious to the gloom and its reason. Carrying a gathering pack, she caught up to J'erik as he steadied the stone. She tugged at his breeches. "You forgot your pack. I'm so glad you came home. I missed you. Will you bring the berries this time? They were so good."

J'erik looked down at her. The innocence in her tiny face sparked a new pain. "If they are near what I seek, yes, Star-ii."

Beaming, hands clasped behind her back while he put on the pack, she said, "When I grow up big, like Fir'ah, I'm going to be a Betweener, too, just like you and her. And I'm going to Choose you so we are all Betweeners and can go get berries."

The child's black hair felt slippery and thick when he touched it. "When you grow up you will be beautiful, like Fir'ah, but never a Betweener."

"Then I will go to the Techi and ask for a baby Betweener." The defiant thrust of her lower lip hardened when Cor-ii, her mother, pulled her away.

An old woman and a young child—was that the sum total of their alliances in the Ah-te? Head shaking, J'erik left the Hold and rolled the gray slate back into place over the tunnel.

The circular door did not roll open again until long after Uli lit the other side of Cassilee. Ulni-da waited beside the small caldron simmering upon the gas flame nature graciously supplied.

J'erik dropped the pack onto a food-preparation table and pulled out gadid and herb leaves. A stalk of berries was shoved to the corner.

"For Star-ii," he said.

Ulni-da grunted and stirred the broth.

J'erik sorted utensils in the near bin. A heavy spoon

and shallow bowl were brought to sit beside the leaves. He unsheathed his knife and sliced small bits of each one, set it down and began pulverizing the bits in the bowl.

"Many times I have wondered where you got that knife."

The metal spoon clanked against the ironwood bowl. J'erik did not look up. "I found it, grown with rust on the handle. Fir'ah and I made a new one and chipped off the rotten parts."

He saw the shallow cave in his memory. They were on the beginning edges of puberty and trying to hold onto childhood in an unspoken conspiracy. The cave was special, filled with pictures and broken relics of eons past. Nearby was the shattered egg of a Star Demon, brittle with age, pitted by something beyond Cassilee's realm and burned through by another Demon. Everything which was inside had disintegrated into Cassilee long, long ago. It was half buried when they found it.

His mind's eye saw the Betweener twins, holding hands and staring at the awesome thing, half expecting it to rise out of the ground and heal together. Fir'ah had been silent for a long time after they'd left. They went back to the cave and ate. During the meal, J'erik remembered seeing the glint of Uli on an object. It was the knife. Fir'ah dug it out and gave it to him on the condition that they never return. They never did.

"That was long ago, Ulni-da. The place where I found it has been made into dust by the Star Demons." Eyes lifting for a second, "They come often now. They chew up Cassilee with light and noise. When they spit it out, it is nothing but fine dust which makes clouds in the wind. I have seen this. And I have seen clouds in the sky."

Gray powder, dotted with yellow and purple, spilled onto the table. More herbs and a tiny chopped root went into the grinding bowl.

Ulni-da reached for his pack. J'erik caught her wrist. "Don't touch it!"

"I. I meant to help."

The Seeress had never been as subdued as during the time since his return. It was puzzling, though not important until she reached for the stash in his pack.

"Your chance to help Fir'ah came and left when she was taken by T'lar." He spat the name with hatred and threw her wrist free.

Ulni-da rubbed life into her veiny hand and stood as tall as her bulk allowed. "You are of age, Betweener. There is something you should know. I was ignorant of your sister's fate. I could not see the danger. Time lulled me with T'lar. There was no way I could know his thoughts became deeds. The years he spent desiring to be Chosen have twisted his mind. That is no excuse.

"I have never been able to see with either you or Fir'ah. Betweeners are born with closed minds, even to a Seeress like myself. I have tried to penetrate those barriers, over and over, and suffered great pain for the attempts."

She resumed stirring, an unseen burden weighting her sloped shoulders. The low rumble of a boil contrasted with the grinding of herbs. Gloom rose with the steam into silence.

J'erik scraped the last powders out of the bowl, mixed them on the table, then used the blade and refilled the bowl. Half the blend went into the small bubbling caldron, the other half he set aside and covered.

He slipped the pack over one shoulder and scooped a bowl full of steaming broth. It smelled as he remembered from childhood. The taste was better.

"There is an old, old legend which tells of the end of the world," Ulni-da said, stirring. " 'Day will become night, and the screams of all the injustices perpetrated upon Cassilee from the beginning of time will sound as one. They will rise in a fury to the stars and call back the guardian moon. And the seeds of destruction will be sown upon the land as a sign.' "

J'erik fumbled in his shirt and withdrew the seeds he had gathered outside the Ah-te. These he held out to Ulni-da. She stopped stirring and gaped at the seeds, then him. Her pale skin took on a transparency.

"Perhaps it is the end of your world, old Seeress, but not mine. I am a Betweener. I walk proudly upon Cassilee, and my world will not die without wounding the killer. There is more to killing Cassilee than the self-destruction of the Strongholds and a few seeds. The Hold kills itself with isolated stagnation and a blindness wrought from fear." He laid the seeds upon the table and took Fir'ah's bowl. "The Strongholds are not the heart of Cassilee."

"Cassilee has no heart. She is death waiting to happen."

Crossing the room, "Life is death waiting to happen, Ulni-da. Cassilee is the source of both and encompasses everything in between."

"You have changed much, Betweener."

He paused. "I have always been this way. So has Fir'ah. You have been a Seeress blind to Betweeners in more ways than one. A small child sees more of who and what we are than you. I pity you your outlook upon life and Cassilee. The narrowness of one restricts the other.

"Fir'ah and I will be leaving this death place as soon as possible."

"Where will you go? What will you do?"

The concern in her voice was touching. "If I cannot help her, maybe our father can. If not, there is another whom I will seek to ask. You would not understand, Ulni-da."

" 'And the calantani shall be equal to the man and he shall touch the seed of destruction with one of his own kind, who is not like the others.' It is the end of the world," she whispered into the steam after he was gone. "The stars will fall upon Cassilee and tear her apart."

Chapter 6

KALI-TE ASKED NO QUESTIONS AND LEFT IM-
mediately. Hope smoothed the wrinkles on her tired face.

J'erik tied a damp cloth over his mouth and nose. A
blanket helped to prop Fir'ah's head up. Crushed gadid
leaves spread on a parchment draped across her breasts.
The hypersensitizing effects materialized quickly.

Handpainted scenes on the walls ran into each other.
The colors were vivid and alive, taking on a dimension,
distorting, changing into a slur.

Numbly, J'erik stuffed the gadid into his pack and
kicked it toward the door. He opened it and shoved the
pack into the hall, then used the door as a fan, swinging
it back and forth on creaking hinges. The aroma hung in
the air.

He pulled the cloth from his face and tested the special
broth. It had cooled and tasted better than he thought
possible.

The deprivation of food and water, which her body
needed, in spite of her state of mind, brought an eagerness. He spoke gently of the past and a friendship that
transcended the birth bond.

Once, her eyelids fluttered, sending his hopes soaring.

He waited for another sign until his own eyes no
longer could be trusted. As a last resort, he considered
the form of communication employed with the calantani.
Hesitation led to debate.

It seemed wrong to invade another's thoughts. That was a territory so personal, so private, consent seemed mandatory. The incident with Lord Chamblis supported that idea.

He paced the room, wondering if the invention of restrictions was merely a guise for not wanting to see beyond the surface. True, he could not be objective about Lord Chamblis after the slow-running scene he had intruded on. But what about Fir'ah?

"No, there is nothing she could do to become ugly." *Then why hold back? Afraid to know her too well?*

It was more than looking into Fir'ah's mind and trying to communicate as a way to bring her back from the nonliving place. Being *able* to perform such a thing was the crux.

The pride of being a Betweener had flourished out of a defense mechanism strengthened by childhood. That pride capitalized upon the difference. It afforded him the luxury of Cassilee during the day; with Uli, and without the nighttime predators. Cassilee's horizons and a few of her cherished secrets were open to him, and occasionally Fir'ah, because of the difference. What he understood, he could accept and take pride in.

But to look into a mind . . .

He could not really see into Diearka or Ladida, just communicate. It was not the same.

A doubled right fist pummeled an open left hand.

Fir'ah did not move. Beauty that the ugly splotches of color could not touch cast a serenity framed by light-brown hair highlighted in gold. She was as opposite as it was possible to be from Lord Chamblis.

The stillness, bordering death, refused to yield to the physical difference.

J'erik sought another answer.

What was so offensive about the vision in Chamblis's muddled thoughts? Objectively, the taking of a human life for food could not be condemned any more than a human taking one of the special calantani's lives for the same reason.

Was it because the victim was a Betweener? A young woman?

Or was it really because he could invade that supreme

privacy of an intelligent being and rape the mind when the body was incapacitated, defenseless?

"No better than T'lar in that respect."

J'erik spent half the night searching a soul he did not know he had and examining each side of the arguments he produced from every conceivable angle. He managed to forgive himself for stumbling into the Lord's mind and the realization of how intelligent the calantani were. At least Chamblis's subjects.

Decision, the agonizing aspect, evolved. Action was the easy part.

He slipped into Fir'ah's mind, wondering why he could not do this when they played games aimed at this prospect. There were no complexities on the plane her mind clung too, only shadows of fear, remorse and an incredible sorrow.

Slowly, he charged her memory to relive the time since she had last seen him. A sluggish response balked at the need to change planes, but moved through the maze of nonsensical thoughts and memories to a time he remembered.

They were standing together at the mouth of the Ah-te as Uli began to light the morning.

"I do not feel good about your leaving this time, J'erik. There is something on the land." Fir'ah shook her head and now strained to identify the apprehensive feelings imparted to J'erik. "It will change the way we live for the rest of our lives. It frightens me."

"Come along."

She smiled, warm and vibrant. "I must tend Kali-te until she is well. You be careful." The pride she felt for him heightened when he kissed her cheek before leaving.

He shared her daydream of a time when another would kiss her in a manner symbolizing a love and emotion steeped in hormones. It was a mutual dream.

The mundane chores sped by; days filled with added work when she worried. The heaviness feeding her depression urged her from the Ah-te.

Carrying a pack, she left by way of the lime forest before dawn. She walked half a day and stopped at a shelter they had used previously. After checking it, she moved onto a long butte. Her urgency to find him cost time with careless mistakes. Twice she fell on the scree

51

and banged herself severely on the rubble. As dusk began to settle, she searched out and found shelter.

J'erik recognized the place. It was a little under half a day from where he had recuperated.

Early the next morning, before Uli lit the east, noise and light bombarded Cassilee. Fir'ah was terrified. She fled to the deepest part of the recess and huddled against the rocks, hands pressed over her ears, eyes wrinkled shut, but unable to restrain the flood running down her cheeks.

The Star Demons did not stay long. She felt them leave and knew they would not return for a while. J'erik found this amazing. Fir'ah acted upon feelings and relied on what they dictated, regardless of how illogical it seemed.

Callused hands gripped the rocks and hauled her up the escarpment to the plateau. At the top, she looked around, greatly disturbed. Something was out of place and she could not put her finger on it.

She scrutinized the plateau.

It seemed right; iron trees in clusters, olca bushes, azaix plants, kaloer bushes, and in the distance, clumps of winding gadid vines.

She turned to the valley. That was it! The long mesa which once had paralleled the plateau was missing. The whole thing was gone! The valley lay flat until the next distant escarpment rose in the east.

He tried to make her skip over the morose implications.

She moved through the memory of the day.

Uli looked straight down, warning Fir'ah that it was time to cut across the jut of the plateau and descend. Running part of the way, she could make the Ah-te by dark. The vastness of Cassilee had swallowed her brother.

She was struggling with herself when her attention was drawn by something glinting in the brush. She called out J'erik's name.

No answer.

She called again.

A scraping noise bounded along the anemic breeze.

A flood of jubilation started her toward the noise. Then an odd combination of fear and curiosity J'erik knew so well possessed her. Cautious, she changed to an

52

inland course and moved forward. Her steps were light, just as he had taught her to stalk a panaver. Her breathing was controlled and inaudible. Loud heartbeats pounded in her ears and J'erik's mind, accelerating his as he eavesdropped on the memory.

Carefully, fat branches of a tall kaloer bush supporting a tangle of gadid parted.

J'erik shared a terror with Fir'ah that ravaged his muscles. His blood turned to hot iron. The vision disappeared and reappeared as enormous eyes, all staring through Fir'ah at him.

Somewhere there was a scraping noise. Faint at first, it echoed until it roared and scratched all his nerve endings simultaneously.

For an instant the vision returned. Something had slithered along the ground, formed mounds at irregular places, gouged holes on the trail, and oozed a sap which dotted the marks in globs.

The vision flickered out and in.

The pattern led to the bushes.

The scraping sound obliterated the scene. J'erik grabbed his head. It felt as though a fingernail was digging away the center of his brain.

Next came a touch. Something cold and slimy grabbed at Fir'ah's/J'erik's foot.

Fir'ah was running.

She wiggled out of her pack and kept on running until she reached the ledge trail winding down the scree and across the slim valley neck to the Ah-te.

Yet, as she crossed the flat and looked down the valley, she experienced a new shock. The Star Demons were chewing up Cassilee. A second landmark butte was gone. On the other side, to the south, the valley opened again. The only thing standing in the way of a connection was the exterior of the Ah-te, worn smooth by weather and sculptured sharply at the same time for the same reason. The world was ending, just as the old legends and prophecies in the ancient books said it would.

The Strongholds had been dying since long before her birth. Their pending demise led to the intermingling of two completely different races who had warred with one another since the beginning of time. Even a Betweener would be swallowed by the Star Demons on Cassilee.

She entered the maw, still running, weakened to the point where her feet barely cleared the ground. She staggered into the darkness and fell against a luminous column.

Her aching lungs filled and refilled, gasping for more air to compensate for all they had been deprived of during the flight. The cool limestone warmed wherever her perspiring body touched.

Something touched her shoulder.

More terror seized her being.

She screamed and screamed, hugging the stone pillar.

T'lar lit a calidrium and coaxed it up to maximum brightness. He was speaking, but she could not understand the words. There was a shade of relief in recognition, but why didn't he speak so she could understand?

She let go of the column and slouched to the ground, hands over her face.

T'lar set the light aside, crouched down and followed the curve of her shirt over her breasts with his finger. She slapped him away. He smiled and continued speaking.

I can't understand! I can't understand! No! Don't touch me! I'll kill you if you touch me! I'll kill you!

Fir'ah's mind went on and on, threatening, pleading, protesting. Not a word escaped her lips. She crossed her legs and tried to hide her breasts from the prying hands so much stronger than hers.

In the flickering light she gazed at her foot and saw something she could not recognize, but felt she should. The flash passed too quickly for J'erik to place it too. The vision was filled by T'lar, grinning, eyes twinkling, removing his clothes, spreading them on the ground, speaking all the while.

Rough hands grabbed Fir'ah's shoulders and lifted her from the column, then deposited her on the clothes. A knee forced her legs down, wheedled, and pried her thighs apart. One hand held her arms over her head while her clothes were ripped away.

The vision formed knots in J'erik's bowels.

T'lar lunged on top of her, knocking the air out of her. The frantic grappling, prying, probing, brought out a strength she did not know existed.

In the midst of the fight came a pain that wouldn't go

54

away. Fir'ah began to fall; down, down, forever and ever, never landing, denying the horror in reality, the loss of her brother, her world, her life.

J'erik turned active in her mind, speaking softly, slowing her descent, finally stopping it and coercing her to abandon the velvet limbo.

He worked through the suffering of T'lar's release from a forced celibacy. He cried with her and shared the agonies, physical and emotional, each time she was violated. The ambiguities and horrors on the plateau remained in the hazy background of memory.

He spoke optimistically about good times to come and promised that she would meet her Chosen unafraid, eager, and able to persuade him when the time came. He took sides between that part of her mind which balked at the thought and the part wanting to believe the old dream, cajoling her fears into submission.

When he had accomplished all he thought possible, J'erik sagged onto his heels and rolled over to the empty bed. Exhaustion killed his curiosity about what Fir'ah had seen on the plateau which her mind refused to recognize, or think over, in harmless memory.

Kali-te tapped on the door and opened it. She was carrying two bowls of herb broth on a tray.

J'erik shook his head, too tired to eat. Lying on his side, he watched Kali-te's feet. The marks on Fir'ah's foot loomed up in his mind. Strange. Familiar. Just out of recognition's reach.

"Ulni-da says the world is ending," Kali-te said, settling on the edge of Fir'ah's bed. "What do you think?"

"Her world may be ending but mine is just resting." He closed his eyes and fell asleep.

Left-handed, Fancher worked on the recycler, trying to coax the broken parts to hold for another day. Time raced and dragged alternately, blending night and day, punctuated by the sounds of terraformers reshaping Cassilee. So close. So far away.

Sapped by the effort, he rested against a bulkhead, breathing hard. He watched the thick bandage wrapped around his chest and wound behind his neck. The wounds hurt. The bandage did not change color this time. He sighed, glad the hole was remaining closed.

The front part of the ship was demolished. The rear—analysis, storage and living quarters—had fared better. The Star III Recon Prober would never be salvaged, nor was it worth the costly effort. The seven days marked as gone by Fancher's wrist computer testified to its immediate value to the survivor. No longer airtight, the doors still operated and the cracks were small enough to keep the kodjelu out. Their scraping and scratching clashed with the thump of armored bodies against the hull when they gathered around the scent of death.

The noise added a frightening kind of sanity to the first few days when Fancher lived in a nightmare delirium rooted in an absolute refusal to die.

Now he thought about the strange dreams and the bronze skin he had reached for after crawling out of the ship.

The Destro-Lase II had severed the branch that impaled him and the chair. It required three attempts and subsequent blackouts before it was pulled free. How long he writhed on the ground before a short lucid period he could only guess.

Sometime, before he lost contact with the real world beating outside the ship, he managed to seal himself in the back section and medpack his major injuries, starting with the hole in his upper right chest. A long gash ran from his hairline, above the right eye, across the bridge of his broken nose and onto his left cheek. A line of sealer tape kept the wound clean while it healed. The scar he knew would result was one of dozens. His main objective was to live long enough for them to become scars so he could count them.

For the most part, little bothered Fancher. Cassilee was already testing him for worth. The hot days and cool nights carried death creatures which could not touch him. He slept most of the time, rebuilding the thread of strength which refused to snap, and floating in the days of childhood. Only in the dream mists did he associate the similarities of Palama with Cassilee. Faces came and left. Mostly there was a brief scene with his sister, Kreista.

He was thirteen again, standing at Kreista's side. Her hair was dark snakes coiled and writhing on a pillow. Cries for Alva through clenched teeth opened her eyes to

Fancher. "You have to do it," she said, panting. "This one's not like the others."

The scene moved, skipping time.

He was kneeling between her legs, heart pounding, sweat running freely in the cold room, mouth dry, hands ready. Kreista screamed, close-mouthed, panted and then pushed with her hands on the bulge in her belly. A bloody little foot wiggled out of the opening.

A clap of thunder shook the house. The four little ones in the next room began to cry. Wind rattled the triple thickness of the storm windows.

"Help him, Fancher! Help him!"

He took the foot, reached up, groping, and found the second one. Each time Kreista grunted, he pulled. What seemed to take hours passed in minutes. The baby was on a short cord. Under Kreista's panting instructions he tied off both ends and cut it. He held the child by the feet and used his finger to clean out the tiny mouth. Then the babe cried. It was the most beautiful sound Fancher had ever heard.

The scene ended with a rush of cold air as Alva barged into the room in a rain-soaked flight suit. The settlement medic went to work on Kreista. Fancher wrapped the baby, held him close and sat on the floor, staring at the little boy with wonder.

Fancher changed daily on Cassilee. Memories of life and death gave him a determination to live and face the enemy riding safely in space at another time.

Outside, the uppermost viewpoint tilted to the sky, the sunrise lightened the fog, caressing the land with a gray-on-ocher haze.

Fancher returned to work on the recycler. If the equipment held long enough for him to heal, the Star III would have proved its worth by him. The day before, during sunset, he had ventured out to gather amilglibs. The ocher dust coating the ship in the waning light turned it a glittering bronze. He christened the ship with an amilglib—the *Bronze Foot*, after the fleeting illusion.

Chapter 7

J'ERIK ABANDONED THE SLEEP WORLD DE-
pressed. His groggy state was filled with uncertainty. He
rubbed the tiredness from his eyes and opened them.

Fir'ah was sitting up, watching passively.

J'erik grinned. The ease of tensions slackened his rigid
muscles and allowed his shoulders to relax. He exhaled
loudly, blowing away the weight; he felt lifted.

Slowly, the jubilation faded.

Fir'ah looked at him as though he were a stranger.
The sparkle in her eyes was gone. No smile turned the
corners of her mouth. A mask of nonexpression covered
her face like a second skin. Her hands lay opened, the
right resting in the palm of the left. They were centered
in a cradle formed by a tight blanket drawn over her
crossed legs. One of his shirts hung loosely over her shoulders and scooped low along the top of her breasts.

"Fir'ah? Are you feeling better? Can you move around?
Can you walk?" J'erik scrambled from the bed to sit beside her.

Eyes frontal, her head moved to monitor his approach.
Something in the way she gazed back without blinking
kept him from embracing her.

"Fir'ah, will you answer me?"

She looked away, turning her head instead of moving
her eyes. Her hands balled into fists.

The old door hinges creaked. Kali-te shuffled through

and closed the door with a swing of her heel. J'erik glanced over, noticing the black mantilla of mourning still around her shoulders. He looked back at Fir'ah, sickened, and hid his face in his hands.

Kali-te set two hot bowls on a rock slab separating the beds and began digging through her robes. "Feed your sister, J'erik Betweener. She is at least among the living. She does not need pity, she needs food."

J'erik thumbed tears from his cheeks before they wound into his beard. Guilt, that he had trespassed upon the sanctuary of her mind and produced a havoc she could not tolerate, enveloped him. He felt he should have known better than to fool with something he did not understand. The cost had been high. Too high. In the name of love, he grieved, in the name of love I have destroyed her mind by forcing her through those memories. I am worse than T'lar. His lust did not kill her body. I have made her a walking ghost.

Dutifully, he retrieved the bowl and fed his sister, then himself. Kali-te roamed the cubicle gathering one thing, then another, and shoving the items into packs and duffles.

Fir'ah allowed J'erik to assist her from the bed and across the room. Her coordination had not suffered; though the movements were lackadaisical, the muscles were rigid, ready to strike out at the slightest provocation. Her head remained turned to watch her brother.

"Take care of her personal needs and wash her up. Get back here as soon as you can," Kali-te said, folding blankets still warm from the girl's body heat.

The old woman was sitting on the foot of his bed when they returned. "Bolt the door."

J'erik did so, looking questioningly at her.

She did not speak until he had moved close enough for her to whisper. An old kaloer parchment filled the hand brought from under her overlapped robes. "Take this. Follow the markers and get Fir'ah to your father.

"When I was a girl and taken to my first Meet, I saw another who once spoke and laughed, but no longer remembered how. Many cycles later, I saw her again. They had taught her her memories again.

"You must go now. Ulni-da is in a trance. She cries much and is afraid." A mass of grayish hair swung over the

60

black robes when her head shook. "It is not good. Take Fir'ah and go. Go as fast as you can from here. The Hold is dead. Nothing can save it." Kali-te pressed the map into J'erik's hand. Tears brimmed her red eyes. "You and Fir'ah are the Ah-te Stronghold. You are the future. If there were some way to save Star-ii . . . but there is not. Uli does not favor the light-skinned."

J'erik squatted in front of the old woman. "You have seen something. I know you have the Gift. Tell me."

Head bowed, "I have seen Cassilee swallow the Ah-te. I have seen death, J'erik." Looking up, a tear working along the deep wrinkles in the hollows of her eyes, "I did not see yours or Fir'ah's. Go now, and lend truth to my vision."

"Come with us, Kali-te. There is a way." He grabbed her hand in both of his.

"I am old. I cannot be anything but a burden. If there is such a way, Betweener, take Star-ii. You must hurry. Time is short."

"I will take you and Star-ii. Dress in all your robes and mantillas. Cover every part of yourself; fingers, toes, everything. Only your eyes may show. I will find a barrow cart for you and Star-ii to ride in."

"No. You will have three burdens then."

"You will not be a burden, Kali-te. I will need someone to look after them while I sleep. I can't do both."

She wiggled her hand free and stood. "I will prepare Star-ii. Her mother must be consulted. When she is ready, you will have to hurry."

As soon as Kali-te left, J'erik strapped packs on Fir'ah and himself. A quick check substantiated Kali-te's usual thoroughness.

Carrying the duffles, he escorted Fir'ah out of the room they had shared for as long as he could remember. The emptiness of it matched the stark furnishings. Pictures carefully drawn and dyed upon the walls bespoke the growing years. The early ones were darkened by the residue of each new calidrium that was lit. The one of their mother, drawn and dyed jointly, between their sleeping places, looked back. She had been a direct descendant of the Hold founders and always seemed to impart a sense of age. Now, J'erik thought she did not look any older than Fir'ah.

Mentally, he said goodbye and thought he heard an echo from his sister. Her expression did not change. Imagination, he decided, and closed the door.

The silence over the Hold whispered doom. Walking the corridors, J'erik wondered if his depression and guilt concerning Fir'ah obliterated the tiny amount of precognition he may have held in common with those in the Hold. Just as well, he mused. I am different enough without something else I don't understand.

Star-ii, her mother and Kali-te huddled across a table in the Common. J'erik stopped short. Fir'ah took six steps then halted.

Cor-ii stood, secured her robes and worked on Star-ii's. "You offer hope for my daughter, Betweener. Do you also offer hope to me?"

"I cannot offer you the same promise of safety as Star-ii, but you are welcome to come. Kali-te? I need you. Please come with us."

As an answer, Kali-te lifted a pack from the table and strapped it on. The tremendous sorrow remained etched into the lines on her face.

"I would take any who would travel with us," J'erik said.

"No others will go," Cor-ii answered. "I go with Star-ii. If you are wrong, Betweener, I will find a way to kill you before I die."

"I'm gonna be a Betweener," Star-ii sang, excited. "I'm gonna be a Betweener."

J'erik smiled at the child and took an extra duffle sack from Kali-te. "Step inside, little girl. You are not a Betweener, so we must hide you from Uli. You will ride." He pulled the bag up to her neck and explained what could happen if she decided to peek out before he declared it safe. Cor-ii placed a kiss on the child's mouth and lifted the ends over her head for J'erik to fasten.

J'erik lifted her, unable to suppress the smile her contagious giggle instigated. Her delight penetrated the cloth and broke the solemnity in the Common. He placed her in the foraging barrow among the extra duffles stuffed with climbing gear, removed his burdens and used them to pad the high wooden sides. Kali-te packed pots and utensils into the corners and motioned for Cor-ii. Separate pouches of dried kodjelu, panaver strips, gadid raisins and dehydrated amilglib slivers were stashed through the booty. Waterskins were placed around the sides and lashed to the packs. The last item was a container of grease. The four wheels moved without a squeak.

J'erik rolled the escape stone back and checked Cor-ii and Kali-te, tying off their garb securely against the wind. The women took opposite ends of the harness and pulled the barrow through the opening with little room to spare.

Fir'ah followed, eyes straight ahead and expressionless.

J'erik waited beside the stone. As Fir'ah walked ahead, he knew his business with the Ah-te was incomplete. T'lar lived and breathed. He wanted revenge. And perhaps killing T'lar might absolve some of the guilt he felt.

The women whispered for him to hurry.

J'erik stared over the empty tables, beyond the wall hangings decorating the Common, to the slender gap leading to the caverns.

He heard the cart bump over the uneven passage worn smooth by sandals and the thousands of wheels passing through over the centuries.

T'lar waited.

"There is something I must do," he said to the women.

Kali-te's voice wound out of the shadows. "There is no time for revenge now, Betweener. Cassilee will deal with him."

"It is a matter of honor. Fir'ah's honor. And my honor."

"Will there be honor when we are among the dead?" The cart stopped. Kali-te continued speaking. "Will wasting the time to kill him restore Fir'ah? Will it make her whole? Will it put distance between us and the Ah-te?" The cart started with a rattle. "Come Cor-ii, Fir'ah. We have a journey to make."

J'erik crossed the Common with long strides. Instinct filled his right hand with the knife. He would settle up with T'lar. Maybe it wasn't the ideal plan he wished there were time for, but it was a settlement nonetheless. The rage driving him quieted for the hunter to stalk his prey. J'erik climbed the steps to the caverns. Not a sound betrayed his advance. His eyes adjusted to the shadows and patches of complete darkness. He listened, sorting the normal sounds of dripping water and gurgling pools.

In the cavern he clung to the blackness, using all of his

instincts in the search for T'lar. He wound through the back trails, moved closer to the maw and crisscrossed a second pattern.

There was a familiarity in the exercise which made him think he had lived through it before. He tried to shake it. The *déjà vu* lingered.

"T'lar! T'lar!" He waited out the echo, listened hard for a new sound.

Water dripped down the stalactites and onto the limestone piled below. The pools bubbled undisturbed. Luminous columns stood mute and glistened in solitude.

He ran down the main path to the entrance.

Wind sideswiped the rocks. The hot blasts pulled air from his lungs. He turned back, sick with the realization that T'lar had escaped, unpunished for the atrocity. He wanted to blame T'lar for everything. Guilt refused acquiescence to rationalization. The choice to experiment with what he did not understand had been a conscious one. That he had to accept without knowing what went wrong.

Slowly at first, then running, he left the cavern, descended the steps and crossed the Common. He rolled the stone into place and ran through the passage. The women were struggling with the cart half a kilometer ahead. He caught up and donned the harness.

Another half a kilometer passed silently. Resignedly, he took a bearing. The old map was worthless in the wake of the Star Demons. Even the direction to the Techi was distorted. The changes in Cassilee obliterated at least the first two sanctuaries noted on the route.

Majestic buttes connected to mold a solid wall on both sides of the vast lowland they walked. The Star Demons' sculpting had removed the taluses built at their bases for long stretches. J'erik angled southwest at a diagonal to take advantage of the easy traveling on the flat, hoping to end up near a climbable scree at the escarpment.

As Uli moved into the west, the small caravan crossed the valley floor. The women, driven by an unseen panic, shoved and pulled the cart, talking to Star-ii when the trek eased in spots. The double-banded harness cut into J'erik's chest and shoulders, diverting rivers of perspiration into the folds of his shirt. The leveling of the ground made the mountains appear higher, jagged, not rounded by weather and time. Darker rock showed where the softer edges and mounds ceased to exist. An ocher film shifted in waves along their ankles in the wind. Small plants fought grit for a share of Uli's light.

Once, J'erik looked to the north, thinking about the calantani and the adventure he would have chosen under different circumstances. Cor-ii brought water, refusing alternate shares herself and urging him to consume enough to maintain his strength. The women balked when he suggested they stop and eat. When Star-ii sided with him, Cor-ii gave the girl a stern tongue-lashing which kept her silent for a hand against the sun. J'erik turned quiet also, sensing the force driving the two women as relentless.

When long shadows stretched from the tops of the western escarpment, J'erik became the one who drove them. A kilometer away, a rock slab rested over part of an eroded talus. The women pushed the cart, Kali-te goading Fir'ah into action.

At the edge of the slab J'erik unstrapped the harness and sat. Cor-ii, Kali-te and Fir'ah slumped beside him, too tired to complain about the wasted time. They rested and drank sparingly.

"Where do we go now?" Cor-ii asked.

J'erik pointed to the sky.

Relief and worry crept into her words. "It will take us all night. Perhaps the next generation of Betweeners will have wings."

Thinking of Diearka, "Perhaps one day this generation will, too." He studied the sky. First-magnitude stars were fighting with Uli. "I have ridden with the calantani through the day. Once I touched a cloud."

Cor-ii and Kali-te became statues etched in disbelief. Fir'ah wandered up the rock.

"Get Star-ii out of the cart. She'll have to walk now. We must climb this tonight. Then we can rest." J'erik unlashed his packs and pulled out coils of rope and tackle. Fir'ah ambled back to the cart. Three packs were strapped to her back. The older women each carried two, as did Star-ii, whose energy was boundless.

J'erik scrambled to the top of the scree and climbed the face for twenty meters before finding a strong outcrop to fasten his pulley network in. It took a quarter of the night to hoist the cart beyond the scree and up to the first ledge a hundred more meters up. J'erik left the group and attacked the next section.

He found a cave sufficient to accommodate them and the wagon. The hoist-and-pulley system was set into stone again. The women would not be able to climb. The facade was difficult for him, an experienced man.

He called down to Cor-ii and had her fasten the rope lattice he made around her. She was strong and could help pull up the rest.

Star-ii and half the duffles were second, then Fir'ah and her burdens. Kali-te was last.

J'erik used the pulleys to slide down to the cart. The women worked the remaining packs and duffles up. Pots clanged against the stone. Utensils clattered like muffled chimes.

The cart was easy to tie off. Getting it up the face in one piece was another matter.

The first rays of light were poking into the black night by the time the group settled. Star-ii slept with her mother, sharing the tiredness all of them felt.

J'erik watched the valley for a while, too exhausted to sleep.

It bothered him.

Twice he thought he detected movement on the lowland. T'lar was on Cassilee's skin. Somewhere. Worse, he had not seen any calantani. It was difficult to believe they had fled, territorial creatures that they were.

He rubbed his forehead. Nothing fit into carefully labeled bins anymore. Lord Chamblis and his tribe had a home, yet they wandered, belying the little he really knew about the species as a whole.

One thing became clear in the mire. If the calantani were still in residence, then the Star Demons were coming, or they were already here.

J'erik glanced at the heights, hoping to find food and nothing else waiting when they climbed again.

Chapter 8

A BASS RUMBLE CURDLED THE SURFACE OF Cassilee. The vibrations reached a magnitude sufficient to disturb her bowels. She snarled back, exposing her fangs. Screaming earthquakes rocked the vertical escarpments on both sides of the lowland. Far in the south, a fissure opened, a narrow ribbon at first, then stretching, unraveling along the flats, groaning and protesting, pushing the rift wider and farther.

Steam belched through the wound, whistling and roaring the ire of Cassilee imprisoned within the depths. Pungent air ate the drier atmosphere and coated the buttes with a hot moisture. Billows rose, so many clouds freed to look down upon the ruins. As though content with the extent of her assault, Cassilee ended the rift two kilometers north of where her tirade was witnessed by a lone Betweener protecting his traveling Hold.

Before the awesome noise trapped between the high walls escaped, a second sound mingled with it. Through the curtains of steam racing in all directions, three bright stars blinked alive. The noise changed.

J'erik scrambled back into the cave's protection. Curious, Star-ii tried to get around him to see the chaos. J'erik scooped her up and carried her under his arm shouting orders to Cor-ii and Kali-te. Seconds later they were huddled as far into the recess as it went. The cart afforded a scant amount of additional protection.

The light came, prying, poking, turning into the nooks and crannies, seeking to touch the sample of humanity pressed into a corner. The intensity of the small finger groping the opposite wall caused Kali-te to cry out in fear. Star-ii whimpered, caught in the panic of the two older women. Fir'ah watched, unblinking.

Cassilee rumbled and groaned. Her cries muted. A fury possessed the land, shaking the looser rock from the ceiling and bouncing the ground as though it were a sea cresting full waves during the height of a storm. Dirt-laden air choked their dry throats and triggered harsh coughs.

Despair lodged within J'erik. Surely Cassilee had turned against them and sided with the Star Demons to rid her of the life plaguing her skin. He was a parasite she wished to be rid of and she had finally found a way to do it. If she could not panic them into the terror by ravaging the flatland, she would choke them to death with the remnants.

The cacophony lapsed. The particles swirling through the air began to settle as an ocher film painting the land inside and out. By the time J'erik ventured to the mouth on his hands and knees, the dust outside had cleared.

The eastern rise had changed little. New screes had accumulated at the bases, as was the case with the section they occupied. The stone slab used as an aid during the climb was covered. To the south, the land was as flat as the day before; not a seam showed where Cassilee had belched a protest.

For a moment, it occurred to him that he was losing his mind. Star-ii's whimpering and Cor-ii's soothing croon laced with fear assured him that the events were real. Only the major proof was absent.

He leaned out to see north. The Ah-te was too far away and behind a lazy meander.

The sound of crying, deep sobs, touched his ears. It was distant, muffled, yet close simultaneously. A wind swept up dust devils and carried the lament away. He listened hard, wondering if it was T'lar or a figment of his imagination playing with the erratic gusts.

Finally, he turned back to the group. Fir'ah stood immediately and began pulling on backpacks. If she was willing to move onto the surface, perhaps the same sensations which told her it was safe before were still in play. Hoping, he trusted her ability to detect the Demon threat. He helped the older women adjust their robes and load burdens.

Star-ii followed the women up a ledge which brought them within reach of the top of the cliff to a plateau twenty meters up. The realities of the dangers found on the surface temporarily vanquished the joys of childhood. She carried a pack and held the safety rope, her small fingers barely fitting around the wrap protecting her skin and the line.

J'erik employed the ropes and pulley rig to get the cart topside. At their present speed, barring more outbursts perpetuated by the Star Demons and too drastic a change in the topography, he felt they could reach the Techi in nine to eleven revolutions.

Fancher welded a patch onto his spare ground suit. The silvery luster was out of place on the dull surface. It reflected sunlight, which otherwise presented a problem when he embarked on the journey he had in mind.

Armed with the Destro-Lase II and a sling box over his left shoulder, Fancher sealed the ship from the outside. The morning sun bleaching the land was shielded by a light helmet he had worn on roving expeditions before the crash. The suit helped keep him cool without the power pack it connected to under normal circumstances.

The waking periods had melted away during his familiarization with the surroundings. He spent hours extrapolating the conditions and their changes. Whole days fled while he tried to needle bits of information from the nearly destroyed data banks in the cockpit.

Today, instead of walking circles around the ship and adjacent areas, he decided to go south, the direction the Bronze Foot in the illusion took. Loneliness had a way of solidifying his dreams. He did not want to believe that there were no humans, but without a confirmation in hard facts, he was too much a realist, afraid to hope. Even the incidents leading to the *Minaho*'s override left a doubt.

While the wounds healed, his health improved and the time became more difficult to fill. As he waited for his strength to return, acute aloneness was harder to bear.

Walking south, he thought of Mikel, and wondered if

his friend thought about him. Ironic, he mused. If he finds out anything, especially about the crash, he's gonna have a rough decision.

Fancher's sardonic laugh gushed out of the helmet. "You don't expect him to cut his financial throat, do you? No . . . Poor Mikel's about to find that not everybody is a humanitarian." Muttering, "About time he learned a few things," he kicked a rock and looked up at a clear sky, a paler blue than when he first arrived on Cassilee. "You hear me, Mik? I miss you . . . I miss everybody."

He kept walking and checked the time. Another twenty minutes before turnaround. Tomorrow, the target would increase by two hours, doubling today's.

The geography varied little from the view near the ship. The depth of the lowlands was impressive on foot. It imparted a sensation of his insignificance that the ship had protected him from during fly-bys. He tried to imagine the barren rocks as green and fertile with an array of grasses, fruit-bearing vines, trees and shrubs; with the first strain of herbivores roaming the highlands, multiplying their numbers until the second, third and fourth lines were brought in with carnivores.

Cassilee was difficult to imagine any way other than how she was.

He approached an iron tree. The trunk diameter was an easy seven gnarled meters. The monster looked able to withstand the harshest of Cassilee's moods, but could it survive mellow kindness and an abundance of water and nutrients?

He kicked at a clump of leaves. A large object jumped and thudded.

Fancher bent over and picked it up. Heart beating rapidly, he turned it over and over. Tears stung his eyes.

Fir'ah's backpack was primitive by his standards, but it was the most beautiful thing he had seen on Cassilee. He removed a glove, letting it dangle on the suit sleeve. Touching the rough, dung-colored material was to touch viable hope. Even if the Bronze Foot was illusion, here was a tangible; proof someone, or something, intelligent dwelled in the hostile environment.

He glanced around, desperate to find a sign of life or a hint of an abode. It took several minutes for him to think rationally and begin a systematic process of elimination.

He continued south, holding the pack to his chest, running flights and surveys through his memory. The last scan, the most important one, had indicated one life form in the cliffs and another on the lowlands. It seemed likely he would have received readings earlier if they were cliff dwellers.

Calculating, searching, Fancher had moved quickly while the sun climbed. He was ready to turn back when a jag in the cliff exposed a mound and rugged hill formation on the lowland. A pair of binoculars came out of the sling box.

Great cracks and several deep chasms appeared as dark streaks in the sun. There was something unnatural about the mound. It took several seconds for it to register. The chambers deep in the far center were too regular.

He readjusted the binoculars.

What was that in the largest pockmark? "Is that a table?" He looked again, trying to distinguish the ruins with an unbiased eye. The table no longer looked like one. Even so, a pattern of destroyed halls and rooms was evident.

Time and distance since he started were greater than Fancher had planned on for several days. The steepness of the cliff plummeted to the lowlands, curtailing further explorations. Fatigue oozed over the exuberance that hope had nurtured.

Fighting depression and the pain in his shoulder, Fancher retreated to an iron tree and dropped in the shade. He rested against the trunk. Idly, he opened the pack; a thin coil of crude but strong rope, three pouches of dried food, a waterskin and a long-sleeved robe. The fabric was unlike any he had seen on either civilized or colonized worlds. The weightlessness was incongruous with the thickness and size. Dyed threads formed pictures of the surface, as it was before the latest phase of development, and symbols of a culture. There were no people depicted. The scenes were uneven, those down the left side showing outer Cassilee in more detail, less quantity, than those on the right portraying domestic items.

He wanted another look at the table that wasn't a table. Maybe it really was. He pushed to his feet, leg muscles twitching a protest. He held the robe for a comparison.

The valley groaned alive. Rock slides and an abrasive clatter summoned him to the edge again.

Water moved down the center of the great riverbed. From the heights it looked unhurried and benign. Behind the moody spearhead, a dark body fanned out to the cliffs, teasing the screes and coaxing the supports to journey along the newest change.

On the edge of the creaking plateau, Fancher watched the muddy death in the chasm. It moved steadily, changing the spearhead, meandering lethargically toward the bend where the ground humped over the Ah-te. From the mound came an earsplitting roar. Water shot into the air. Debris belched up with the force and scattered before landing.

Quickly, the binoculars tried to focus on the remnants. After one look, they dropped painfully around Fancher's neck.

It was a table.

The hand of death reached from the heart of Cassilee and spread a depression across the land. Fancher felt the ominous weight and responded by shaking his fist at the sky, yelling, while the tears stinging his eyes fell to the ground. Hopelessness woven through the presence of death increased the anger. That anger cursed the terraformers, proclaiming their ineptitude and lack of human parentage.

Eventually, the ire played out. Water bubbled near the top of the mound, fighting the geyser into submission. Fancher staggered back to the iron tree, retrieved the pack and started home.

A shadow flew over the land.

Numb, he gazed over the river valley.

A monstrous orange creature flew circles at the center near the geyser. Hard musical notes sounded as a cry. The beast dipped and soared, searching for something he could not find.

Fancher continued walking in the open. The beast ignored him, though part of Fancher wished the thing would attack and relieve him of his life.

Long after the orange thing had disappeared, Fancher wondered if he was the larger, stronger reading in the cliff the day of his crash. If so, then perhaps the weaker one was human. The idea appealed to him. The *Minaho*'s top officers did have something to worry about if he lived. It lent a tiny comfort that some other life form shared his misery and rage at being left alone.

They traveled by night and by day, stopping to sleep when J'erik could pull no farther. Cassilee remained quiet. The calantani flew against the stars and the bright fuzzy light cluster moving with the night across the southern section. They too seemed wary and kept a distance from J'erik's party, which would have seemed easy prey a short time ago.

The days passed, uncounted by any other than J'erik. The iron trees became more abundant, the trunks larger than around the Ah-te. Vines—not gadid, some other kind he was unfamiliar with, possibly ilankor—grew between the trees, tying one trunk in with the next like a net. The fleecy purple leaves twirled in the smallest breeze. They bounced back and forth between coiled tendrils. Huge yellow fruit hung below the thick purple ceiling, double globules connected by a thin red fiber a couple of centimeters long. The areas where iron branches hung out amilglibs were empty of the vine, as though an invisible hand had reached down to define the growth areas. Below, tunnels wound into foreign mazes. The thickness overhead denied a glance at Uli which might lend a sense of direction.

J'erik scouted both directions and found no way around the purple, short of a three-day detour back into the valley they had just crossed.

They ventured inside the eerie world, Kali-te making marks on the gargantuan iron trunks. Soon, multilegged creatures, ten to twelve meters long, watched from the lush walls. As J'erik penetrated, they became braver. The most brazen one, larger than the others visible, came up to J'erik and bent to his hip with the side of a furry face. The two-meter-high head was slightly larger than the long convoluted body striped with alternating moppy chartreuse and bright yellow against deep-green body fur.

The legs were a series of right angles, out from the body, turned down and finally straight on the ground. Twelve-centimeter barbs, black, the color of the legs, formed alternating rows on four sides of each leg. The wide earthpads at the end of the legs supported the body weight. Barbs peppered the tops in all directions. Exactly how many legs the creature possessed was difficult for J'erik to estimate, but a couple of hundred seemed a reasonable guess. They were well spaced and appeared to close, forming a phalanx, if the furry body contracted.

He stroked the long-haired chartreuse stripe near the beast's solid-green eyes, each one the size of his spread hand. A narrow area of long black bristles separated the eyes and reached into circles. Two dark holes in the fur under each eye inhaled and exhaled. Crouching down, J'erik saw the mouth. He continued petting, far more gently than previously.

The mouth could have belonged to an herbivore and a carnivore at the same time. It opened the full width of the head, the lower jaw flatter and shaped like a shovel at the bottom. J'erik wished he could take the creature out to the light in order to see how the fangs and molars fit together amid the smaller blunt and pointed assortment. A flat tongue rolled into the top of the mouth. With astonishing speed, it unfurled and licked J'erik's hand.

Star-ii squirmed away from her mother and ran to J'erik. "He's pretty," she said, reaching out to the creature.

Cor-ii ran to grab the child.

The creature's legs began to close as the long body contracted. A low growl erupted from his mouth. Green saliva drooled from between two bottom fangs. The faster-than-light tongue retrieved it before it hit the ground.

Cor-ii froze in terror, able only to gape at the threat to her daughter.

Fir'ah dropped her packs and sauntered into the tableau. As soon as she reached Cor-ii, she shoved her away from Star-ii and began stroking the chartreuse mop. The beast tilted his head, nuzzling her, and lifted off the first two sets of legs, still managing to keep his head low. He gave her his undivided attention. Fir'ah's facial muscles worked in tiny jerks and spasms.

Star-ii giggled and petted the soft underneck. Two tendril feelers shot from both sides of the beast's face and petted the child in reciprocation, knocking the head covering away to expose the thickness of her jet-black hair. Her laughter floated through the winding tunnels and inspired an imitation of the sound from the onlooking creatures. Delighted by their participation, Star-ii departed from the leader and ran to the nearest one in a connecting tunnel. She petted him along the yellow stripe, then moved on, as each lowered his head to receive the touch.

Soothed by Kali-te, Cor-ii managed to contain her fears into small sobs muffled by the back of her bound hand.

You have traveled far, Betweener. Have you much to go before reaching your destination?

J'erik drew back.

The creature weaved upon his legs, his tremendous head higher than J'erik's.

This second of Cassilee's creatures intelligent enough to communicate was magnificent. They seemed to have no shame when invading another's mind to convey messages. He glanced at Fir'ah. She looked back at him for several seconds, turned away and retrieved her packs.

I am called J'erik of the Ah-te Hold where the flatlands are many levels.

Forgive the intrusion, J'erik Betweener. We have been expecting you for many of Uli's journey. I am Lorff, Master of the Zanstyrs.

You've been expecting me?

The head swung to the side. *Perhaps not exactly you, but a Betweener like you.*

J'erik was confused. Why should they expect anyone?

The onlookers moved in beside the leader. A circle formed around J'erik. Star-ii called for them to come and play. None gave her a second glance. They rose upon their third and fourth sets of legs, totally obscuring J'erik from his group.

J'erik looked from one to the other, noting the variations in the head stripes and first sets of legs. Slowly, his hand crawled up his hip to his knife.

Yes. That is part of it, conveyed Lorff. *We can afford no weakness in the Betweener we follow. I have tried to probe your mind and found nothing but barriers. Will you not let me in?*

J'erik's eyes narrowed. The furrow in his brow deepened.

Lorff issued the equivalent of a sigh. *Disappointment would have been mine if you had agreed. Now, I must ask if you are willing to fight one of my warriors.*

And if I am not?

You and the other Betweener are free to leave the way you came. Do not venture into our domain again.

The two women and the child of the Ah-te?

They will stay. They are not Betweeners and should never have left the Hold. The terms are simple. If you win, you are Master of this domain and we are bonded to you. If you lose, the Betweener woman goes back to where you entered the maze. The others will not see Uli on the morrow. If it is a good fight and you manage to score before the warrior kills you, your friends will greet death swiftly.

J'erik fought the rage boiling inside. He was trapped, and the weight of his party's fate burdened him greatly. A snarl hardened his mouth.

You are disturbed, Betweener. Do you not live life on an all-or-nothing basis as does the rest of Cassilee?

No, I do not. Even Cassilee compromises.

Very well. The child may leave with the Betweener woman in any event. Is that sufficient compromise?

No. I am Leader of this Hold. I alone am responsible for invading your territory. Therefore I alone should pay the consequences of that act. Is that not all or nothing and to your way of thinking? If I fight and win, I am the undisputed Leader and share that command with no one else. If I fight and lose, you have my life and I have nothing.

Lorff considered for a moment before speaking to the gathered zanstyrs. His voice transcended octaves from low-toned guttural utterings to high-pitched squeaking.

J'erik glanced from one to the other, trying to guess which would be his opponent. All looked formidable.

We have reached a consensus. The lightness of his communication denoted either mirth or amusement. J'erik did not doubt the agreement was reached prior to Lorff's poll of the other zanstyrs. *I think perhaps it is us who live with compromise, not you, J'erik Betweener. It will be as you request. We will see if you are as good with your knife as you are with words and leadership. Be it known that you have my respect.*

And I have your word my Hold will be escorted out of the maze before Uli sleeps tonight, in the event I forfeit my life?

76

Lorff bowed and lowered onto all of his legs. *You have my word.*

J'erik had trouble understanding why Lorff's word for the safety of his Hold made a difference. But it did. The weight of leadership lifted a yoke, balancing the burden. They were close enough to the Techi for the older women to take charge and arrive safely, barring additional encounters such as this.

The zanstyrs withdrew slowly, their barbed legs clattering against their neighbors'. J'erik moved back also. Beside the cart where Cor-ii held a firm grip on Star-ii and Kali-te waited with Fir'ah, he dropped his packs. He took Kali-te aside and explained what had transpired as rapidly as possible. As he spoke, he stripped away excess clothing, keeping only his loincloth.

A flurry of noise and creaking vines yielding to the zanstyrs enlarged the clearing into a fighting arena. A shallow gully defined the limits.

J'erik looked at each member of his small Hold. There was a freedom in fighting for only his survival which made part of him look forward to the battle.

Cassilee had tested him many times, many ways.

He looked across to Lorff.

She had never tested him in this manner.

Chapter 9

THE RANKS OF ZANSTYRS PARTED. A BROWN-striped warrior moved from the rear. His size was comparable to Lorff's. He moved rhythmically, keeping his body contracted so his opponent could not fit through his legs.

J'erik studied the beast, searching for vulnerable points, limitations and advantages he might capitalize upon. Logic denied any shred of hope for a victory on the physical plane. Cunningness became his best asset. He would have to outmaneuver and outguess the warrior. Warrior. The title alone put the fear of a premature union with Cassilee's ground into him.

The warrior waited at the edge of the arena.

J'erik tossed the knife from his right hand to his left, flexing his fingers and gauging the grip. He shook his shoulders and legs, trying to work his tensions into a lower key.

Fir'ah approached, holding out the calantani rope. He took it and slipped it over his neck, managing a feeble smile in the process.

There was no return smile. She stared at him as though wanting to say something which refused to be vocalized. J'erik took her hand and pulled her to him. The response to his embrace was forced, as though it pained her to be touched in any manner. She ran to the cart as soon as he let go.

Whooping and low rumbles marked the zanstyr's readiness for battle.

J'erik turned his undivided attention to the arena.

The warrior began crossing the gully, spreading the convolutions of his body to breach the gap and keeping to the perimeter as he moved.

J'erik waited until he was halfway into the arena before leaping the boundary. Contracted as he was, J'erik figured the zanstyr's length at an easy twelve meters. Stretched, he could be as long as fifteen or twenty.

The warrior moved cautiously, sizing up his opponent as he was being sized up. Feelers were halfway extended from the sides of his face, twitching.

The legs were an army of soldiers, armed and ready for attack, always prepared for a defensive role. Watching the move, J'erik saw no way to break through to the soft body riding above and below. Even were he to reach it, he had no idea where the vulnerable parts were located or how to kill the beast. He too kept to the outer part of the arena, watching, figuring, looking for an edge. He moved as the warrior moved, maintaining a distance between the maw and the lightning tongue it housed.

A translucent membrane blinked over the warrior's eyes. The zanstyr's head dipped.

J'erik kicked up dust and dragged his feet as he followed the circular retreat pattern between the front and back of the warrior.

The beast blinked again, bowing his head in the process.

J'erik feinted an attack.

The warrior's head stayed bowed, the mouth opened to the restless flicking of the tongue.

The back legs of the warrior continued moving when the front ones stopped.

J'erik backpedaled hurriedly. The beast was about to spring. He grinned, noting the tension ripples in the high fur along the brown back. He angled toward the center, diminishing the warrior's strike effectiveness. The massive body did not seem agile enough to throw a springing thrust on an acute angle.

The zanstyr sprang. He shot into the air and lunged for the angle J'erik had chosen. The maw opened to the full extent, dislocating the hinge bones at the jaw. The feelers whirled, whips singing in the air. The tongue shot out and wrapped around J'erik's thigh as he dove into the center of the arena.

Instantly, he began slashing at the tongue. It dragged him four meters before he cut through. The main part retracted into the safety of the maw. Dark-green syrup oozed from the injured end. The warrior began to reposition for the next assault.

The tongue section around J'erik's leg remained fast, tightening each time he moved. On his feet and watching the opponent, he slipped the tip of his knife under the edge of the segment and sliced downward. The piece fell away. An angry red-purple ring throbbed around his thigh. The self-inflicted gash stung mildly in comparison. The remnant writhed violently on the ground for several seconds before it stiffened in death. An exaggerated limp made the warrior brave. He moved closer.

J'erik waited, wanting the beast to lunge again.

The zanstyr anticipated the Betweener and refused the bait at the last instant. He backed away and assumed an it's-your-turn-to-attack attitude.

The mood of battle changed.

Each time J'erik moved, the zanstyr countered defensively, too swiftly for a reflex action. The warrior was just too big to be able to react that fast. It seemed the beast knew his plans before they became actions.

Suspicious, J'erik reinforced the barriers of his mind and reexamined his qualms concerning the invasion of another's thoughts. Seconds later he experienced the invisible pressure of one trying to probe the barriers. Furious, he struck back at the warrior, venting his rage.

The zanstyr reared back. His head cut hard arcs in the air.

J'erik moved swiftly, running at the exposed underside, shifting the knife to his left hand, where it plunged into the fur and sliced half a meter before he twisted and spun into the center of the arena.

The warrior lifted higher, the hundred legs acting as a catapult which hurled the bulk at the smaller target.

J'erik ran at him, both hands holding the knife high so it cut into the underside. The force unbalanced him. Shock rocked his left shoulder and arm. A snapping in the wrist made his hand useless. The right hand com-

81

pensated. He held the knife tightly as he cleared the body.

The beast's legs closed in midflight.

J'erik ducked and rolled along the ground. An earthpad barb caught him across the back and laid open the skin from his left shoulder to his right hip. The blow halted a momentum which would have carried him out of the arena and into forfeit territory.

The warrior oozed thick green blood from two places on his body and drooled it from his mouth.

Any reservations over using the mind link to destroy the opponent evaporated when J'erik realized his position.

The zanstyr occupied the center of the arena. Though moving slowly because of his wounds, the warrior was stretching out his body to seal J'erik against the boundary. The legs worked like well-oiled machines gauged to precision and maintained an equidistant tolerance not allowing the penetration of a man. J'erik did not have to probe the beast's mind to know what came next.

Sidestepping, he closed in on the head.

The warrior could not expand and seal the area without breaking the uniformity of his legs. He hesitated, undecided in his fear of the small opponent.

J'erik continued to approach the head.

The near feeler extended and began to spin.

J'erik tightened his grip on the knife pressed against his thigh. Quickly, he brought it up and stabbed at the invisible circle. The force shook his arm into his body.

The maw opened with a roar. Green saliva coated the molars and fangs. The tongue stayed retracted.

J'erik sidestepped again, not giving the beast an angle, yet careful to stay beyond the reach of the legs.

The warrior shook his massive head from side to side, the brown stripe flinging his length the opposite way in long, snapping whips. J'erik pulled free of the beast's mind, the frustration and terror more than he wanted to know of the warrior. Death hovered over the brown hunk, though not so close that his course was unchangeable.

The head jerked left, then right, and left again.

J'erik charged, the knife in his teeth. He straight-armed the neck, grabbed a handful of fur and hurled his weight onto the zanstyr. He scrambled for the top.

The warrior lifted, trying to unload the burden, coiling as tightly as he could, nearly coming back on himself. He sprang from one side of the arena to the other, flailing his legs and head, spewing green blood onto the spectators.

J'erik held with his good hand, knees and feet. For the moment, his attack had reached maximum effectiveness.

The hindquarter sagged and fell. The front teetered until the line of feet formed a prod against the hindquarter. The slight lull in the frenzy let J'erik catch his breath. He steadied behind the head, leaned forward, grabbed the knife from between his teeth and sliced it through the zanstyr's lips and cheek where the jaw hinged. He flipped the knife into a stabbing grip. He opened his mouth and clamped his teeth onto green-splattered brown fur. It took three tries with the lurching warrior fighting against him to shatter the dislocation hinge on the right side of the jaw. The skin tore into the fur as the weight of the teeth dragged the shovel mouth to the ground. The left side snapped, but did not tear.

This time when he invaded the warrior's mind, he listened to a plea for a swifter, kinder death. This he promised. The zanstyr's legs buckled, first the left side, nearly unseating J'erik.

Holding the knife in his teeth, green blood running down his chin and onto his chest, he felt for the life column at the base of the skull. His useless left hand dangled over the mark. The knife slammed point first into the center of the column. A geyser of green shot two meters into the air.

The warrior collapsed instantly. Death was his.

The digestive system excreted body water and matter to mingle with the green river flowing into a lake at the center of the arena.

Slowly, J'erik got to his feet and walked through the fur on the warrior's back. He looked at the spectators, who had not uttered a sound, not even Star-ii. He shook his head, sending green droplets into the air. Not a centimeter of his bronze skin was untouched by the blood he had spilled.

His eyes met Lorff's.

Lorff led the zanstyrs in a subservient bow. *It would appear that you are truly Master.*

J'erik shook his head in disbelief. Winning had not

eased the burden. It had restored it with the end of the battle and increased it.

Whatever I am or am not, Lorff, this day has had a hand in molding us with the battle forced upon this warrior and me today. I do not condemn your life code. I state what is true. He glanced down. A warm breeze whispering in the vines overhead reached down to ruffle the brown fur. *It seems wrong for a life to be thrown away like this. I held no grievances with him.*

Nor did he hold any against you, Master. It is the Order of Life here.

J'erik sighed, giving up the dregs of anger. *Now I am Leader of the Zanstyrs.*

The chartreuse stripe jiggled centimeters from the dirt. *You are Master.*

Looking at his sister and the two women, *I will need an adviser whom I can trust. One who knows the customs and rituals of the zanstyrs. We will require transportation to the Techi. Is there a waterhole where I may clean this warrior's blood from my body?*

Water is a short way to the south. Master, I would be honored if you considered me as a candidate for your adviser.

Nodding, J'erik started to dismount the carcass. *Lorff?*

Yes, Master J'erik?

Does your Order of Life provide for a ritual or burial for this warrior?

Yes, Master.

We will not leave until that is done. He slid off the fur, splattering the green mud with his landing. The strain of the battle began to demand a price. He straightened and crossed the arena.

Kali-te waited at the edge of the gully filled with murky green-brown. "Is it all right?"

J'erik leaped the boundary and nodded. He removed the hair rope and handed it to the old woman, asking her to make a noose on one end and attach the other end to the cart.

The noose tightened around his left hand. Holding his left forearm in his right hand, he pulled against the cart. Sweat popped into the green covering his face. He kept pulling until the wrist straightened and snapped at the joint. He removed the noose and painfully worked the hand and fingers. Suddenly, his whole body ached.

The old woman turned to leave.

"Kali-te? Have I seen all the ancient legends and writings? Is there one which prophesies a Betweener expected by both the calantani and the zanstyrs? Is there one which mentions the zanstyrs?"

"If your destiny were foretold in the legends, there would be nothing you could do to change it, would there?" She did not turn to face him.

"No."

"And did you not just complete a battle which changed your status and destiny?"

J'erik nodded and headed for the waterskins.

"The legends are old dreams written by fearful men."

He would get nothing from old Kali-te today. She required levers, quick wits and a press before yielding information she did not want to give freely.

The cool water helped wash the foul taste of death from his mouth.

Legends, he mused, wiping his beard, have all been lies or clouded truths written by madmen and retold and rewritten by every generation. What difference does it make? What will be, will be.

Rustling leaves beside the cart distracted him. The knife filled his hand.

Star-ii looked up, big black eyes filled with tears, her chin quivering. She brought a hand from behind her and stretched it to J'erik. Little fingers balanced a yellow il-ankor fruit by its red connecting cord. A small bite was missing from the side.

J'erik crouched and reached for the offering. She stepped forward for him to take it. As soon as he did, she ran against him, crying, nearly toppling him as she hugged his neck. He soothed her quietly, stroking her head and assuring her that he was fine. When he glanced up, Cor-ii was standing at the back of the cart, her mouth pinched so tightly that the lines from the corners to her nose had disappeared.

Chapter 10

BY THE TIME FANCHER'S PHYSICAL CONDI-
tion neared a point where he could travel, he had been
ready for well over eight days. Now, the shoulder and
chest wound stayed closed during exercises and trial runs
with full packs. Red scar tissue contained the usual throb.
The deep facial laceration melted to a light pink with
white bridges where the healing was best.

His hatred for the location, which served as a perpetual
reminder of lost hope, spurred his anxiety to get underway. The river, licking stone walls a few meters from the
top of the plateau, whispered at night. And the stone answered back, wooed into the deceptive calm where the
only journey ended at the bottom, not quite so deep as
when the first waters had explored the porous bed.

It took time to strip the Star III Recon Prober of
usable parts, and more time to reassemble them into
what he wanted. Early in the planning, he discovered the
impossibilities of taking along all the things he needed.
More hours went into analyzing and reworking what he
had into at least dual if not three- or four-way functions.

Adapting the force field into a portable unit for protection from any hostile life forms and the weather became the most vital and time-consuming project.

As an experiment, he killed a kodjelu and cooked and
ate it. He strained his memory for bits of information so
easily fed back to the terraformer. Gradually, he re-

membered which plants were edible and what parts. The next kodjelu tasted better in a stew. Efforts to dry the leftovers met moderate success. It was an alternative should the varmints get scarce during the journey. He hoped to acquire a taste for it. It did not seem a realistic hope.

Flexible cable rigging, knotted and wound into coils, sat on the "must take" pile. He decided to wear the coils and the rope found in the backpack. An added hook on his utility belt held the coils. They bounced on his right buttock. An elastic strap took care of the thumping problem without costing mobility.

Several days passed while he made a large pack from fabric and a couple of sections of lightweight, high-strength supports. He was less concerned with making long distances once he started than with establishing a steady pace. In this, Fancher deemed time an ally.

The last night beside the river was the longest one he had spent on Cassilee. Sleep eluded him. Memories of Kreista, Alva, their children and finally his parents and Mikel took turns crowding his thoughts. When the inner visions focused on the one person still alive, Mikel, he thought about Commander Satow and the *Minaho*. He was a cold, cunning man whose personal discipline canceled out emotions.

Watching the parade of stars, it seemed odd that he and Mikel had shared a cabin. Mik could have picked just about any cabin on the ship, considering what his father was at New Life Enterprises. Strange that he would want to bunk with a Colonial. Fancher grinned, remembering a time when he had spoken of his partial investigation of Palama to Mik. The grin faded. It now seemed that Mikel had expected, even anticipated, the revelation.

"Time distorts everything," he whispered into the night.

The river whispered back and seemed to laugh at the idea that one of its spectators would consider leaving. More cliff walls groaned into the watery depths.

Even the kodjelu managed to disappear before dark, and the calantani maintained a distance.

Before dawn, Fancher loaded his packs. The clatter of

each step took on a rhythm beyond the old camp boundary. The Star III was closed for the last time.

He looked back once, gave a mocking salute to the metal friend and the liquid death, which pulled a quarter kilometer of cliff down as a return farewell.

During the middle of the night, J'erik answered Lorff's summons. He crept out of the waterhole camp and into a tunnel where the zanstyr's stripe glowed like a decorative calidrium.

The ritual for the warrior required the Master's presence. The chanting, which had begun before Uli left the sky, continued, softer than at dusk. The tones lacked remorse. The peacefulness, at times joyfulness, cast an impression of celebration, not at all similar to the dirge associated with death in the Ah-te.

J'erik climbed Lorff's face and rode into the gathering. He sat erect, allowing all the curious, young and old, large and small, a glimpse of their new Master. The pride he felt was new to him. In time, he would learn all there was to know about the zanstyrs. In time, he thought.

The arena had been expanded. A circle of light marked the boundaries and framed the brown striper's carcass. Purple leaves overhead formed a ceiling which stretched endlessly without a sag. The walls beyond the gathering closed in and lent privacy to the ceremony.

Prompted by Lorff, J'erik entered the arena and stood next to the warrior.

The chanting took on a new tone filled with reverence and a touch of awe. The zanstyr multitude alternated bobbing up and down by stretching and contracting their collective thousands of legs. The ceremony lured a greater iridescence from the head stripes, regardless of color. The effect produced tongues of fire licking the air between ceiling and ground.

J'erik looked around, then down at his chest.

The hair rope of the calantani Lord glowed brighter than any of the zanstyr head stripes. Grinning, he listened to Lorff.

Abruptly, the chant halted. The silence became absolute. Cassilee held her breezes at bay, lest a leaf should rustle to interrupt the ceremony for the warrior.

New directions from Lorff weakened J'erik's grin. He

walked to the front of the beast and looked at the gaping maw. The wrong angle dragging the near side to the ground was grotesque even in death. He unsheathed his knife, knelt beside the jaw and began to carve into the upper gums. The rigid outer layer turned mushy once the knife penetrated. It held the tooth he was after with roots J'erik was sure extended to the beast's hindquarters. He knew he was taking a long time to cut out the five-pronged anchor, longer than the battle, but he could work no faster in the dim light. Green slime continued to cover the area. It drooled down his arms and ribs and formed a pool around his shins.

With the slurp of air gushing into the last pocket, the tooth fell. J'erik had to use both hands to pick it up and carry it to a point midway between the carcass and the border.

He returned to the warrior and ran the knife around the tip of the head stripe. The bristles circling the eyes poked and stabbed when he ventured too close. Some quick climbing, more skillful bladework, and the section was outlined from the rest of the body fur. Caked blood matted the brown shag. Clotted balls crumbled and grated his flesh. Fine powder mingled with his perspiration and turned him green. Carefully, he started at the stripe tip and skinned the section away from the warrior. In death, the zanstyr did not aid his victor.

Half dragging, half carrying the pelt, J'erik maneuvered it beside the tooth, fur side down. Hands on hips, knife sheathed, remnants of blood and tissue clinging to his arms, chest and beard, he waited for Lorff's next instruction.

The zanstyrs resumed chanting, bobbing and weaving from side to side, this time in unison.

The night rolled by. J'erik put the time to use by testing himself and his new realm. Each mind he contacted revealed more about the zanstyrs.

As dawn peeked over the east, J'erik contemplated the zanstyrs and himself in another waking light. He felt more certain about his abilities and strengths. The power to look inside to see what the calantani Lady called "soul" and know the truth value in each communication made words spoken by individuals pointless and shallow by

90

comparison. The zanstyrs were a world he could understand, and therefore accept.

When the light brightened the ceiling and the chanting abated, J'erik felt an unparalleled serenity. He reveled in it. There were no complications, no interpretations, no misunderstandings with the zanstyrs. They looked upon him as Master, holding no malice for the taking of a cherished life. The incongruity escaped him. Life, a highly prized commodity, was lived with purpose. The warrior had sought and found his.

The Order of Life was simple: both violent and non-violent, dependent upon the Master and the situation. Their territorial prerogative encompassed the area of occupation, and woe to the intruder, whether man or beast.

His new subjects approached the pelt in single file. Each took a turn licking the underside of the head stripe as a tribute to J'erik and a gesture of homage to the warrior.

Before the ceremony ended, J'erik came to think he had only scratched the surface of his manhood.

When the last youth of the zanstyr horde had departed, J'erik carried the tooth and the pelt out of the arena.

A dozen blue stripers converged. They burrowed with large shovel-formed front earthpads. Streaking from one quadrant to another, they seemed to be everywhere.

Moments later they pulled away. The warrior had been rolled into a grave and covered. The mound of excess soil was smoothed over the arena and left no actual spot to indicate where the bulk lay. A blue wrapped his tongue around the tooth and planted it in the ground, roots first.

Six red stripers with front pincers worked on key walls and dropped the ceiling over the clearing.

The warrior ceremony ended.

J'erik climbed Lorff and rode back to camp.

Star-ii was delighted to see him. She dragged Fir'ah toward the zanstyr, skipping when one of Fir'ah's long strides allowed slack.

"Can I play with them now? Can I pet them? Can I?" She let go of Fir'ah and folded her hands under her chin in anticipation. "They're so pretty. And I'm not afraid of them. I promise, I'll be gentle."

J'erik slid off Lorff. "First, you must help your mother

and Kali-te prepare a meal. Later, you may ride on Lorff with me."

Star-ii, delirious with excitement, ran back to the wagon, where Cor-ii watched with cold eyes. Single-handed, she set about fixing a meal.

Fir'ah had retreated as soon as Star-ii let go. She returned carrying a bowl of water for J'erik. She handed it to him, her face a jigsaw of complexities and contradictions. Her eyes locked on a linear vision with his, unblinking, searching.

"What is it, Fir'ah? Talk to me. Say something. Have I so damaged you that you will never forgive me?" He took the water, holding onto her fingers for several heartbeats before she wiggled them away. After the touch, an impression that she was trying to communicate lingered.

Her lips parted, then closed. Contortions played havoc with her face. These stopped as unexpectedly as they had begun. Two streams of tears rolled down her cheeks. Her head lowered in defeat.

He set the bowl aside and instinctively embraced her. She cried against his chest, sniffing and sniveling. J'erik held her, wondering how a gift that permitted him to conquer the zanstyrs and communicate with the calantani hierarchy could have such an ugly side when it was applied to the one person on Cassilee he loved.

Again, he thought of T'lar, speculating on whether or not it was he who followed at night.

He hoped it was.

Fir'ah stopped crying and wiped her cheeks on the insides of her wrists, and pushed the moisture clinging to her lashes away with dry fingertips.

J'erik smiled, realizing that this was the first time she had sought comfort from him. "Forgive me, Fir'ah," he whispered. "Forgive me, Fir'ah."

In less time than it took to blink an eye, Fir'ah's arms surrounded his green-crusted chest. Her face, still damp with tears, worked up and down.

J'erik held her very close, his own eyes stinging. A weight lifted on one part of his heart and came down heavier on another. "I love you, Fir'ah."

Her arms tightened, a response her mouth was unable to make. She clung for long minutes, atoning for the times past when her body had abhorred all contact.

The embrace slackened. J'erik responded in the same manner, not wishing to stunt the headway his sister seemed to be making. A shred of the predawn pride sparkled as the depression of guilt scurried to a dark shadow of his mind.

Fir'ah moved away, not looking into her brother's face. Methodically, she retrieved loose articles scattered around the camp.

J'erik dismissed Lorff temporarily and sought the waterhole. A few days' rest might do us all good, he decided. It sure couldn't hurt us.

Chapter 11

FOUR DAYS LATER AND HALF A KILOMETER from the waterhole camp, morning fog rambled through the purple mazes. The moisture felt greater than any they had encountered on the journey. J'erik figured the proximity of the vegetation contributed to the change. But when they left the growth behind, the open land was humid.

"Cassilee is indeed changing," he said to the squirmy child between his legs and wrapped in layers of skin protection.

Traveling on the zanstyrs was the easiest part of the long journey for J'erik, Fir'ah and Star-ii. Kali-te accepted it with the wisdom and philosophy of age, stating that she had never expected life on the surface to be like that in the Ah-te. Death was not a fear, but there was no reason for it to come a split second earlier than necessary.

Cor-ii became a blatant problem. Sullen, reluctant to get near the beasts, she preferred walking to riding one of the monsters. The pace, very slow for the zanstyrs, who were used to high speeds, was too fast for Cor-ii on foot. Begrudgingly, she conceded and rode a brown-striped warrior with Kali-te.

The pace quickened to a medium clip for the zanstyrs. Cor-ii muttered and grumbled until noon, when the fog thinned and Uli coaxed steam from the rocks. By then, the distance was greater than J'erik and the Dwellers would have been able to cover by dark.

Midafternoon brought the first break. They ate while the beasts foraged the sparse land for nourishment. The green stripers worked hardest, that being their allotment in the task distribution designated by the color of the head stripe.

When Cor-ii resumed the complaints laced with threats, Kali-te launched a tirade of her own and vented accumulated hostilities at the woman until Cor-ii was subdued. Through it all, Star-ii clung to J'erik and Fir'ah, never looking at them or her mother.

The zanstyrs returned and loaded their cargoes. Purples scurried ahead, scouting, marking the way through the rising mountains dotted by iron trees and variations of gadid spreading over endless kilometers.

Shielded by J'erik holding a robe over her, Star-ii ate her fill of berries.

Lorff followed a trail over the mountains which J'erik would have had to go around. The women and wagon required the low elevations and smooth terrain when on foot. Kaloer bushes grew as large as trees. They towered over the zanstyrs and their riders. Bits of green velvet freckled the hollows in lumpy black trunks where Uli no longer managed to poke a finger. The fog rolled in again long before dark. It added a new dimension to the unknown highlands.

The zanstyrs were prepared to go for as long as J'erik wished. It was slow traveling due to the treacherous heights. Whole mountainsides were carved away from the main bodies. Narrow, bottomless chasms ran for kilometers and stopped without warning. Steep cliffs of dark rock plunged like giant steps leading to the lowlands cloaked in fog.

Twice after dark, the purples returned and sent the horde in a different direction. The third time, J'erik told them to find a safe place to stop for the night.

Purples left to scout. The Dwellers of the Ah-te waited. Cold seeped through their damp clothing. J'erik huddled closer to Star-ii for warmth.

Sobs muffled by the vapor made him hold the small child tightly and whisper, "We're going to camp soon, Star-ii. There's no need to cry. I'm here."

A little hand pulled down the face wrappings. "I don't cry. This is fun." A yawn her hand could not cover breathed out to the fog.

"Stay here with Lorff. I want to check on the others."

"I love Lorff." She leaned forward and nuzzled the chartreuse mop.

Take care of her, Lorff.

He paused halfway to the warrior carrying Kali-te and Cor-ii.

"I tell you, Kali-te, the Betweener is possessed by Cassilee's ancient demons. He wants to steal my daughter. Look how he has turned her against me. See how he keeps her close to him and away from me. He wants to kill me. I know he does." Fright laced Cor-ii's anger.

Scornful, Kali-te replied, "You're like the rest in the Ah-te. You fear what you don't understand and want to be rid of it." One of her disgusted sighs penetrated the night. "If he wanted your child, all he had to do was take her. He could have left you and you would be dead right now. It's your own hateful actions which have turned your daughter away. He offers her kindness and love. You do not own that child, Cor-ii. You didn't even in the Ah-te."

J'erik turned away, saddened by the woman's attitude. He walked around the back of Lorff to where a blue carried Fir'ah.

The crying grew louder.

"Fir'ah?" he called softly, not wanting to alarm her. A choking sob bit off the sound.

The blue lowered for J'erik to climb up. Beside Fir'ah, "What is it? Are you afraid?"

She clung to him, holding so tightly that her trembling shook him. Her arm jerked toward the sky.

"What do you see?" J'erik looked where she pointed, following the arm with his fingers.

She weaved, forming arcs in the night.

J'erik forced a calm over himself and took her face in both hands. "Star Demons?"

Eyes closed, she nodded vehemently.

Clattering rocks and clanking barbs on boulders cut through the silence. The purples were back in a hurry. In seconds the zanstyrs panicked and fled the open space.

J'erik pulled Fir'ah from the blue, dragging her when

she stumbled. The blue turned and disappeared into the night. J'erik goaded Fir'ah up behind Star-ii and sent Lorff to find a temporary sanctuary for them.

Next he summoned the nearest purple. The success of his journey hinged upon knowing where the Star Demons were and where they were going. The Techi was close. Safety was a promise, one that could not be fulfilled if the Demons stood in their path.

Kali-te and Cor-ii were gone before Lorff turned around. The fog swallowed their retreat.

J'erik stood alone until a scout returned. He crawled over the bristly face and onto the leading edge of purple, entrenching firmly into the shaggy stripe. Legs spread and toes dug in, he stretched his arms and charged the purple to take him down the mountain to a place where the fog broke.

The purple, called Chacon and the leader of the scouts, turned on himself, practically completing a circle in a rush to obey the Master. The small, flatter area gave way to a plunging mountainside. J'erik grabbed larger chunks of purple and pressed his knees tighter to the body. Head up, all he could see was one rolling fog bank after another. He began to feel as though he were walking on the sky again.

Chacon moved straight down the mountain. He took the vertical cliffs by using the barbs and folding his legs under his belly. The contraction/expansion movements rippled along his length in a series of three to get the desired speed. Shards of rock flew out and down the cliffs. Some pelted the furry zanstyr and his Master.

The purple traversed a quarter of a kilometer, then attacked the cliff vertically again. The sector Chacon moved from moaned and crackled. He traversed a second time, taking them farther from the horrendous noise under the rock veneer.

J'erik held to the beast, using hands, knees, toes and teeth. The illusion of skywalking became fact when Chacon stopped traversing away from the weak section.

The fog thinned. Chacon crossed a step plateau in a matter of seconds. Upon command, he stopped. J'erik lurched forward, sliding down the beast's head and over one eye. The snake tongue wrapped around the Master's waist and put him back into a respectable position.

Erect and shaken, J'erik surveyed the five lower steps. The right angles and smooth ledges defied natural occurrence or a series of coincidences. At the base of the structure the land was fuzzy. Iron trees were distinguishable in the glow of the star cluster not yet blotted by the cloud line stretching to the south.

Out of the west at the leading edge of the fog came a flash, followed by a second and a third.

J'erik directed Chacon against the cliff.

Specks of light darted between the stars, flickering back and forth in a crisscross pattern. J'erik counted twenty-eight before giving up. They moved too fast.

Larger craft descended through the light specks. Their sudden proximity piqued his caution. They swooped down in the west, traveling east at awesome speeds. Their enormity left J'erik gaping and Chacon recoiling against the cliff.

Another group approached from the east. As though cued, lights came on, shocking the night with an intense brilliance.

J'erik covered his eyes. Chacon turned his entire head, lowering it into the angle crook of the cliff for added protection. Though stunned, J'erik wanted to get moving and out of the light. He communicated with Chacon, desperation gnawing at his concentration.

Slowly, the zanstyr progressed up the perpendicular face. The Master held on with blind trust. The ascent was not the straight line used on the way down. Chacon struggled, weaving from side to side in halting surges. He stopped a few times, but finally reached the upper step ledge and slipped into the cool darkness.

The roar of Star Demons felt a thousand kilometers away in the mist swirling around them, antagonized by gusts of wind. They spent a few precious minutes adjusting before pushing upward. A refreshing certainty returned to Chacon's climb. He navigated the last section as adroitly as the descent.

Noise came and left. Each time it sounded more distant. The dense fog could not alleviate the nakedness J'erik felt on the mountain. He and Chacon were alone. No hard rock protected them from the Demons. Cassilee's mists were fickle. They threatened to roll back and expose them to the alien eyes from the stars. The Demons had only to shine their brilliance at the heights and surely they would melt the security blanket and see the vulnerability racing over the rocks.

Chacon sped over the flat area the group had vacated a short while ago. Loose rocks bumped under a hundred barbed earthpads. A few larger ones clattered after the zanstyr, unable to attain his high speed on the steep slope. Chacon veered north, then down another vertical slope. Half of his body clung to a semihorizontal ledge for a kilometer. A hard right brought them into total darkness.

Chacon's stop was less abrupt than on the mountain. Nonetheless, J'erik slid forward. He climbed down the zanstyr's face and stroked the beast while their eyes adjusted to the new surroundings. Ragged breathing steadied to normal and quieted. Even so, the zanstyr's rhythm was loud in the shelter.

J'erik began to explore. The cavern was large, much larger than the Ah-te. It carried the familiar Hold odors and feelings. He wondered if this was one of the ones marked on the ancient map. The name refused to be summoned out of memory.

He returned to Chacon, knowing how a Hold would view an unannounced visit by a Betweener and only guessing how they would receive Chacon. He glanced through the opening. The sky was alive with colors flashing in all directions.

We would not be welcomed here, Master. It is the only place near that I know existed.

It is good, Chacon. We will wait until the danger outside passes and hope that one inside does not happen.

It is too late for hope. They come.

We must go. Quickly! J'erik catapulted atop the stripe and held fast as the zanstyr backed out into the night.

The heights flowed through a shroud boiling along the rock. A steady hum filled the sky. Screeches and rocks belched from out of the cavern mouth. A rain of knives, sharpened to razor edges, befell J'erik and his mount. Thick fur and a tough hide were a form of protection for Chacon.

J'erik was not as fortunate. The pain in his right thigh was someone's triumphant score.

Several minutes passed before he realized how bad the wound was. He waited until Chacon found a more level tract and tried to reach back for the knife to re-move it. The penetration angle was bad.

Take us straight down.

Chacon obeyed in a literal sense. He put the strength in J'erik's arms to a test, as well as the roots of the purple stripe the Master held.

A blinding light flashed on the right oblique. Chacon slowed. J'erik willed the dots floating on his eyeballs to go away. Rocks, bits of iron trees and tons of dust hailed from above. The hope for safety was cruelly obliterated.

Chacon did his best to line up with the fall. He took advantage of an outcrop and used it as a deflector. Even so, the efforts were near futile. Rocks, debris and grit poured out of the ugly night without an end.

J'erik resigned himself to the inevitable.

Fancher erected his mobile camp near a collage of gadid vines and iron trees. The night began strangely. The calantani remained in the highlands at dusk. The kodjelu disappeared at midafternoon and had not shown their beady red eyes even when he baited a trap with dried meat.

He ate slowly and sipped water between bites, stretch-ing the meal out to make him feel full before he actually was. The unpredictability of the land imposed meat-conservation measures he had hoped would not be neces-sary until much later in the journey. It had been days since he last saw a panaver. They were strange creatures. He wanted a better look at them.

Bleaker than the forced conservation measures was the emptiness around him. The trees and assorted foliage be-spoke life, which in turn imparted a slim hope. Seeing the monstrous winged beast soar and dive through the twi-light before the mists crawled over the land was some-thing he could relate to. If there was a human in the cliffs with a beast like that usually gracing the night skies, then a possibility of intelligence existed within the creature. He wanted to hope so.

The skeptic proclaimed: No such luck.

The isolated man pleaded: Maybe. Just maybe.

His efforts to capture and train a kodjelu that morning failed. The creature took off at the first opportunity, not even staying around as a luncheon guest.

Fancher stretched out in the dome created by the force field. He was warm, secure and lonely. He watched the stars, brighter and clearer than from his homeworld of Palama. For lack of anything else to do, he chose them as an audience for the trick which usually worked him out of depression or box-canyon thinking. He assumed both sides and sought a rational solution to the problem.

"Funny, though, how I play tricks on myself," he said in an abnormally high voice.

A low tone answered. "It's not funny. It's rather sad."

High-pitched: "But I did so well at this during training. Ninety-five days in isolation under worse conditions than these. Another sixty in sensory deprivation. Why is this so hard?"

Low: "Nobody's going to come and get you, Fancher Bann. Nobody's going to send in supplies at the end and tell you what a fine boy you are. Nobody cares if you make it. They wrote you off as fertilizer." He rolled over and adjusted the field for maximum. "You always wanted to be independent and totally self-reliant. Now you are. Don't like it? Too bad. You're in the arena and it's the spectator's move."

Looking back at the stars, the high-pitched voice said, "Independent, yes. Totally alone, without another living soul on the whole planet—no."

A sad laugh preceded the low return. "Some people don't get fifty percent of what they want out of life. You did. Why complain?"

Fancher's normal voice cut in. "This isn't working and it's sick."

He tried to concentrate on sleeping. Long, deep breaths slowed his heartbeat and shoved drowsiness over his eyes.

In limbo, just before real sleep conquered, the southern horizon started moving around the stars. His eyelids opened a crack.

Another disturbance in the south poked his brain. Acknowledging it meant coming awake.

The second time his eyelids flickered. Fancher was awake.

Star III Recon Probers were fortifying the ozone layer, finishing the work begun over a century ago. The massive iron-tree branches heavy with amilglibs and fat supple leaves hindered his view. Quickly, he shouldered

102

his packs and strapped the mobile force field to his waist. He grumbled, not seeing a clearing ahead and knowing there was none for an hour's walk behind.

The packs went back to the ground. He rummaged through the disarray for a light. Cautiously, he checked the iron tree for hazards. When nothing foreign was detected, he expanded the field to encompass the whole tree.

He lassoed a broken center leader and climbed. His boots slipped on the glassy bark. Two near falls convinced him to go barefoot.

At the top of the tree, he watched the southern light show come through the clouds. Beyond the shield, wind stirred the gadid and knocked amilglibs to the ground with unpredictable gusts. Nothing touched him. He was isolated from the growing maelstrom, just as isolated as he was from his comrades working overhead.

"Three days," he muttered. "Three days and they'll be gone for years. . . ."

He began to realize just how long those years would be when his sinuses began burning. He watched, growing more angry.

"I'll be waiting for you, you butchers! I'll be waiting! Hear me, Satow?" A fisted hand shook at the sky. He kept yelling.

Chapter 12

THE AMOUNT OF TIME J'ERIK CLUNG TO THE zanstyr became immeasurable. It seemed forever that the air was choking thick with grit and dust. Chacon was bent to the left, easing the Master's precarious hold on his fur. Numb spots where parts of the mountain grazed J'erik's body creeped into awareness. They vied with locked muscles agonizing their own fate. Bloody perspiration wept across his legs, saturated his clothes and worked down his back. It formed a pool against the brown-striped hide, then trickled over his shoulders to his arms and into his hair.

He wandered in and out of limbo, instinct the only ally holding him onto the zanstyr.

By the time he was able to view their predicament with clarity, the sky had cleared of lights other than the stars. Rocks no longer careened down the decapitated mountain. Dust rose when he breathed. It sat upon the land and the survivors in thick, delicate layers.

Uli crept above the horizon. The east was unfamiliar after the night's siege. J'erik basked in the dawn, hoping it would restore sense to his muddled state.

Carefully, he pushed up to see over the dusty clump of fur which no longer was purple.

To the right, it was an easy hundred meters straight down.

Chacon.

He experienced the edge of a deep pain inside the animal's brain. It burned like the cooking fire in the Ah-te.

Take us down. The order was conveyed with a force designed to reach a place where Chacon had no choice but to obey. J'erik twinged, reminding himself that they had to get down before Uli baked the last iota of strength from them.

Chacon moved with difficulty. His head bobbed, taking the Master up and down, side to side, opening the mud-caked wounds wrapped in pain. Through clenched teeth, J'erik cursed the Star Demons for his wounds and that of the zanstyr, for their assault upon the traveling Ah-te, and for the brutal rape of his world.

The tumultuous descent ended. Chacon pushed off the wall and leaped to the ground with an ungraceful thud that deposed the Master into a dust pit.

The sky fought with a hundred bright colors, won and turned black. J'erik felt as though he would fall forever. The ground closed over him. Something wrapped around his midsection and jerked upward.

Chacon set him behind his head and held on until the Master was stable. J'erik spat mud balls into the filling pit and listened to the zanstyr's profuse apology. He stopped short of lashing out, mindful of the tremendous pain Chacon suffered.

They moved west for half a day to a waterhole surrounded by vegetation. J'erik's tongue had begun to thicken. Uli's heat robbed him of more water than he thought would ever be replaced. He and the zanstyr drank sparingly at the well. Still thirsty, J'erik turned his attentions to the knife in his thigh. Mud scabs had formed a rigid seal.

He tore a gadid leaf off a vine and folded it into a cup, which he filled with water. By loosening the folds, he produced a regulated drip around the wound. It cleaned slowly, but well. The awkwardness of bending back added to the discomfort. He tried working the knife out, then resorted to amilglib spines to kill the pain.

The knife pulled free. The wound was a clean one and bled well. Gadid leaves served as a temporary bandage, though he knew he would have to take care not to open the wound once it scabbed. It was deep and unlikely to withstand much stress.

He scooped another cup of water and washed the weapon. The familiarity intrigued him.

Chacon sidled up as close as he could without crushing the Master. He implored J'erik to remove the thorns from his hide. J'erik shaved away crusty hair from around Chacon's wounds. He cleaned them as he had his own, using ten times the water for each. He spread his fingers around a curved handle, pushed in on the swollen area and drew the knife out. Chacon heaved an audible exhale. He repeated the process nine times. The rest of the zanstyr's pain could not be helped. There were missing tufts of fur where large rocks had scraped down to the skin, several to the bone; healing needed time. Both of them needed rest.

J'erik crawled back to the water and molded another cup. The knives were interesting. The style and design were similar along the blades. The curved-handled ones were a finger width shorter than the straight-handled one. The markings on the curved knives indicated that they had been belt knives of successful hunters. The flat, straight-handled one told another story. He recognized the marks.

How many times had noise in the distance caught up to them on the journey?

J'erik shook his head, admonishing himself for not doubling back to confirm his suspicions. Simultaneously, he defended himself, remembering the fatigue. He wondered how many had changed their minds and started out of the Ah-te, all heading for the Techi.

He studied the knife.

Traveling to the Techi would have been less difficult for a man alone, or a group of adults with several men along. Old Kali-te, sour Cor-ii, young Star-ii and unpredictable Fir'ah were hardly a strong group, nor could they share the tasks demanding brute strength.

J'erik slipped a curved knife into his belt, flipped the other in the air and caught it several times before banishing T'lar's weapon to the opposite side. T'lar seemed to have a propensity for survival. The four days' rest in the vine forest could easily have given him time to reach the Hold, J'erik reflected. And rather than conclude the obvious fate of the Hold he and Chacon had visited, J'erik preferred to consider him alive. It would be nice to return the knife personally, he thought with a cold smile.

Rest now, Chacon. We are traveling all night and tomorrow until we reach the Techi.

If they are still there, we should make it before Uli touches the east, Master.

In ubiquitous darkness Fir'ah soothed the whimpering child clinging to her. Lorff was barely moving to breathe under them. Star-ii had cried herself to sleep half a dozen times since the holocaust. Hard as Fir'ah tried, the words refused to sound. They were trapped by an invisible wall in her head.

"Is there anyone here?" came a weak voice out of the far darkness.

Both sat up, the child wiping her nose on her sleeve.

"We're here," whispered Star-ii. Excited, she screamed, "We're here!"

The noise roused Lorff. He heaved, lurching upward, pulling and contracting those parts of his body not pinned by the collapsed cavern mouth. Loose boulders crashed to the ground. Elevated slabs, half exposed, groaned under the shift and gave centimeters grudgingly. The echo filled the blackness and drowned the voice.

Star-ii kept yelling until dust filled her mouth and Fir'ah covered her face.

Lorff struggled for half a day and rested periodically. Fir'ah and Star-ii huddled off to the side, afraid to venture too far away from their only hope of rescue. The voice did not return. Fir'ah was relieved. She preferred the solitude of darkness and her faith in Lorff to the voice calling in the distance.

Star-ii ran the gamut of false optimism and tears. Her frustration at speaking to one who could not speak back expressed itself at intervals marked by a growling stomach which had not known food for nearly a day.

Fir'ah worked into cold sweats trying to force the locked words into freedom.

Desperate and tense, she patted Star-ii in a signal the child had learned to mean: Stay where you are. Fir'ah climbed on Lorff's back and crawled along his spine to where the fall pinned him. She slid to the ground. Using her hands, she explored the width of the barrier and noted which rocks might be pried loose to help Lorff's efforts.

The zanstyr rested while she worked, conserving his waning strength for the right time. Soon, Star-ii groped her way to the noise and lent a hand by rolling what rocks she could away from Lorff's feet.

Fancher packed his gear and chewed on the soft fruit of an amilglib. The day was half gone, a circumstance which added to his foul mood. A fitful sleep deprived him of rest. Anger heightened his determination to be ready and waiting for the time when Satow and the terraformers returned to establish a base.

He walked, charging his shield. He had no illusions that New Life Enterprises representatives would welcome him with open arms.

On the contrary.

A new thought crossed his mind. The absurdity of it made him laugh. Toying with it, his anger changed to irony.

According to the schedule, it would be a minimum of three years before work started on the base. He counted on their eagerness to open Cassilee and subtracted a year.

Two years constituted possession. Harsh as Cassilee was, there existed only a small possibility of anyone recognizing him, except perhaps Mikel. But Mik thought him dead. And the probabilities of Commander Satow opening his personal log to the scrutiny of the Allied Worlds Federation before the ambitious Commander met his demise did not exist. No. Officially, Explorer First Class Fancher Bann was deceased and every effort had been made to rescue him and his defective ship.

The idea appealed to him more and more. Just seeing Satow's face would be worth it. The record undoubtedly named a couple of men who "personally" confirmed his remains. Satow had a reputation for leaving nothing to chance. Nor could he afford to.

Yes. Rather than present himself as a survivor to show up Satow, he would change the story just a little and become the survivor of an entire species and claim sole ownership of Cassilee. That would accomplish even more.

His step lightened. The sun no longer felt as hot. The justice in his plan set him grinning. Truly it was a day to dream about while he worked toward the goal.

A breeze caressed him, seeming to whisper encouragement for the plan which would keep the Star Demons off the surface of Cassilee a while longer. He breathed deeply. An inner peace blossomed from his lungs and spread over his entire body. For an instant, the loneliness melted and the planet became a living friend. Cassilee empathized with his plight. His tiredness vanished.

The land took on an incongruity void of logical explanation. Mud bubbled in pools, emitting steam into the dry air. It was a narrow strip along the north side of his course. The steady plop of breaking bubbles took on a bass rhythm. Beyond them the land had been lifted to form gigantic step pyramids missing the upper sections. Veins of crystalline minerals flaunted rich colors in the sun.

South, the beginning edges of a forest rippled purple and green. It was the thickest growth Fancher had seen on the journey.

He checked the compass reading on his wrist computer and changed direction to the west. Ahead, the land looked different, though it was more familiar and in keeping with what lay behind. The strange formations on each side of him seemed alive and watchful as he passed the hurdles it imposed.

A herd of panavers rambled toward him. The leader paused, then continued. The wrinkled fold across the top of his tapering head focused on the traveler. His snout was oblong, easily the length of Fancher's forearm. Two nostrils flared at the end over a spreading mouth. The panaver's neck was thick, yet graceful. His head remained steady as the six-legged body ambled along without much rhythm. At best, it was a gawky-looking creature.

Fancher watched them change color as they skirted the forest. He whistled.

Ears, one on each side of the fold and a third behind the slit on the crown of the head, came to attention. They were cupped into points. Fancher considered it a sensible arrangement. They could hear in all directions without turning their heads.

"Yeah, two, maybe three years," he said quietly to the herd. "There's a lot to do and much more to learn."

The leader stopped a couple of meters from Fancher. He was easily as tall, and the wide, heavy body supported by stilt legs was twice as long.

For an instant, Fancher wondered why he had not activated the shield. The beasts could trample him if they chose to. They might not walk gracefully, but they ran like the wind. Also, considering his meat rations, he was uncertain why he did not single one out for dinner. Dried, it would last a long time and be far more than he could carry.

The leader continued peering at him with eyes located deep in the forehead fold. He lifted his right front leg. A forked hoof that looked too large for the leg stayed in the air for several minutes. The panaver turned when he moved and kept going.

The strangeness of the encounter puzzled Fancher briefly before the wind applauded his actions with a soothing whisper. Smiling, feeling better than he had in years, and enjoying the day without his usual depression, Fancher moved west. For the first time since touching Cassilee, he was glad to be alive.

Chapter 13

THE TECHI ROSE ABOVE THE MELTING FOG and into the near morning. A granite giant, cragged by wind and sand, it stood over the slopes Chacon crossed. Rolling knolls dotted with ilankor and gadid vines lay far behind them. The scent of amilglibs had been scarce during the night's journey, which had taken longer than expected. As they closed in on the lone upthrust, almost no vegetation grew.

J'erik was more than a little disappointed that they had not encountered another zanstyr on the way. Anticipation honed a sharp edge as he neared the Techi. Rumors and stories from childhood flooded his mind.

Chacon stopped, waiting for instructions.

The face loomed straight up, retreated along a shelf, then continued to the top. A series of switchback paths, broken at the necks to thwart the kodjelu, led to the shelf.

Chacon's cold, wet fur turned to mud where J'erik slid down. The impact was taken by J'erik's left leg, cushioning the landing for the right one. Petting Chacon, he released the zanstyr to forage.

As he disappeared into a thick patch of fog, J'erik turned toward the path and picked up two full kodjelu traps similar to those used by the Ah-te. He walked up the first section slowly, thinking of the differences that existed inside the Techi. Bronze skin, light hair and pale-gray eyes were the opposite of what he had grown up with. That's the easy part to get used to, he mused. They have no Seers, only machines. None of them has the Gift so common in the Dwellers.

He crossed a switchback, changed hands on the traps and looked up at the shelf.

Hand-drawn pictures of machines hung in his mind. The old books stashed in the study rooms of the Ah-te had been filled with accounts of what they could do. But some of the journals were so old that the kaloer parchment had blackened and crumbled.

They were histories, thousands of generations old, dating to a time when everyone lived upon the surface in places filled with buildings and machines. Then came the wars. War was nothing new. According to the books, the two species had been battling since the beginning of time. But the war to end all wars had happened. The damage to Cassilee had been done. Those who could, fled to the stars in droves. Machines took them.

J'erik climbed the last break. Legends, all legends, he decided. Only part can be true. Which part?

"There is only one war now. The one for survival against the Star Demons," he muttered at the raised kodjelu traps.

He entered a recession on the shelf and rubbed his leg. Mud and blood trickled down his calf. A second wall blocked his progress. He looked outward and saw Chacon moving north in a clear area.

"State your name, please."

J'erik's neck became a swivel.

The rocks repeated the command.

Hesitant, "I'm J'erik, a Betweener from the Ah-te. I come to see my father, J'osh-uah."

The rocks split at the center and rumbled aside. J'erik glanced around, then limped forward, conscious of the ache in his leg. The dark interior took a bit of adjustment. As his vision changed, J'erik began to grasp just how different the life-style of the Techi was.

The walls were high and smooth. Steel corners and flat lines defined the boundaries ending at the cold floor he stood on. It was a burnished metal without seams. The room showed no doors and was large enough to house a couple of full-grown zanstyrs.

"Please move to the front wall and center yourself equidistant from the corners."

He complied, looking for the source. Concentrating, he searched for a common denominator such as the one used with the calantani and zanstyrs.

The rock yielded nothing, nor did the metal in front of it. He turned back to the wall and realized he did not know how to find what he sought.

The metal parted to a corridor similar in size to those in the Hall of Rooms. Bright colors formed partial designs on the smooth walls. Streaks of red-brown made more recent headroads. The faces on the first mural were corroded by the growth eating the floor and ceiling corners. Impulsively, J'erik touched the wall. It was as smooth as it looked. Amazing.

As an afterthought, he set the kodjelu traps near the closed entrance.

He returned to the artwork. What remained fascinated him. A feeling of age clung to it. The colors were vivid, sharp. Flat, even surfaces aided the artist in perpetuating continuity. It was so different from the rough walls in the Ah-te, where fungus was hedged back as a frame for an artist's endeavor.

The voice guided him to an open room and gave instructions for the use of the sanitary facilities. The door closed when the voice stopped.

A small amount of rust patterned the wall opposite the door. The whiteness in the dim lights radiating from nine spots in the ceiling made the room feel clean. An above-the-floor bed sat in the far corner. A chest of drawers without handles hung on the wall below a mirror.

J'erik looked at himself, a grizzly sight covered with dirt.

Following the instructions, he entered the side room and stopped.

A water pool bubbled and gurgled in the center. A smaller pool clutched the wall, and yet another sat on the floor. Never had he seen such a flagrant use of water.

"Voice? Answer me."

"Yes, J'erik Betweener?"

"Did I understand correctly? I am to contaminate the large pool with the dirt I carry?"

"The water recycles through a purification system.

Grooming articles and a change of clothing will be brought to you momentarily."

"Did you answer my question?"

A tinge of amusement crept into the tone. "Yes. Get in the water. You will contaminate it only temporarily." After a pause, "Your concern is appreciated, Betweener."

The water was a luxury unparalleled by any physical indulgence to date. The pools outside the Ah-te proper were mostly acid. This was clean. The slippery substance making bubbles along the top ate the dirt and stung his wounds, particularly his leg. The water drained at two places in the bottom and entered from two more near the top. It was neither too cold nor too warm. He submerged, vigorously rubbing his scalp. When he surfaced and opened his eyes, the possibility that he was being poisoned crossed his mind.

Lord Chamblis's Betweener stood at the door holding a pile of clothing and a decorated box. A small grin parted her lips and put a twinkle in her aqua-colored eyes. She held up her hand and gave him a half-nod.

Stunned, J'erik did not need a key for silence. Speech was out of the question.

Her smile stayed bright. She set the pile down on a counter beside the small pool and approached the tub.

The initial shock wore thin. A million questions bombarded J'erik's mind. Then a new sensation washed them down the drain for recycle.

The girl sat at the side and watched. She reached out, touched his forehead and moved a shock of wet hair to the side. Her head tilted for another perspective.

"I'm a guest here also. Your name is known in places which I travel, J'erik Betweener of the Ah-te. I am Lor'ee." She stood and left the room, touching the wall on the way. The door closed.

For several minutes after she left J'erik studied her in his mind's eye—the shiny hair, shades lighter than his own, curling over her shoulders and peeking at the full beginnings of breasts hidden by a white robe tied at the waist. His forehead tingled where she touched. Every nerve in his body was alert for the next contact.

The water lost its appeal. He scrubbed quickly and climbed out. Waiting to dry, he scraped his face with his knife. Next he trimmed his hair to above the shoulders and the front above his eyes.

Dressed in a white tunic and short pants, he left the side room, eager to see Lor'ee.

She was not there. An elderly, gray-blond man sat on his bed, waiting. He stood when J'erik entered. He was nearly as tall as the Betweener. A strength that age had not touched showed in his build. The long, even lines creasing his forehead and reaching to the corners of his eyes were stern, but not unkind. They added to the authority of his appearance and denoted years of wisdom.

"I am J'osh-uah, your father." He bowed slightly.

"I am J'erik, the Betweener who is your son." J'erik returned the formality and ended it. "Where is my sister? Can you help her?"

Concern deepened lines around the Techi's mouth. "I have bypassed regular procedure to ask the same question of you. Where is Fir'ah? And the girl child of the Ah-te?"

"I had hoped they would be here."

"They are not. There is an accusation against you which claims that you abducted the child for yourself."

Bitterness hardened J'erik's expression. "Is that all Cor-ii had to say?"

J'osh-uah shook his head. "Your accuser also charges you with plotting her death. However, you did not have an ample opportunity to carry it through because she did not allow you near her."

"What of Kali-te? Does she not speak up? Does she not explain what our circumstances have been these long days? Does she not—"

"Who is Kali-te?" J'osh-uah interrupted.

For a moment, J'erik returned the leader's gaze, then strapped his belt tighter and replaced the souvenir knives beside his own. Dust flew when he shook out the brown stripe. He rolled and fastened it around his neck. The calantani rope was last.

Stoic, J'osh-uah watched. "You are planning to go somewhere?"

"I'm going to look for Kali-te, Star-ii and Fir'ah."

J'osh-uah hesitated a moment, then said, "You can't go out the way you came in. It is watched."

"Then I will find another way."

"Where will you look for them?"

"Every place between here and the mountains which the Star Demons chewed up. There was a Hold there. That is where the pattern ends."

"Was? The Tor-ad-ih is dead?"

"Perhaps a few survived. I don't know." He touched the knives. "Their hospitality left much to be desired." He pulled one out and cut a strip from the bottom of the tunic. This went around the leg wound for support.

"There are few Holds left."

"Right now, I'm not concerned with how many are scattered over Cassilee. I want to get out of this one." J'erik rushed to the side room and took a long drink of water. Coming out, "You will let me out to find my sister, the child and the old woman?"

J'osh-uah did not answer. His expression was one of contemplation.

"Send out searchers after dark. If I have not found them by then, I will appreciate the help. But I can look now. I also travel faster. You would be giving them an advantage, even if you doubt me."

Slowly, "Have I your word you will return, in either case?"

"You have my word."

A reserve in the stiff nod betrayed the Leader's inner conflict. "Very well." He motioned to the door and walked out, with J'erik following.

J'osh-uah moved quickly through the turns. The corridors took on a forlorn look. Neglect had taken a toll. Few of the lights shone from the ceilings. Deterioration ate at the walls and left jagged sheets which looked as if they would crumble if touched. He stopped beside a door, took a plate from his pocket and inserted it into a narrow slot.

The interior was vacant. J'osh-uah pointed at a rusty panel. "Pull it out, go through, then replace it on the other side."

J'erik worked on the panel, finally resorting to his knife to pry it from the broken holders rusted together.

"May the spirit of Cassilee go with you," the elder man said.

J'erik glanced up, thinking it an unusual thing for a

Techi to say. "If not, I'll look for her, also." He smiled and pulled the panel back.

A shaft of light wormed through a narrow opening high overhead. The close proximity of the walls helped J'erik's climb. They allowed the usage of all sides. Once on top, he found Uli coming to her uppermost point. The heat struck him immediately.

He scrambled over the rocks and found a place where ledges wound down the facade and were close enough to drop on.

Chacon was nowhere in sight. He summoned the beast and any others near enough to hear the call. By the time he reached the base, Chacon and half a dozen others led a dust cloud toward the Techi.

Above, pebbles grated off the switchbacks. Dust billowed down twenty meters to the left.

Pressed against the cliff, he looked up, unable to see much.

A second flurry descended. Someone was coming down rapidly, too much so for safety.

J'erik stepped out, hand resting on his knife handle.

Lor'ee jumped down and landed beside him. "Two can search quicker than one." Grinning, she straightened her shoulders. "Especially if they are Betweeners."

J'erik shrugged. "We must hurry." He began examining the approaching zanstyrs for their directions and activities since the night of the holocaust. None had seen Lorff or the old woman after scattering. A blue held a vague impression of a cavern, but it had not existed when he sought it as a refuge. He ended up outrunning the rock-and-fire storm.

J'erik summoned the blue.

"When did Cor-ii reach the Hold?" he asked Lor'ee.

"A foraging party found her at the base when they went out last night. She was dazed and talking nonsense about a Betweener who held the power of life and death. One who commanded the beasts of Cassilee without a word." She started for the blue. "Of course, they did not believe her." Over her shoulder, "I did. That's why I stayed. There's an orange calantani who searches the changing land for you and a Lady who refuses to mourn. They have great faith in you, J'erik Betweener."

He held the thousand questions about her and the

calantani for a better time. "Let's find the three who are missing before the kodjelu do."

The zanstyrs spread a search pattern, J'erik on Chacon in the center, where he could maintain contact will all of them, except the blue Lor'ee rode. She lay upon the stripe and held on as J'erik instructed. The zanstyr chose his pace and traveled slightly under top speed to the demolished Tor-ad-ih. It was easily more than half a day at the blue's pace.

J'erik and the gathering horde scurried over the flatlands. Irregularities were visible for distorted kilometers shimmering under heat curtains. There was something vaguely disturbing about the new contour of the land. It was difficult to place why it bothered him, other than the increasing scarcity of vegetation away from the Techi lands. The nagging impression blackened his mood. He pushed the zanstyrs harder, using his allies to their utmost capabilities.

"Fir'ah, I'm hungry. And I'm thirsty. And I'm tired. My arms hurt. There's sticky stuff on my hands." Star-ii sank onto a rock and waited for Fir'ah to produce a solution.

Fir'ah groped through the dark to where her pack rested against the wall. The waterskin still held a few drops. She took it to Star-ii and shuttled her off to their resting spot between the wall and Lorff's head. She returned to work on the rock fall once Star-ii was settled. It was hard work for a team of men and an impossible feat for a woman alone. Most of the rocks were too large to budge without a lever. She settled for moving the ones she could, hoping Lorff's strength lasted to make another new headway. Her main objective was to create holes between the boulders in order for Lorff to move them with less effort.

The job became harder and harder. She stopped often. Fatigue disconcerted her efforts. Rocks Star-ii had moved became too heavy.

When the child woke, Fir'ah rested beside her, half asleep, hands wrapped in rags in her lap.

"Are we going to get out of here?"

Fir'ah took her hand and led her away from Lorff.

The beast struggled, snorting volumes of foam and

120

moisture. The rocks groaned and moved in jerks as they loosened. Lorff paused, breathing heavily, turned on himself and tried to reach the barrier with his front legs. The frustrating effort fell a couple of meters short.

Fir'ah tenderly stroked the side of his face. Star-ii too petted him and wiped her hands on her robe often to be rid of the foam. "We won't leave you, Lorff. I love you. And there is nowhere to go in the dark."

Fir'ah hugged the child's head with her elbow. Star-ii's bravery and ability to express the words were a good sign. They petted a few more minutes and stood back.

Lorff tried again. He gained another meter, pulled down boulders which thundered in the cavern and smashed against the walls. Without warning, he collapsed. Earthpads turned every which way at the end of his legs.

Star-ii began to cry.

New sounds wound through the dark and sparked a memory.

Fir'ah grabbed Star-ii and ran toward Lorff's head. They were almost there when a light flickered in the cavern.

"You, from the Ah-te, come out."

The light reflected off the walls, seeming so much brighter than it actually was after the hours of darkness. Fir'ah jerked Star-ii around Lorff's head and clamped her hand over the child's mouth.

"Is there anyone here? I will help you. Just make a noise."

Star-ii grappled with Fir'ah's hand. She held tighter and brought the girl to the ground, trapping her legs. T'lar's voice sent a convulsive tremor along the bronze skin. The child's terror grew also. Star-ii clamped her teeth into the wrappings and bit, opening and closing her mouth until her teeth found flesh.

Fir'ah's hand stayed fixed, shaking. Star-ii fought her, using fists, elbows and body. The child's refreshed strength was too much for Fir'ah's depleted condition. Star-ii wormed her way out of the Betweener's grasp and ran, screaming, "T'lar! T'lar!"

T'lar swept the child up with one arm. "Star-ii." He looked around and backed away from the unconscious zanstyr. "Are you alone?"

121

"No! Fir'ah's here, too. I think she must be scared, 'cause she scared me. Maybe she doesn't know it's you."

Fir'ah's heart skipped two beats and sank.

"Fir'ah." There was a longing in his voice which drove the Betweener into a mental frenzy.

T'lar skirted Lorff and extended the calidrium high above him and Star-ii. He set the child down and gave her a little shove to direct him. "Fir'ah? Come out. There is only us, now. We are the Ah-te." He followed to the place Star-ii pointed and stood before the Betweener cowering against the wall. He grabbed her forearms crossed at her chest and pulled until she stood.

"What about Lorff? Are you going to help us get him out?" Star-ii leaned on the zanstyr and stroked the area around his feeler.

"Who?"

"Lorff." Star-ii pointed. "He's sleeping now."

T'lar considered for a moment while looking at Fir'ah and said, "If I leave a calidrium will you stay with him until I return? Will you promise not to move from beside your big friend?"

Star-ii pouted, then brightened. "I will if you give me something to eat and drink and promise not to be gone very long. We ran out of everything."

"Certainly." T'lar handed her the calidrium and held Fir'ah, changing hands to remove his pack. "There is food and a waterskin. Light a fresh calidrium. You can keep it here. Fir'ah and I are going to find more food. We'll return very soon."

"Get lots of food. Lorff'll be hungry." She tore into the pack. "He needs me. I'll wait."

T'lar pulled on Fir'ah. She held her ground, resisting with the last dregs of strength she possessed. He yanked harder, grabbed her head and whispered into her ear. "If you'd rather stay, I'll take Star-ii. She is a bit young, though."

Fir'ah glanced at the child tilting the waterskin, then back at T'lar. For an instant, she was able to muster the concentration required to see the truth in him. It was ugly and chaotic, making no sense. Head bowed, she followed him into the darkness.

Chapter 14

CHACON SPED TOWARD THE BLUE WORKING on the rock fall. Lor'ee was nowhere in sight. The blue's legs functioned in conveyor fashion. For each boulder pulled down, another rolled with it. These were shifted along the outsides and pushed away. The blue was careful to leave the inroad wide.

J'erik sent the group off to continue the search, keeping Chacon and another blue with him. Chacon started to help the blue. J'erik ordered him back to rest.

A rock hit the cliff, careened off and hit again before it rolled to a stop at the bottom. J'erik looked up. Lor'ee stood at the top, waving. "I think I found something. Can you send help?"

J'erik waved back, wishing she would get away from the edge, and sent Chacon. The zanstyr went up the face. The cliffs were as steep as the one he and the zanstyr spent the night on, but not as high. He stepped back to see what remained of the mountain on this side.

The western escarpment he remembered as straight up. The top had risen an easy three hundred and fifty meters before the Demons sliced through the midsection and pulverized the millions of tons of rock. Now there was nothing. The cliffs still rose, but with an unnatural rigidity, never narrowing or flaring.

He moved back farther. The outcrop which had sheltered him and Chacon was barely visible. On the first of four levels where the mountain took on the guise of giant steps, Chacon disappeared over the top.

Activity around the blues increased. The two worked fast. A brief communication from both was jumbled, but concise enough to know they had found something. Abruptly, their pace diminished to a crawl. The blues alternated tunneling, moving man-sized boulders gently away from the area, then hurling them aside.

The first blue called again.

J'erik passed between them. At the site, above the heads of the zanstyrs, was a barbed leg. It fell at the touch of a tongue.

Another meter of excavation exposed the hind end of a zanstyr, crushed by the fall. A green crusty powder mortared loose stones together. The work faltered for a moment.

Gingerly, the Master brushed the edge of the stripe. His heart beat into his throat as the chartreuse was unveiled. He tried to clear the lump, nodded and backed away. The blues proceeded, working around a granite pillar which held the precarious matrix overhead in place. Several meters later they hit open space.

Lorff! Lorff!

A feeble response stirred the beast. He tried to hoist himself onto his legs. They did not seem to want to support the mass.

"J'erik!" Star-ii ran from behind Lorff's head, arms extended. "We were here forever!" She slowed, then stopped before getting too close to the dying sunlight.

"Where is Fir'ah? Is Kali-te with you?" He spoke to the child, staring at the calidrium she clutched.

"No. Kali-te was with my mother. Remember?" She hugged the Betweener with a vehemence. "Fir'ah's safe." Her smile became a grin when she let go of his legs and he picked her up.

The blues issued a harsh summons.

"Stay here. I'll be right back." He placed her on a boulder, turned and ran through the passage.

"That's what everybody says. I always have to wait." She folded her arms, stuck out her lower lip and bowed her head.

Once atop a blue, they were already scaling the cliff up

to Lor'ee. The blue was quick and reached the top without slowing.

He slid down and hurried to the hollow Chacon cleared. Lor'ee waved and started into the hole as soon as the zanstyr moved the last boulder.

J'erik followed, admiring her agility. Grease-blackened sides were slick and made dangerous by the years of cooking in the lower Hold. Layers fell away from the sharp juts which were the best handholds. The fifteen meters down to an open kitchen seemed longer than it was.

By the time he dropped to the floor, Lor'ee had found a calidrium. She lit it from a gas flame struggling at the end of a broken pipe. More pipes were scattered across the floor. A second fixed one was at the central cooking fixture, where a caldron was tipped on its side. The broth sat in murky puddles around cracks in the floor.

The earth motion which had shoved up half the floor a meter higher than the original also affected the natural gas flow. That fact alone killed the Hold for future use. The trickle of gas was insufficient for cooking or smelting.

"Look," Lor'ee said, pointing at the floor, eyes darting at the erratic shadows.

J'erik took a calidrium off the floor and touched the flame. A spark flew.

"Come on." Lor'ee gestured to the dark trail leading into one of four corridors. An aisle through debris lay clear where the pattern moved along the floor.

She led while he followed, guarding. Both were apprehensive exploring the halls of a strange Hold. J'erik recalled how welcome he had been under desperate circumstances, then thought of Chacon. He tried to rationalize their reactions and hoped a difference did exist.

Doors broke the wall formation twelve meters into the corridor. A few were closed. J'erik pushed the open ones aside and checked for survivors. The closed ones were another matter. He slid outside bolts into place on those that had them. There were two in need of checking. For the most part, they were storerooms. Others were completely empty. He noted the age of the Hold by the smooth walls carved out of the stone by legendary machines long since decayed into dust.

"J'erik," Lor'ee whispered, head tilted at the ninth door. "In there."

J'erik glanced at the closed door, then down at the knife in his hand, unable to remember drawing it. He moved in front of Lor'ee, handing her the calidrium. A quick wave positioned her on the other side of the door. His hand rested on the latch for a few beats while they gazed at each other.

When he moved, it was with speed. Latch up, he kicked the door. It banged the wall and swung halfway back.

Lor'ee reached around and pushed near the hinge. It creaked back and stayed.

The room was totally silent.

"Throw one," J'erik said, holding his hand out to the side.

She took a step back, separated the calidriums and tossed one. He caught it easily, continuing the motion by moving into the room. The light stayed high, off to the side as he crouched, peering into the darkness.

The room was large and empty. J'erik moved cautiously along the wall. At the far corner, ready to make the turn along the back wall, he heard a moan. He froze, trying to locate the source.

He called out, gauging the distance to the door in heartbeats.

No answer came.

Another long silence passed. J'erik continued along the back wall. The sound came again. This time he found the direction before the stone walls confused it. The calidrium arced high across the room.

A rumpled mound of hair and rags lay stuffed in the corner.

J'erik ran to the calidrium, picked it up and scoured the area. No other doors led from the room. Satisfied that they were alone, he went to the corner.

Carefully, he turned the heap over.

"Oh, Kali-te, Kali-te."

She winced. Pain deepened the age wrinkled at her temples. Her left arm rose, the wrist bent the wrong way.

"It will be all right. We go to the Techi now."

Tears caught in the corner of her swollen right eye.

Tenderness in the way he picked her up bespoke

affection. She moaned several times, but managed to cling to him with her good hand. He carried her out to the corridor, motioned with his head at Lor'ee and followed, pausing only when she unlatched the locked doors. Halfway through the hall, Lor'ee ducked into one of the storage rooms for rope and blankets.

In the kitchen, he laid Kali-te on a clear spot and straightened her fouled robes. Some of the wounds had scabbed; those were not the ones worrying him. The way she clutched her abdomen and tried to keep doubled over scared him. Open gashes, still oozing, had left the trail they followed. A mottled plague of bruises covered her face and hands.

Lor'ee lost no time in lashing three short pipe lengths together. J'erik tested the knots, then moved Kali-te on top of them.

"Listen to me, Kali-te. We must tie you to these. I know it will hurt, but there is no other way to get you out of here."

They covered her with blankets and doubled spare ones to use as padding against the ropes. J'erik placed the strain on her arms and legs, avoiding her midsection. Two leader ropes looped through his belt. Benches were piled onto the old hearth until he could reach the vent shaft.

Going up was as difficult as the descent. The soot fought him every bit of the way, coating his hands, body and the rock. At the top, he crawled out and checked the surroundings. It was dusk. Chacon and the blue waited patiently off to the side. He gave them instructions and freed the ropes.

Chacon's lightning tongue whipped around the double ropes. He backed away while J'erik peered into the vent and told Lor'ee to start guiding Kali-te into the opening.

She held the two bottom ropes to keep the litter from spinning. The pipes screeched against the walls, making black rain fall below. While they hated the noise, it was a better alternative than an up-the-middle ascent which might injure the old woman further if the carrier shifted.

J'erik grabbed the pipes at the top and helped pull it over the edge.

"J'erik."

He leaned over the shaft and whispered loudly, "Yes?"

"They're coming."

He pulled out his knife and cut a dangling rope from the litter. "Grab the rope. I'll pull you up." He wound the end around his shoulders and right hand, then set his feet.

"I can climb faster than you can pull."

Already he felt her weight and heard the melee grow out of the shaft. She was heavier than she looked. The rope worked into his flesh. Each new grip she took shook his arms.

Another weight on the lifeline taxed his strength to the limit. *Chacon. Grab and hold.* To the blue: *Move the rock over the hole as soon as the Betweener is clear.*

Chacon and the blue complied instantly. J'erik leaned over the edge, one arm extended for Lor'ee, the other braced against the rock cover.

Lor'ee stretched and grasped his hand. Soot blackened her face and hair. She released the rope and grabbed onto his wrist with her other hand. Suddenly, her eyes widened and her weight more than doubled.

"Hold onto me," she hissed through clenched teeth.

J'erik tightened his grip, feeling hers tighten also. She hung free for a minute. The greater part of the struggle became the hold on her foot. She blinked hard, threw her head back and shook her body. Simultaneously, she delivered a hard chop with her heel to the hand pulling her down.

A yell, and she was lighter. J'erik hauled her out of the hole and rolled them both away. The blue dropped the cover. Angry sounds leaked through the gaps.

J'erik and the woman lay on the ground, breathing hard, clinging to each other. Chacon let the rope slip down slowly, giving the climber time to find the rock holds. It slackened and wiggled into the shaft.

Lor'ee did not hurry away. She lifted to look at J'erik. "I thought they had me. Many of the Holds blame Betweeners for what is happening to Cassilee. They believe we have disturbed her balance by going out to the surface." A white smile flaked soot onto him. "We'd better hurry."

J'erik let her go, wishing the circumstances were different and he did not have to relinquish her closeness. Together, they lashed Kali-te to Chacon and rode down a more gentle slope to Star-ii.

The blue remained near the shaft. His instructions were to remove the cover when the Master was well onto the plains.

Chapter 15

LORFF STAGGERED IN A CIRCLE OUTSIDE THE cavern. His last three sections, twisted, denuded and legless, dragged on the ground. The blue stood guard over Star-ii, though the child did not understand why he blocked her exploration of the large area illuminated by the last dregs of daylight. She talked incessantly to the beast. In turn, he spread his body to confine her to an area against the wall where Lorff had been.

Faint noises, suppressed by distance, trickled through dark channels. As the rantings increased, the blue closed the boundaries around Star-ii and opened an exit to the outside.

Star-ii gave ground reluctantly. The steady approach of the barbs won out to hedge her toward the exit. She looked around, listening to the noise. There was a fear riding the inner tunnels which prevented her calling out and halted protests.

Lorff wagged his head, flicked out his tongue and caught the child around the waist. One arc deposited her onto his stripe. Hobbling, dragging the dead weight off-setting his natural rhythm, he sought to put distance between them and the cavern. He summoned the Master, conveying urgency in a single thought.

Scattered zanstyrs returning from exhausted search patterns caught the danger expressed in Lorff's broadcast. They crossed the open land at top speed to converge at the demolished mountain. Rising dust clouds hung in the air against the ribbons of light in the west.

Chacon too quickened his pace. His arduous labor maintained a smoothness for his riders.

A calidrium-carrying group oozed over deposed monoliths littering the floors and partially blocking passageways. The blue recoiled.

For a moment the sight of the zanstyr hushed the people. Someone in the rear yelled, and the cry was taken up. They spread along the wall and over debris. Rocks hurled across the open space, a few hitting the zanstyr.

The blue held his ground.

J'erik leaped from Chacon, sending the beast on to the Techi as he touched the ground. He charged the closest zanstyr with the care of Star-ii to relieve Lorff and waited until she was transferred before asking about Fir'ah.

"She went with T'lar. They didn't come back for me like he said. He promised! I'm not going to believe him ever again." Lower lip pouting, she looked away. "He lied to me." Back to J'erik, "Didn't he?"

J'erik could neither confirm nor deny. Sick with dread, his stomach began a slow roll. "T'lar . . . " His love for Fir'ah coupled with the experience he had relived with her in the Ah-te produced a hatred greater than he thought possible, outstripping the emotion in their small room. It engulfed his entire being.

Star-ii was trembling, her gaze fixed upon the Betweener when he managed to regain a semblance of self-control. Calmly, "Stay with Lor'ee and Kali-te at the Techi until I get there." He sent the zanstyr on his way.

J'erik started toward the Tor-ad-ih. His heels thundered on the ground and agitated the dust. His right hand rested on the hilt of his knife, his eyes narrowed and straight ahead. Only once did his concentration deviate. He glanced back to be sure Lorff was getting safely away from the area. He stomped between the zanstyr-made mountains to the entrance.

The blue flexed sections, giving the Master as wide a path as possible. When he reached the zanstyr's head, he catapulted to the top of the stripe and stood erect, hands on hips, for all to see.

The noise quivered and died. Rocks and knives hung in raised hands, ready to be launched.

"I am J'erik the Betweener of the surface lands. I seek another Betweener, a woman called Fir'ah who does not speak. Bring her and the kodjelu's waste of a man, T'lar from the Ah-te, but no longer, for he was dead to the Hold before the Hold died."

An absolute silence was broken by a voice from the shadows. "And if we do not?"

Cold, calculated, "Then Cassilee will swallow you like spittle upon the plains when Uli stands overhead."

A murmur passed over the group as they shrank into dark places. A man stepped forward and tossed the rock he held to the side. "I am N'oblic." In the eerie shadows cast by the calidriums, the speaker's head bowed in respect. "There was a man called T'lar with us for a very short period. We have not seen him since the upper Hold was destroyed by your spirits, Betweener."

"He is here. He holds my sister captive and I will have them both. You have until sunrise. Find them. I will return then." He took a deep breath and exhaled slowly. "Though my sister does not speak, I will know if she has suffered ill treatment by any from the Tor-ad-ih." He paused, pressing his fingers into his hips. "Uli is unkind to the light skin stretched in her brightest light. That will be T'lar's reward, and any who help him from this moment on. Understand this."

"The Tor-ad-ih is large, very large. There are tunnels and passages leading farther than we are able to walk and carry supplies. What you ask of us is not possible if they have found the lower levels where the mazes are. Were we sixty times as many, we could not explore them all.

"We will search all the areas we know, but we will not enter the mazes. We would be lost there. If we find the man T'lar and the woman, be assured that they will be returned to you at sunrise. We have no wish to interfere in the justice of the Ah-te. If we do not find them . . ." N'oblic shrugged. "If we do not, then they are not in what is left of the occupied areas."

The speaker took three steps toward J'erik. "Cassilee will not swallow the Tor-ad-ih easily. There will be a price if your vengeance is false or without justice, Betweener."

J'erik's words hissed through clamped teeth. "Find them! At sunrise, the zanstyrs begin another search of your Hold." He sat on the blue stripe and watched those watching him, the isolated man in particular. "There is no escape from the Tor-ad-ih. You will be watched. When you find T'lar, throw him into the night."

It was dark by the time J'erik and the blue retreated into fresh air. He stationed zanstyrs around the mountain in pairs so that they could alternate foraging and watching. All knew Fir'ah on sight and, with an image projection, what T'lar looked like, also.

He charged the blue to take him back to the Techi at his best speed. He kept an eye turned to the sky for invaders. The stars remained fixed. The cooling night air rushing at him could not touch the anger and depression eating at him.

Fir'ah dressed quickly in the dark. The ache in her hands increased as she tied a cord belt around her waist. Her fingers seemed either frozen or independent of what she wanted them to do. Once the first waves of panic had run their course in the big cavern with Star-ii, resignation brought its own salvation. She endured.

The air was stale in the depths T'lar used as a refuge. It conjured something vile: T'lar. She could hear his approach through one of the dozens of tunnels before light shone against the walls. She stood, feeling the overall strain in her muscles, and glared at the spot where he would enter the circular anteroom.

He stopped short when he saw her, as though surprised. Fir'ah noted his face change expressions, realizing for the first time how deranged he was. Lines in his forehead, around his eyes and at his mouth were deeper than his years should have made them. The time since the Ah-te had strengthened him physically and deteriorated him mentally. It was as though he sacrificed one for the other.

T'lar took several steps and dropped two heavy packs onto the floor. The thud changed his mood. He put the calidrium into an ancient wall holder that crumbled, but held the light by one of three bands. Trancelike, he moved to Fir'ah and tenderly placed his hands on her shoulders.

"We could have a good life, Fir'ah. If only you could

care a little. . . . It doesn't have to be the way it is. You could change it. We need each other now."

She met the rheumy gaze upon her without blinking. His hand wandered into her robe and closed around her right breast, squeezing, nails digging into her flesh until blood trickled down her ribs.

She continued to stare, expressionless. That part steeled by the silent barrier worked for the part writhing in pain, calming, absorbing it in a dark void. She yielded nothing. The passivity forced to the exterior built upon the hatred inside.

T'lar's eyes brightened. A grin spread across his face in pleasure. Saliva gleamed in the corners of his mouth until he licked his lips and wiped the grin away. At the same time, he released her, only to grab her by the shoulders again and throw her at the packs on the floor.

"Pick one up and strap it on."

Instinct sent her hands flying to break the impact. For a second she was glad for the exile to silence. It kept her from involuntarily giving him the satisfaction of knowing how much pain she was in. Carefully she selected the lighter of the two packs and strapped it on.

"Come on." He hoisted the second one and retrieved the light. "Some of these passages must lead to the surface. A few have wall torches which haven't been used for a long time. It looks as though it was abandoned eons ago."

Checking to be sure she followed, "This is some Hold, nothing like the Ah-te and their few people. More than a hundred survived the Star Demons in the lower elevations. They are above us now. They don't come down here.

"Star-ii will be taken care of. They'll find her soon." The wistfulness in his tone when mentioning the child seemed out of character for the man Fir'ah hated. She watched his back, thinking how easy it was to forget the sorrows and frustrations in his life when he incited terror, pain and hate in hers.

The walls glistened in the light, changing texture and color as they passed. Dripping water labored to close the passage with lime deposits. Thus far it had succeeded in narrowing it in places and making it slippery.

T'lar's eagerness to put distance between them and the

Tor-ad-ih allowed no rest periods. Fir'ah procrastinated. The day and a half digging around Lorff had sapped her energies. Nausea jabbed at her stomach. She continued to put one foot in front of the other, unwilling to suffer T'lar's wrath for stopping. A sensation of limbo where everything was suspended in darkness, in front, behind, on every side, acted to halt time and life. It was similar to the nothingness J'erik had forced her to give up.

J'erik.

She stumbled.

Why did he not cover the whole distance? Why did he retreat and never finish what he had started?

Her legs buckled, refusing another step. She grabbed for the wall, missed and fell.

T'lar turned back and sat beside her. He removed both packs. After putting out the calidrium, he lay back and rolled Fir'ah onto his shoulder.

"Sleep now."

Fir'ah slept and dreamed of better days.

A few kilometers from the Techi, J'erik caught up with Star-ii and Lor'ee. Searchers kept a wide girth from the zanstyrs, though the Betweeners and Star-ii called to them repeatedly. Zanstyrs not carrying passengers changed to a northern course where grazing promised to be a more worthwhile endeavor. Led by Chacon, the three crossed the last of the open plains.

Lor'ee ran up the rock face and returned with ropes, a litter and men to raise Kali-te before J'erik freed the old woman from the zanstyr.

With Star-ii on his back, J'erik climbed into the Hold proper, simultaneously dismissing the carriers for their own protection against the fearful hunters roaming the night.

J'osh-uah met him in the metal entry. He nodded, beaming approval that lit his aged face when he saw the child. "And Fir'ah? Is she yet to come?"

He set Star-ii down and waited for her to join the bustling group converging on the interior. "No." He walked slowly, head bowed, and gave a brief account of her condition when he returned to the Ah-te. The partial recovery he attributed to time and the special broth. He could not bring himself to bare yet another difference to

136

the man who was his father and Leader of the Techi. Before he finished speaking about the Tor-ad-ih, Lor'ee met them in the corridor.

"She asks for you, J'erik."

Nodding, he followed Lor'ee down a series of straight corridors to a large room filled with elevated tables, lights, shiny instruments and neatly folded linens. Two men were bent over Kali-te, mumbling as they examined her. The closest one shook his head continuously during the conversation. He adjusted something near Kali-te. The machine was linked to her arm by a red tube.

The shorter man looked up and motioned to J'erik.

J'erik met him halfway across the room.

"You are the Betweener, J'erik?"

"Yes."

"She asks for you when she is conscious. There is nothing we can do for her."

J'erik surveyed the room. An expression of incredulity settled over him. "You have all of this and can do nothing for her? Nothing?"

The man looked down at the glowing white floor. "We have all of this, but the ability to use it has been lost over the generations. Not all of it functions. There was a time . . ." He sighed. "There was a time when all the secrets were open. No more.

"Too many breakdowns, too much knowledge lost in the machines, or by the great ones who understood them."

Meeting J'erik's gaze, "If she were my own mother, I could not do more to save her. I am sorry, Betweener. Please, stay. Listen to her. Talk to her. The time is short."

Hearing such words spoken with such total sincerity, J'erik felt he had come upon the lowest point in his life. Numbly, he followed the medic over to Kali-te and did not notice that the man had left until he returned with a damp cloth. J'erik wiped his hands on it. The black soot on off-white contrasted to birth and death.

He stood over Kali-te for long minutes while the two men labored with the few bits of existing technology prolonging her life. Her chin quivered and her mouth twitched. Fluttering eyelids opened as she whispered his name.

"I am here, Kali-te. I am with you."

". . . not the death I saw," she whispered so softly he had to put his ear to her lips.

"Perhaps it is not your time, old woman. I still need you." The words came from his heart as a truth finally acknowledged. All the years of her devotion flooded back with a realization of how much he loved the old woman. Not once had he told her. His right hand upon her forehead stroked the soot-blackened gray hair.

Her eyes closed as though resting. Her mouth moved without making sounds.

J'erik stiffened and looked hopefully at the two men watching. Both shook their heads. Machine noises changed pitch. The taller man began to unhook the lines running to Kali-te.

Panic jangled his insides. He felt as though he could not survive another loss this day, bowing to the slim expectations of seeing Fir'ah again. It hit like a raging storm. The black weight stepping on his heart shoved it into his bowels.

"Kali-te? Listen to me. It is not your time. Fight the devil . . ." His voice broke. Tears washed soot and dirt from his face. They fell to stain the clean linens draped over the frail body.

"Help me." The words came hard and sudden. They burst upon J'erik with an added force. All senses rose with an awareness of the plea. Without hesitation, knowing all was lost for Kali-te, he tried to intervene in the same manner as he had for Fir'ah at the Ah-te.

The lines of pain melted from the old woman's face, only to reappear on the young Betweener's. He crossed the threshold and touched her mind, ever so careful not to touch too heavily, lest he eradicate the fragile essence that was Kali-te. He tried to leave the mind and enter the inner physical world existing by the tenacity of willpower and the old woman's stubborn disposition.

He no longer registered blinking lights or bright machinery in a clean room. Broken bones and torn tissue, shrouded in red hazes, overtook his vision. He moved inside the pain, seeking the centers, feeling death squeeze at the tenuous fiber of life linked to him.

Energy levels accelerated. Cells regenerated at a rate which reached exponential levels. Tissue built layer upon layer, mingling and reworking healthy solidity over the opened gaps and deep bruises. A lung birthed a new chamber as it pushed back the ribs penetrating the old damaged area. The bones molded along the breaks to begin the long healing process with a rapid head start to hold them in place.

Torn capillaries, ripped veins, collapsed arterial walls required time, guesswork and more concentration than the major wounds threatening to cancel out Kali-te's life. The tortuous complexity of those areas, where he knew nothing but the need of her body to mend itself, sapped him to exhaustive limits.

Body shaking, his legs neared collapse. Slowly, he withdrew from the physical world of Kali-te and lingered in the aura of her thoughts.

He felt the hand push her from the warrior's back, knew the desperation to find shelter and the fall through the open shaft.

Yet the love and gratitude radiating from her brought repressed sobs from his throat. The sounds were not a conscious thing, rather distant, disassociated with what, and who, he was at the time. The old woman loved him and Fir'ah as her own, just as she had always professed. She shared the heartache of Fir'ah's lot in life, but felt a joy in the silent Fir'ah which shone a far more hopeful aura than the withdrawn state.

Gradually, J'erik departed. There was a consolation that if his intervention resulted in a permanent silence, as he believed it had done with his sister, Kali-te would live. The old woman cherished life and had accepted the probable consequences without a qualm.

Lights registered in the room. Hissing and humming machinery conversed off to the left. A touch of vertigo descended and melted away. The solitude isolating him from everything began to crumble. He looked tenderly at Kali-te. Her puffy eyes opened. Her voice was weak, but clear. "Betweener," she said, then smiled feebly, mouth corners twitching from the strain.

"Old woman."

Her smile broadened, strengthened, as her eyes closed for sleep.

The joy of having Kali-te for however long and able to speak overwhelmed him. He kissed her forehead and tucked the linens around her bony shoulders. The impact of what he had accomplished crashed upon him as he straightened. He glanced around for Lor'ee. She was beside him and seemed to have been there for some time. The two medics were at the entrance with J'osh-uah, Cor-ii and a dozen other witnesses.

Lor'ee slipped her arm around his waist, steadied him and walked to the group. Their looks were grim as a whole, bordering fear. Cor-ii's eyes widened.

J'erik turned to the medic he had spoken to earlier. "When she wakes, you will help the bones to mend properly?"

"Yes, I will. I will take very special care of her, Betweener." Both manner and tone oozed respect and more than a tinge of veneration.

J'osh-uah spoke. "When you have rested and taken care of your needs, I have much to speak about with you."

Nodding, J'erik searched for Cor-ii. The woman tried to shrink into the gathering. "Cor-ii!" Her name echoed throughout the Techi.

The group parted, leaving her nowhere to go and standing alone. Chin up, she glared back.

"You have falsely accused me of stealing your child. There is much I know about you." A quick glance at Kali-te and he resumed the boring stare at Cor-ii. She trembled visibly. "Cor-ii of the Ah-te, you are dead to me. You are dead to Kali-te. Should you venture upon the surface, stay clear of the zanstyrs who once were friend to you. It is no more. You are fair game to them and the other beasts of Cassilee. It is only the grace of the Techi that keeps you from the land . . ."

A murmur flew over the spectators and died quickly.

Turning to J'osh-uah, "Would you keep someone you trust with Kali-te until she is able to care for herself?"

"It will be done." The leader pointed to the medics, who nodded in agreement.

J'erik shuffled through the people-lined wall, feeling their eyes upon him. He tried not to lean too heavily upon Lor'ee until they passed the last one. "Will you lead me out of here?"

Chapter 16

JOLTED AWAKE, FANCHER GLANCED AROUND, seeking the reason for his wakeful state.

The wind had stilled at evening and remained a quiet breeze. The soft glow of flowing lava out of a growing volcano cast a ghoulish light in the distant east. Nothing to worry about. No kodjelu ran in armor-bumping hordes. The few skimpy iron trees were empty. A thin fog from the west lay in sporadic wisps on layers of air.

Resting back onto one elbow, he checked north. The panaver herd which had been keeping pace with him stood fifty meters away, watching in a line.

He had not slept long, and his legs agreed more rest was in order before starting again. Even as he thought about it, the toll of the day's journey lessened and a new strength developed.

The panaver leader brought the line closer. Their colors changed to an iridescent blue. They reminded Fancher of a holograph at an artists' convention.

A sense of urgency overcame him. He gathered his belongings and readied to journey. It seemed an insane thing to do, but he knew he was going to do it. Mumbling, he shoved articles into the packs. "The natives seem friendly enough. May as well travel with them as opposed to being alone. Nothin' to lose but time. And I got time."

He embarked on a northerly pattern. As usual, the panavers closed ranks and refused passage.

"All right," he said to the leader. "West it is—again. You lead. I'll follow."

The leader raised his oversize hoof for several seconds, moved to the head of the column and set a southwesterly course.

Fancher looked to the south. Streaks of light fell from the stars. He watched passively and kept walking.

The fog turned cold and heavy. Slippery rocks, darkness and fatigue complicated J'erik's descent. He had to wait for Chacon to come in from the fertile grazing lands. The zanstyr signaled when he neared by bumping his legs together. The barbs clanked loudly in a series of hollow notes.

"If one of us is to be rested and full of food, it's best that it's you, my friend." J'erik patted hunks of fur dripping cold moisture onto the ground. Wet, the zanstyr was hard to mount. After more effort than he cared to exert, J'erik settled on the purple and hoped that the Tor-ad-ih would have Fir'ah and T'lar waiting.

The mystery of what had happened with Kali-te stayed in his mind with a sense of wonder. While he loved the old woman, it did not explain how he could help her in such a manner, on such a grand scale, and harm Fir'ah with a permanent silence using even less penetration. The more thought given to it, the less it made sense. It was impossible to accept.

Chacon galloped through waves of mist. Occasionally, it thinned enough so he could see all of the beast's head. Silently, he thanked Cassilee for the excellent vision she provided to her surface creatures. The zanstyr held his head higher than normal. Chacon was becoming a better mount each time he carried a passenger. The bobbing and weaving were minimal. It was easier to hold the fur on an uphill grade. J'erik rested in a state of almost sleep with his eyes closed.

Some time later Chacon intruded upon his quiet. *Master. Much is wrong here. We have traveled upward since leaving the Techi. This place was level in the day.*

Awake immediately, J'erik sat and peered into the fog. Through the wall a line of gray infiltrated the east.

Can you see the mountain?

142

No, Master. We are where it should be, but it is not here.

You are sure? The mist is heavy. Could your direction be wrong?

Chacon did not answer immediately. *Master, I am sure. The mountain is gone. It is likely that we have been traveling on what remains for most of the journey.*

The enormity of such a complete obliteration of matter was incomprehensible. A big Hold like the Tor-ad-ih? Pulverized? All the people? Fir'ah!

Nothing could be so fast, so final. Surely some had escaped. . . .

He attempted to communicate with the zanstyrs left to watch.

Nothing.

Star Demons. Did you see them, Chacon?

We saw their signs early in the night at a great distance. The stars fell and moved north. They did not stay long, for we saw them leave before we reached shelter with Lorff.

They stayed long enough to eat the mountain. None of those I left guarding returned to the main group? Not one, Chacon?

No, Master.

Our losses are tremendous. We must send out purples. All twenty-eight cannot be dead. . . . Even as he formed the words, the vastness of the devastation registered and snuffed the hope of finding a single survivor. The Demons struck viciously on a grand scale. Their swiftness was unfathomable.

J'erik sat motionlessly for the time it took Uli to climb the horizon. He saw her through the fog as a great weeping eye whose sorrow dulled her brilliance. The water running down his body was a solid cold tear of shared misery. Erratic winds moved the fog around in moody swirls. The patterns changed rapidly and shrank under the relentless stares of J'erik and Uli.

Chacon?

Yes, Master?

Forgive me for questioning your judgment.

I also questioned before voicing it to you.

Where we are standing now? What was here yesterday?

The cavern where Lorff was trapped.

The area was smooth. No boulders larger than the height of a man remained. The few that did were widely scattered over the flatland. Concoidal fractures shot through all the exposed facets.

Somewhere in the Tor-ad-ih was a place with many, many deep passages. J'erik stood and looked around. *If any escaped the Star Demons' wrath they would have to be there.*

Chacon navigated the area as he remembered it. He made a lattice pattern while J'erik moved on foot. The fog melted. Uli dried the land and radiated more heat, until tiny cracks began to appear when she looked straight down.

J'erik and the zanstyr searched every meter of the surface where the Tor-ad-ih had once risen into the mountain, level after level. A brown, five blues and two yellow zanstyrs galloped in from the northwest, claiming to have been sent by Lorff.

J'erik wondered if the old Leader knew more than he let on, or the five blues were a coincidence. He dispatched them to the most likely spots, where they were to tunnel into any open area they sensed. He sent the brown back to the main group with a request for all but Lorff and a warrior to return and help with the dig. If there were survivors in the deep tunnels, they would not last long without food, water and possibly air. He left a yellow on the surface and took a second with him.

Halfway to the Techi where a patch of green seemed to have sprung up overnight he stationed the second yellow as a communication relay.

Chacon returned to the Techi. More strange patches of green flourished in nooks and crannies, against rocks and out in the open for no apparent reason.

J'erik took note, but these phenomena lacked the magnitude of wonder in light of his own experiences during the past revolution of Uli. Chacon sidled up to the wall path where the Master could climb up to the ledge.

I will be close, Master.

I want to know if they find something. Rest well, for I will want to go quickly when they do.

May I suggest that you bring a rope, Master? I believe I could travel faster if you were more secure upon my stripe.

J'erik looked down into the purple's great right eye and smiled. *Then, Chacon, I shall bring a rope. Have you any other suggestions?*

No, Master. Not at the moment. However, I may have some later. Chacon ambled off as though dismissed.

The sky was clear. The blue had a washed-out look. It was lighter than the normal royal blue Cassilee had been covered with for all the early years of her life, prior to the last few months. The horizon edges had lost the deep, rich hue where occasionally a few stars peeked through. It looked as though Uli bleached out the sky with her heat. All that was hanging in the atmosphere made the air a bit harder to breathe, a bit moister, and the heat a bit stickier.

Head shaking, J'erik gave up trying to understand what was happening to Cassilee. The changes were too great, too rapid for assimilation.

Lor'ee waited beyond the metal door, just where he had left her. She did not speak. For that J'erik was grateful. The way she neared and slipped her arm around his waist whenever possible carried a pleasant message all its own. Her clothes were clean. Her shiny hair was tied back, and her scent was one of freshness.

They walked unnoticed to his room, where she left him at the door.

J'erik climbed into the bubbling water, clothes and all. It seemed a waste not to accomplish two things at once with the pure water. He washed the clothes as they came off his body, then slapped them over the side onto the floor.

The warmth made him drowsy. Lulled, he dozed, slipping into the pool until water filled his nose and mouth. Coughing, sputtering, he bolted upright, sending water onto the walls.

A giggle from the main room snapped his head around to see Lor'ee. She crossed the room and whipped a towel from a pile of fresh clothes. It fluttered in the air.

"I think you've been in there too long, Betweener."

He looked at her, then at the towel, shrugged and climbed out. A flush spread above the white tunic she wore. The color in her eyes deepened in contrast to the pink tinge.

J'erik dabbed at his face, then wrapped the towel around his waist. "Why are you here, Lor'ee?"

A quick headshake and she turned back to the main room.

"Lor'ee? Why did you return?"

"I thought you might want someone to talk to." Pausing in the middle of the room, "I wanted to . . ." She took a deep breath, but could not finish the sentence when she glanced back at him.

"You wanted to what?"

Facing the door, she did not move. "Choose you," she whispered.

J'erik grinned triumphantly. At last! Something he understood, and wanted to understand on a more personal level. He closed the gap between them by coming up behind her. "Did you change your mind?"

Startled, she turned, not expecting him to be so close. Her mouth opened and closed before she regained some composure. "When is the last time you slept?"

He shrugged; the grin faded to a smile.

"I have to go before J'osh-uah finds out I've been here."

He held her shoulders until she lifted her head to look at him. "That would make a difference?"

Nodding, "He has given orders that you are not to be disturbed until you have had proper rest. If he finds I've been here, he will ask me to leave and never return. I would be banished. He would be well within his rights, too. I should not be here."

"You risk that and still will not Choose me?"

Her voice was a whisper. "I am afraid."

"So am I. I'm afraid you will leave here and I will not see you again."

He bent and touched her lips with his. He felt her fingers tremble on his forearms, unsure of who was shaking the most. The confidence expressed in words was hollow inside. "Tell me what you fear."

The pink drained, leaving a white pall over the bronze. "I did not expect to ever want to Choose. At least, not for real. I mean, I have thought about you since Ladida returned, and . . ." She stopped, eyes moving rapidly in a plea for understanding.

"Stay with me for now. I would not sleep if you left. You do not have to Choose. Just be near me, Lor'ee."

She chewed her lower lip for a moment. "You will sleep if I stay?"

"Yes." Taking her hand, he led her to the bed and lay down.

Lor'ee found a shred of bravado and took a place beside him. She did not object when he pulled her close. Her smile returned. Two wiggles settled her comfortably. "Sleep."

For biological reasons, J'erik considered the request impossible. But sleep won out before he could think of a persuasive argument.

The light T'lar carried pulled Fir'ah along an invisible string. The nightmare of black noise and gyrating walls, which belched a cloud of dust at them, sent a message denying a refuge where the journey began. The kilometers they had covered since the eruption were filled with groans and threatening noises eking out of a dozen new tunnels branching from the one they occupied. The sour air freshened for a time. Gradually, it fouled and became difficult to breathe.

"Hurry up, or I'll leave you behind!"

Fir'ah smiled in the darkness. It was nice to hear a spark of worry in his voice. Close walls, low ceilings, and darkness did not scare her. It was a separate reality which she could identify with personally. It emulated that safe place she had dwelt in before J'erik coaxed her into the light. Yet now there seemed something incomplete, something she did not want to remember and felt it important that she did.

Her smile widened.

It was there. Just out of reach. Closer than ever. Like the key to a locked door. Behind that: the thing which would free the words, even though what lived there was terrifying. But terror was becoming somewhat of an abstraction. She had already absorbed more of it than she thought humanly possible.

In the end, she would live or die. Presently, there was little difference. The distinction had been swallowed by indignities. If she lived to see the light from Uli, she vowed to escape T'lar. The surface was Betweener territory, not Dweller turf.

Thinking out a future plan, she slowed.

T'lar gained a longer lead.

She noticed the last hint of light die around a bend, then turned around and walked quickly toward the last offshoot tunnel. It did not matter where the shoot led. Even if it became a dead end or a gas pocket, the choice was hers. Not T'lar's. The opportunity was too good to pass.

Fir'ah giggled mischievously. Who said he's right? she thought defiantly. Maybe he'll be the one stuck with no place to go. He'll never know which one I take, and he can't search them all.

She found the last offshoot and stood in the entry, trying to feel the destination and flavor. The impressions came slowly.

It was rejected. She moved on.

The fifth one felt better than the others. Hearing T'lar yell her name made her decision easier. Bits of rock sifted through the pungent air. She removed her sandals and ran with her hands outstretched. The twists and turns were gradual enough so the glancing blows changed her direction without causing injury.

T'lar's voice faded away.

She ran until her lungs refused another meter, then put on her sandals and walked, determined to go until she dropped. Now there was only her life to lose and everything to gain. Reassuring herself, she nodded, feeling death of any kind preferable to facing T'lar's wrath.

Chapter 17

"**A**RE YOU RESTED?"

J'erik was awake instantly. "No."

"Uli is well over the horizon." The amusement in J'osh-uah's tone was not well hidden.

"Which one?" J'erik mumbled, pulled the cover over him and flopped onto his stomach. The sleep left him more tired than the absence of it.

"The eastern one."

Quickly, he checked with Chacon for a progress report. The blues had excavated down to the lowest levels, where three halls of rooms were filled with the remains of the upper floors. Next he reached to his side. No Lor'ee. "Where is she?"

"Who?"

Twisted into a sitting position, elbows on knees, "Lor'ee."

Shrugging, "On the surface, I suppose. She usually goes out this time of day. It is just as well. We have much to talk about."

J'erik watched the older man for a moment, seeing the wheels turn and click. His presence was truly the one of a Leader. Asking for Lor'ee had been a mistake. J'osh-uah absorbed the information as an olca leaf took water.

"All right. Let's start with Lor'ee."

The dark skin around J'osh-uah's mouth wrinkled into a smile which carried the displeasure of a frown. "I would rather not. It is clear she was here against an order issued to the entire population. The penalty is also clear."

J'erik swung his legs over the side, grabbed his clean clothes from the elevated dresser and began to dress. "Then we have nothing to talk about."

The Techi Leader shifted uncomfortably at the foot of the bed. "The child told us more about the man T'lar. The old woman whom you performed a—a miracle on spoke of your journey and the fate she saw for the Ah-te."

J'erik strapped his belt on and slipped the Hold knives into place. He rubbed his leg and felt an old scar. He glanced down, surprised. The knife wound was completely healed. He accepted it without question. The answer well of understanding had long since run dry.

"Is there any chance of Fir'ah's being alive in the depths of the Tor-ad-ih?"

J'erik left for the small water basin.

J'osh-uah rose and followed to the door.

J'erik drank until he could hold no more, then began scraping the growth from his face. "This is easier with a reflection glass."

A certain exasperation marked J'osh-uah's tone. "Our hunting party did not return the night before last. Have you any idea what happened to them? There were twenty men in the group."

"It must be nice to have this much clean water."

"All recycled," he answered with an impatient wave. J'osh-uah's pale-gray eyes met his son's in the mirror. "I understand that the land is drastically changing. Star Demons again?" Arms folded, he continued, "The Tor-ad-ih is one of the oldest Dweller settlements known. It is also the largest on Cassilee. Unfortunately, they have not conceded the necessity of commingling, as we have with other Dweller Holds over the last generation. They too have suffered the malady of birthing few live babies."

J'erik washed his face and rinsed the knife.

"They may be less averse to a Betweener."

Drying his hands, J'erik watched his father in the mirror for several minutes. "What you're saying is that I should go over there, check out any survivors and spread the breed around? Stay away from my own kind?"

"Well, not exactly." J'osh-uah was searching for words, a problem which appeared to be a new experience for him. "Betweeners are the hope of the future. Cassilee is dying, J'erik. We will die with her unless we can overcome our foolish history of prejudice. Time is running out on all of us."

Shouldering past J'osh-uah, he went for his sandals and pack beside the wall. Three coils of rope taken from the Tor-ad-ih lay beneath the pack. Lor'ee, he thought.

"I realize that you are not the average Betweener, J'erik." Calculated, even-toned, "Betweeners are few and scattered over the planet. There was a time when we had communications from the two distant Techi Lodges. But no more. Lor'ee says the one in the north no longer permits anyone in or out. It must be dead."

Sandals tied, rope anchored to the belt, the pack lifted to his shoulders, he settled the rolled brown stripe. "We must talk again sometime."

"J'erik!"

He paused at the door and glanced over his shoulder.

"You are not leaving until we have exchanged some information."

Facing the man who was his father, "I mean no disrespect, J'osh-uah, Leader of the Techi. There are things I must do, places I must go. There is a drive in me which pushes my destiny and me with it. I do not understand it, but what I do comes naturally. It makes me stronger each time I touch what lies inside. No, I don't think I am the average Betweener, as you say. I will live what life I have the way I must. That does not include seeking a Chooser I do not want. Hold life is dead on Cassilee.

"Guard the life which dwells here well. It may be the last."

J'osh-uah came to his side. "All the more reason that you should not set yourself with Lor'ee. Stay. There are women here."

"You still do not understand, do you? It is too late for a future that way. The Star Demons come again and again. Each time they eat a piece of Cassilee and spit out the remains. We are less than kodjelu to them and even more helpless. I wish to find a way to strike back at them. And the woman I take with me will not last three revolutions of Uli unless she is a Betweener."

J'osh-uah shook his head slowly, suddenly very old. "I can keep you here."

J'erik grinned quickly. "As what? A prisoner? No. You can try, but you could not keep me for long.

"I will say goodbye to Kali-te and Star-ii. Perhaps I will return for them one day. I am still the Ah-te, even when I am the last one on the surface of Cassilee. Your rigid code assures that they will be well treated.

"There was a time, after our mother died, that Fir'ah and I needed someone. You would not take us then, but Kali-te cared in your stead. Your words and ideas for a future race on Cassilee are one thing. Living with Betweeners, even those who were a part of you, apparently was another. In my mind, I am not a social experiment.

"Not until this day did I know that what I had hoped for from you as a father could not be found. You do not have it to give, and I cannot pretend indifference. I am disappointed."

The door opened. Lor'ee started to take a step and froze. Color ran from her face when she saw the grim expressions shared by the two men.

"Get your things, Betweener. I am yours if you Choose me. If not, we can at least leave together."

"I Choose you," she said, glancing from him to J'oshuah.

"And I accept. It is final."

Star-ii sat with Kali-te in the room they shared. The tall medic took a silent leave when J'erik entered. J'erik spoke softly and asked each to care for the other. He promised to leave a zanstyr and mate in the area so Star-ii could play at night without a guard. He privately requested Kali-te to send one or both if she needed him.

Star-ii cried out loud, holding onto J'erik's neck while he tried to soothe her. She refused to be consoled and wanted only to have him take her along. Kali-te permitted a tear, but understood. It was a fact for which J'erik was grateful.

Lor'ee led the way to the top, where Diearka and Chamblis waited. It was delightful to see the big orange one again.

Lord Chamblis?

The ringlets jiggled with a formal bow, bringing a

152

giggle from Lor'ee and a smile to J'erik in spite of the emotional scene he had just left behind.

I thank you for the kindness which preserved my life. My Lady and I are in your debt.

The Lady Ladida is well, I hope?

She is eager to see you, Lord J'erik Betweener.

The orange one snapped his tail, demanding attention. J'erik climbed onto his haunch and reached to the forelimbs. *Ah, Diearka. I have missed you. More than a few times, I dreamed of flying through the clouds as we did before.*

Both calantani placed riders behind their heads and in front of the first wing sets. In moments, they were soaring opposing circles.

Diearka labored to carry his Lord into the heights and show Cassilee to him.

Diearka, you do not have to try to please me. Your presence and your belief in me is more than I ever hoped for. Tell me, have you seen all of Cassilee?

It is impossible to see all of her, but I have roamed the circumference several times. It is a long, long journey.

Are there many Holds scattered around?

Twenty-eight or twenty-nine. Possibly there are more. As I said, she is very large and Holds are not easy to spot.

How about other life forms, like the zanstyrs?

There is another, though I have not seen it. He paused. *It is something I have felt. Their presence is powerful and not hostile, yet not benign. It is difficult to express. Twice, I thought I had found the source, but it was only a herd of panavers. You will know when you feel it, Lord J'erik. Your sensitivity has increased a thousandfold since I last felt your touch. Now I can barely feel you in my mind. Before, it was different.*

Grinning into the wind, *Like a landslide?*

Yes. Very much like being under one.

The enjoyment of being airborne had a way of easing his worries. Ahead, Lor'ee appeared to be a part of Chamblis. More than ever he wanted to carve out a niche of Cassilee where life could flourish, safe from the Star Demons. Daydreaming about what would come with Lor'ee ate the time away. Diearka started a half-circle descent to the honeycombed land where the zanstyrs dug for survivors. In the western distance a puff of dust fuzzed the horizon.

Chacon, slow down. There are plenty of workers.

Yes, Master.

The purple kept coming at full speed.

Diearka landed next to Chamblis. The two calantani stayed close. The zanstyrs regarded them skeptically. Each weighed the proximity of a threat.

Master! Fetch the Master! Survivors! came a cry from a zanstyr deep in the ground.

J'erik mounted the closest one, gave a few simple directions and held on. Several dozen strides and over the side they went. The darkness was rough with suspended dust. Straight walls formed thousands of years earlier bore fresh marks from the collapse.

In the depths, crying and hurried conversations seeped out of a very large and dark blotch in the side.

A zanstyr of an indiscernible color, possibly a blue, pulled away the last of the straight slabs which had fallen into the tunnel.

As J'erik's eyes became acclimated, the darkness lost its overwhelming impressions. Shapes and sizes took on distinction. He slipped off the beast and picked a path through the rubble to the source of the noise.

"You, of the Tor-ad-ih, how many of you are there?"

Hysterical sobs rose, then choked off. Whispers were punctuated by a series of high-pitched, loudly spoken conflicts.

"I am here to help you."

"Betweener?"

"Yes. Is my sister with you?"

"No." A man stepped into the brighter shadows. His arm was wrapped in rags. Beneath the dirt, open wounds bled through partial scabs. He stood erect. The squareness of his shoulders, the levelness with which he gazed back at the Betweener carried the certainty of courage in the light of nothing to lose. "We looked until the Demons came. She was not found, nor was the man. Two packs and provisions were missing from the stores we salvaged after the first attack. That is all we know, Betweener."

Nodding sadly, peering into the semidarkness, "N'oblic?" Seeing the responsive nod, "The zanstyrs have begun excavation of two other areas such as this. Is

154

it a worthwhile project? We can only guess how the Tor-ad-ih was laid out or where we might find survivors."

"We are all that is left out of a thousand and sixty-four Dwellers."

The number was staggering, for less than a fraction could be crowded into the anteroom watching in near-silence.

"When Uli begins seeking the horizon, I will call you. The zanstyrs will ferry you to the Techi."

"If we elect to go, we can walk. The Tor-ad-ih—"

"The land has changed all around you, N'oblic. You will not make it by morning on foot. There is no shelter along the way. It is all gone. You will be safe on the zanstyrs as long as no one attempts to harm one of them. On that you have my word."

A sardonic grin deepened the pain in the Dweller's face. "Your word? You, who have threatened to have Cassilee swallow us, give your word that no harm will come to us on your beasts?"

"The offer is there." Turning away, regret heavy, "Your death will not bring back my sister. I have no taste for revenge against the Tor-ad-ih. Let us keep it that way."

Chapter 18

GRUNTING, GROANING, SWIPING AT THE PER-
spiration running into his eyes, Fancher surmounted the
lip of the chasm he had crossed. He crawled half a dozen
meters and rested, panting, holding still while the aches
reminded him that he was not one hundred percent.
Knowing he felt better than he had a right to expect did
not lessen the muscle spasms in his right arm and chest.

On the opposite rim, panavers stood at the edge and
watched. Fancher got his left arm partially lifted and
managed a wave. He was going to miss them. It had been
a long push, but crossing the chasm here would result in
saving an undeterminable amount of time. Days, possibly
weeks, could have been lost trying to go around it. He
knew of its existence from the survey and had hoped to
have a plan by the time it was reached in the north.

He sat up, grunting. A finger ran along the scar over
his forehead and nose to clear the perspiration away. A
snap uncoiled the last loop of flexi-cable from his
utility belt. Gloved hands worked one over the other to
pull up the supplies. They banged against the cliff every
couple of meters.

He thought about Mikel, now on the way home. For
the next couple of years it would be the only planet and
her peculiar inhabitants. Then Satow.

He slapped at the dirt on the supply cover and checked
the panavers.

They were moving along the rim in a single file. The leader continued to radiate an array of fascinating colors. Disappointment registered when their direction changed, and they moved out of sight one by one. The time spent with the panavers was etched in his memory as truly extraordinary. In their company, he had not felt tired, hungry or thirsty. The loneliness was temporarily assuaged and neither hatred nor anger troubled his mind. He liked the gawky-looking beasts and mentally wished them well.

Two salt and protein pills were downed with a sip of water while he surveyed the next stretch of land. It was relatively flat for several kilometers before skimpy mesas fingered the gray-brown desolation. Mountains floated above the heat shimmering in the distance. Where they began was a guess at best. Only the tops poked above the distortion lines.

A hot wind churned up acrid-smelling grit. Fancher rested a short while longer, then moved on, hoping the motion would work out some of the aches from the climb.

A glance back to the chasm brought a smile. Climbing it was one thing, swimming would have been another. It would not be long until what the terraformers set in motion would fill the chasm and spill out onto the lower plains they had leveled to form an inland sea. The satisfaction of putting one over on the godlike powers birthed a smugness in his sudden optimism.

He headed toward the mesas, then the mountains in the distance, humming and whistling alternately.

A gnarled gaint stood nude and blackened in the heat. Fancher changed course a few degrees to see how the old iron tree had died. A dirty barroom ditty faded into the wind. He stood a couple of meters from the tree and listened to the wind blow dust devils into a frenzy.

Dead kodjelu, insides eaten clean, were strewn around the tree. Claw and tooth marks serrated the hard surface where the glassy bark had been consumed. Armored carcasses, half-covered by blowing sand filtering into every crack on the parched land, stuck up as a warning to the traveler.

Fancher swore under his breath.

It was all so clear.

The life-cycle balance had been changed. The kodjelu

hordes were larger than ever and starving. They would eat anything and everything in their path, then each other. Considering the abrupt atmospheric changes implemented by the terraformers, it would get much worse before better times were at hand.

He touched the tree. It swayed in the wind. A hard shove sent it toppling and him jumping to the side.

The roots were eaten away, as was the inner pulp core. More kodjelu armor clattered as the sand moved to fill in the depression.

Ahead, and to both sides, were other dead giants, some already on the ground. The increasing wind displayed and hid kodjelu plates for as far as he could see. Nothing was left alive.

Fancher turned on the shield and walked fast, nearly running. He shuddered at the death around him, checked the compass and moved toward the mountains.

Never had his own mortality registered so keenly as it did here, where nothing survived. Even as he walked, he could not take three steps without stepping on, or having to kick aside, part of a kodjelu. He tried to imagine their numbers and could not.

The blues halted, weaving, one by one, and rested, producing a solid rumble of snores.

Dusk settled over the shreds of the Tor-ad-ih. Initially, only a few of the survivors used the climbing rope. The group was clearly divided into those who refused the aid of a Betweener and his beasts, and those who were resigned to whatever fate held in store.

Lor'ee helped the wounded onto Chacon and showed those riding with them how to unfasten the braided knots of cloth and fur securing them. Chacon carried a total of seven, five wounded. Lor'ee went to his head, patted the face along the side and said, "Take them back, Chacon. They are very afraid."

Chacon snorted an agreement. He moved slowly to be sure the riders were fixed into the purple. By the time he had traveled a hundred meters, the speed increased. The weight was not a hindrance, but a slow gait would be.

Seven more exhausted Dwellers rode the next zanstyr. These were more vocal about their fears, but willing to

159

recognize the necessity of using the beasts to reach safety.

The last ten climbed onto the surface. Among them were N'oblic and an old woman J'erik figured was the Seeress. N'oblic approached J'erik alone. "I am N'oblic, Speaker for the Tor-ad-ih."

"Are there more of you below?"

"No. None that are alive." The dark eyes lowered for a moment. "We have been warned through the generations that one like you would come and it would be the end of Cassilee. Our Seeress is strong. But she cannot see you, nor could she see into you. This phenomenon supports the legends many of us did not believe wholeheartedly."

N'oblic fingered the dirty rag tied around his forearm. Flakes of dried blood crumbled. "Now I speak only for myself, Betweener. I would like to know how one man can be responsible for the death of Cassilee. I would like to know why, Betweener. If you call the Star Demons, why? Why do you do this?"

"I have never met a Star Demon, other than to run from him." J'erik smiled ruefully. "I hope the time comes when I may claim otherwise."

For a moment the two exchanged a quest for truth in looks. J'erik continued, "I have found that people generally believe what they want to. Anything, or anyone, different is something to be feared. Perhaps it is easier to blame the difference, and condemn it as bad, than to look inside and face the thing feared most—self. It is not the fear which forces judgment, but the inability to confront it."

The words spoken to N'oblic held a message for the speaker as well. Pausing, he acknowledged the meaning briefly, then dismissed it.

"You have to trust yourself before you can trust me, or anyone who is slightly different, N'oblic. There are certain things I can do. That is true. The Star Demons? No. I have no control. No say. The answer is not that easy. I wish it were. You will have to look elsewhere, just as I have, too.

"As for the Seeress, tell her to stop trying. Ulni-da of the Ah-te could not see for either Fir'ah or me. Tell her to rest assured that I will do what I can to preserve

160

Cassilee, not destroy her." J'erik gave him a genuine smile. "I live here, too. Where would there be to go?"

N'oblic relaxed slightly. "Perhaps it is time to re-examine the legends and our beliefs in them. You are sure we will be accepted at the Techi? We have not been what you could call friendly for the last few millennia."

"J'osh-uah works for Cassilee's future in another manner. I am sure he will accept you, though how you accept his ideology is another question."

"What way does he work for Cassilee?"

"He is my father."

N'oblic was silent for a moment before saying, "Oh."

"Bargain with him. Survive, N'oblic. Survive. All life is precious. It would be a shame to leave the land to the kodjelu and the Star Demons."

"Yes, it would." Reaching up, he put his hand on J'erik's shoulder. "I would like to speak about this with you again. You will be at the Techi?"

"No." J'erik glanced down into the black pit. "I will go north in a short while with the woman who has Chosen me." He searched for Lor'ee. She was conversing with a pregnant woman not any older than herself. "You should be going, N'oblic. Ride the zanstyrs." Grinning, "Forget the fear and enjoy it. They are trustworthy, also. Rest assured that no harm will befall you. As I have said, as long as they do not have to defend themselves from an aggression, you are safe." The grin disappeared. "Do not hunt them after I am gone." In the last strains of Uli, J'erik's face turned hard and foreboding. "That would be a grave mistake. For I leave two as a guard and playmate for the child from the Ah-te and the old woman, Kali-te."

N'oblic motioned to the nine near the excavation. "It is my belief, after speaking with the Betweener, that we owe him a debt of gratitude and some trust. His beasts dug us out and saved our lives. To question the wisdom of riding, instead of walking, to the Techi, with no water or food, is absurd. However, those of you who wish to walk will not be stopped, nor will you be shunned by us if you are fortunate enough to succeed.

"I do not know how we can repay him for our lives. But I, for one, trust his judgment that we ride. I am riding. Those who wish to do the same, please stand beside me."

Whispers and gestures flew over the close group. The pregnant woman glanced at Lor'ee.

Lor'ee nodded, urging her on.

Rubbing her protruding belly, she started toward N'oblic. A young man grabbed her arm. She pulled, trying to break free.

"Let her go." J'erik said in a quiet voice which carried through the group and brought a silence.

The young man held on.

"Please, C'nuba," the woman pleaded. "I cannot walk that far. My time is too near. The babe still moves within me, but I fear for him if I must walk. Uli will find me." Crying, her voice rose. "I know Uli will find me and the child will die in her light with me."

The man shook his head. "You have Chosen me and I say no."

"Then I choose to be alone. You are not my life. You are not part of me! Another will be the child's father!" Jerking, she pointed to the Betweener. "I Choose him for this night."

The young man trembled in rage at the insult she had dealt him. "Then, I challenge." Shoving her at the Dwellers, he closed in on J'erik.

"No challenge," J'erik said. "The advantage is clearly mine. She rides." Angling his head to the side brought a yellow striper into motion.

The crowd drew back, most of them lining up with N'oblic, the last few waiting to see who would triumph before making a commitment.

The Dweller tore off his tunic and robe. Grasping a Hold knife, bent-kneed, he was ready to spring.

Diearka and Chamblis snapped their tails in the air, heads bobbing as they united with the zanstyrs. Tongues flicked and crackled in the night.

The woman pleaded, "C'nuba, you are in an impossible situation. Look around you! Even if you won over the Betweener, what would happen? Look around you! You wish to walk, then walk. That decision involves only you."

C'nuba ignored her. He stalked the perimeter, circling the Betweener, sizing up his chances. J'erik was easily a head taller and far more muscular. C'nuba did not back down. The scars on his arms and chest attested to a familiarity with the Square. The fact he was alive spoke of his success.

The Seeress began to moan, softly pleading for C'nuba to abandon the pursuit before it was too late.

J'erik shrugged and unsheathed his knife. There seemed no purpose in letting the man advance and score without a struggle.

C'nuba moved halfway around, until he was between J'erik and where Lor'ee stood with the calantani. He jabbed at the air, testing, faking, trying to get a response from J'erik. His expression changed. Instead of lunging at the Betweener, as his last fake had led the spectators to expect, he lurched sideways and grabbed Lor'ee. As soon as the blade was at her throat, she froze into the silence besieging Cassilee. "Start walking. All of you!"

"Let her go now, and I will not seek retribution," J'erik said evenly.

"No! She is a piece of inbred filth, just as you are. Kodjelu dung! No more."

J'erik glared at C'nuba, eyes narrowed into a squint. "Once I allowed a man who had wronged one whom I cared for to go unpunished. Never again. You have had your chance, C'nuba. Now you will reap what you have set into motion." Deliberately, J'erik sheathed the knife, all the while concentrating on the dark-eyed aggressor.

Lor'ee blinked, swallowing. The knife was so tight at her throat that the motion split the skin. Blood ran between her breasts in two streams.

J'erik invaded the opponent's mind.

The knife-wielding arm gave centimeters slowly, fighting to keep a position near Lor'ee's throat.

Holding her breath, she closed her eyes for a second.

C'nuba's arm shook, palsied, moving out and away. His left arm, crossing Lor'ee's midsection and gripping her right, suffered spastic jerks, fingers working irrationally, before it, too, was straightened.

Lor'ee sank between them and ran to J'erik. Automatically, his arms surrounded her, pulling her securely against him.

Guttural noises ground out of C'nuba. His eyes bulged to an enormous size, threatening to pop out of their sockets. His legs shook, trying to run but rooted to the ground. Gradually, the knife turned awkwardly, point aimed at his bare chest. He whooped and screamed, drooling, biting his tongue until blood spurted out. His left hand tried to pull the knife free and force the right into another direction. Slapping at it with his fingers, he flayed the skin to the bone. It hung by threads, glistening ribbons flopping in the starlight.

Steadily the knife closed in on his chest at the left breast.

"Nooooo!" C'nuba managed to scream, teetering back and forth, unable to stand erect or fall to the ground.

J'erik blinked long and hard, nodding purposefully.

The knife plunged into C'nuba's heart. He keeled over, eyes wide as the lungs inhaled a last breath, then let all the air out. Body substance voided, fouling the air. A stream of blood shone for an instant, until the dry land claimed it.

To N'oblic, "Do what you will. I leave two zanstyrs for a hand against the stars." His hand rose against the glowing nebula as a distance-time measurement.

Lor'ee sniffed, holding tighter.

"Come. We'll leave this place now." Lifting her chin, he touched the flood of tears. "You are very precious to me, little Betweener. No one hurts you and lives."

They returned to where their packs sat against the rocks. It was far enough to take them out of sight of the stunned Dwellers of the Tor-ad-ih. J'erik propped Lor'ee against the stone, rifled the packs for a clean shirt, dampened it and wiped the blood trickling down the front of her. She held the cloth at her throat, using the edge to dry the tears. They continued to flow.

J'erik sat on a rock, elbows on knees, fingers running through his hair, and eyes staring at the ground. The power he held was a terrifying thing which he could not begin to comprehend. The scope felt limitless. The way he knew it was there, never thinking about it, never doubting once it was in play, frightened him more. Was there no control? The sensations of C'nuba's death stayed. His body reenacted the trauma over and over without dying.

He did not look up when the zanstyrs clattered and bumped into the distance toward the Techi. A preoccupation with what he had done made him uncaring of whether the rest walked, rode or stayed. He felt sick, but knew he would not be.

It was a measurement of three hands across the sky before Lor'ee knelt in front and touched his face. He looked at her, reached out and felt fresh tears. A hint of fear clouded her expression. He ran a moist finger over the bruise lines on her arm where C'nuba had held her.

"Please, J'erik. Don't shut me out." Moving a cluster of hair away from his eyes, "You look so far away from me."

"You look frightened."

She swallowed hard, holding the cloth tighter to her throat, then nodded.

"Of me?"

"Yes."

"I frighten me, too. What I did—that's something I would not want to ever do again, Lor'ee. I can still feel him dying inside of me, again and again. I should have made him fight in the Square. I would have killed him. But . . . but it would have been different. Different." He resumed staring at a bland patch of ground.

Lor'ee tucked the shirt into the tunic front and placed her hands on the sides of his face, lifting, until he looked at her. "Do you really believe he would have entered the Square? Do you really think I would be here now had you done it differently? Can you tell me you did not have this sorted out *before* you did it?"

He thought for a minute. "No, I cannot. But once you were released, I could have found an alternative. In truth, I saw him as T'lar, and I did not want to give him a second opportunity such as T'lar had. They shared many traits." Hands clasped and wringing to the rhythm of the halting words, "They are not visible things. It is hard to explain. And I could not perceive at the Ah-te as I can now. The similarity existed. I do not want to look inside another person again. Their thoughts are painful."

"Can you not just graze the surface and see where the words match the inner truth?"

"No." Head shaking in frustration, "Only with the zan-styr and the calantani."

"I understand. But, knowing all you know, emotions aside, you can only do what seems right at the time. And that's all you can do. You cannot look back and say 'if' or 'but.' Take what you have learned and we'll go on, together, because we are both still here. Let go of the thing which you allow to punish you. Believe what you saw inside of C'nuba." More tears dripped from her chin. "I will share it with you."

Her mind touch was gentle, subtly flitting over invisible wounds and trying to mend them. He pulled away, startling her, then grabbed her shoulders before she toppled. He stood, bringing her along. Slowly, he smiled.

Lor'ee threw her arms around him and cried aloud. "It's so sad, J'erik. How do you live with it?"

The pain of C'nuba's death lessened slightly. She had touched the trailing edge of agony and absorbed a tiny portion. The willingness to try to ease the burden meant more than alleviation.

"Lor'ee, Lor'ee, your Choice has not been consummated. Do you have regrets?"

She sniffed, looked up, careful to keep the wound closed. "No."

He touched her throat, entering the bodily-function area of her mind which allowed him to accelerate cell growth without becoming entangled with her emotions. "I should have done that before." He was in and out in less than two heartbeats, not allowing time for a backwash. Bent to her upturned face, he kissed her. The salty taste cast a bittersweet meaning. A second kiss, naive and exploring, came naturally.

Lor'ee pulled the shirt free, wiggled away and walked to a smooth place where they would sleep for the night. J'erik followed, untying the brown stripe. He spread it out and offered his hand.

Lor'ee knelt, disrobing while J'erik placed his weapons near the top of the mat. Her breasts rose and fell in the light from the nebula. The folded tunic was placed on top of her sandals.

J'erik went to the packs and returned with a couple of blankets for when the chilly night reached its darkest point. He dropped them at the foot and undressed.

166

Chapter 19

F IR'AH SLEPT, WALKED UNTIL EXHAUSTION
stopped her, ate sparingly, and slept again. It became a
ritual, emotionless, mechanical. She lit a calidrium only
when the tunnel took erratic turns or the elevation
changed. The sound of her bare feet slapping on smooth
floor was a consolation. It also saved the sandals for rough
areas to extend their usefulness.

There were times when she thought someone was
watching. Not T'lar. It did not feel the same. Several
times she ran to where she thought it was. It faded and
evaporated just as she should have reached the strongest
point. During the pursuits, Fir'ah passed up more side
tunnels, knowing they were there, but intent on the present course.

Fresher air sweetened the stale atmosphere she tried
to become accustomed to breathing. It charged her sag-
ging body with a hopeful spirit, quickening the pace.

On the surface, she could cover thirty kilometers a
day. Underground, she was sure the average was much
greater. The terrain was not brutal, nor was Uli's heat
a hindrance. Water seeped through rocks, keeping the
temperature low. Often she jogged to keep warm. Frequent patches of stagnant air set her coughing and tried
to impose a lethargy. Nausea became a normal state,
which, in turn, helped her conserve her supplies.

A hot surface breeze warmed the interior. Fir'ah

panted as she ran, exhaling hard to increase her endurance. Soon the warm light of Uli will give me a direction, she thought.

For an inexplicable reason, she stopped. Emotion charged her to run. Instinct and the abrupt, strong presence engulfing her denied motion.

Ahead was a circle of light, warming the inside, blowing new life through the cavern.

Cautiously, she took a step forward. Moving was like stepping into an invisible barrier which bounced her back.

The presence grew even stronger. She felt as though she would see the source any moment. She turned from the light and peered into the darkness behind.

Nothing.

A half-burned calidrium came from her pack. She lit it and began to search the expanse.

The light reflected on rich ore deposits. The tunnel had not changed much in composition since the calidrium was last fired.

She turned toward Uli's glow, yearning to stand outside and bathe in it with her clothes off.

The tunnel fanned out, tripling in width. The ceiling disappeared as completely as the floor did. Ten meters beyond the near edge, the tunnel returned to normal. Twenty meters later, it opened to the outside. So close.

This time when she tried to move forward, she met success. Using the techniques J'erik had taught her, she removed the pack, lay on her stomach and inched to the rim, the calidrium stretched in front.

The void swallowed light without yielding depth. The sides were straight down. The solidity was impressive; not a granule crumbled when her hand passed over the side.

She crept along the rim, first to the right, then to the left, trying to find a ledge that afforded a passage. There was nothing.

The tunnel had proven to be a dead end in a manner she never expected. Resigned, she retreated to the pack and sat crosslegged against the wall, hands resting in her lap.

The light of Uli eventually dimmed. The opening was slanted, keeping the stars from showing themselves. She sat there the entire night, dozing once in a while, waiting to see Uli once more before returning to the black maze.

When morning came, Fir'ah watched the light grow. Some of her frustrations melted in the brilliance. She ate slowly, thinking about the amilglibs dropping from iron trees and gadid berries full of juice.

Rumbling, like a distant rock slide, bounded into the tunnel. She stopped eating, looking around at the walls. The light circle remained solid. Reflexes had her checking the black ceiling, as though she could see through it to detect Star Demons. Strange not to feel their presence first, she mused.

The noise intensified. She watched the cave mouth, expecting it to be closed by the massive landslide which surely was coming down the mountain. The light flickered, changing the shape of the opening, obscuring it, and carving a new variety of shapes.

Fir'ah shoved loose articles and uneaten food into the pack, rose and swung it over her shoulders. The noise was deafening. Even with her hands over her ears, the screeching and thundering claws against the rock clashed with banging armor.

The chasm had become an advantage. The kodjelu kept coming on an endless stream. After the shock dwindled, Fir'ah became curious. She lit the calidrium and held it high, watching the stream of red eyes fixed on her from across the chasm. The hollowness of the shells grew even louder.

A new concern materialized. Could conditions have changed that drastically in such a short time? Why were there so many in the horde? A feeding frenzy was one thing, but mass suicide in order to reach her, one lone individual who would hardly feed twenty kodjelu for one meal?

It did not make sense. Worse, if the kodjelu committed genocide, what would she live on?

Fir'ah turned into the darkness and stifled the calidrium. The death cries of thousands rang in her ears. She walked half a day before coming upon the first tunnel that felt safe. A right turn set her course.

Optimism filled her mood. She had found Uli once; she could do it again.

Fancher Bann stood on a rise and gazed into the valley below. His field was set at max, the charger opened to the sun. Half the day was gone before the last kodjelu disappeared into the slit at the base of a plateau.

He drew out the Destro-Lase II, checked the setting and charge, then sat, bracing his arm on his left knee. He aimed for an outcrop above the opening and fired.

A sheet of mountain crashed into a cloud of dust. He fingered the safety and replaced the weapon, then watched until the air cleared to be sure the opening was sealed.

Eventually he rose, stretched and saluted the mountain. "As the skinny Aurigian said to his obese wife when he locked her in the steam room, 'Hope to see less of you in the future.'"

Fancher entered the ravaged valley where only wind, rocks, sand and carcasses, both kodjelu and vegetation, were left. If he could make the opposite rim by nightfall, it would be excellent time.

He strained to make the distance.

By the time Uli had settled in the west, he was well beyond the rim and onto semi-flatlands again. Sculptured cliffs stood ragged on his left and stretched into infinity both ways. Starlight played with shadows and formed eerie shapes in the crevices.

Fancher set up for the evening, lay back and watched the clouds blot out the stars.

He thought about the panavers, the kodjelu and Mikel. The shield erupted in blue light.

Fancher bolted, frantically looking around, thinking that more of the little beasties were around.

He listened. Something was out there. Not the little beasties.

The shield turned blue again, followed by the hiss of disintegration.

He snatched a beacon kept beside the control and aimed it in the direction of whatever had touched the field. He waited until the third time before flicking on the light.

A scream carried through the night. Twenty meters away stood the grotesque image of a man, bloodied arms thrown over his face. Shreds of skin and clothing hung from him as though he had been a target in a glue-and-confetti game. The hands were big, as though swollen. Most of the fingers were missing down to the knuckles. He turned, hobbling to the rocks in front of the cliff.

Stunned, Fancher thought of the beasties, part of him wondering how the man had survived them, the other part marveling at the sight of another human. It took him longer than it seemed to get his mind and body coordinated enough to call out. Independently, his eyes and the light followed the man until he disappeared.

Fancher sat for a long time after turning off the beacon, listening for the tiniest noise. Where there was one man, possibly there were more.

It seemed a sensible piece of logic, just as not trespassing in the dark did.

The man needed help, especially if the logic was in error. And Fancher wanted company, without risking a battle if there were others.

At dawn, the cliff would be explored. He settled down and tried to rest.

Fir'ah too rested for a short time and traveled on. The glimpse of Uli had given her a hopeful inner light which kept the blackness from becoming overwhelming. When the air sweetened with the coolness of night, she trod carefully with the memory of the hole severing the last passage heavy on her mind.

She lit the last bit of calidrium and gasped.

The walls were lined with holders and calidriums tied together for wall torches. Some were still useful. She lit them as she passed, discarding hers for a torch. The sputter of dust indicated a prolonged idleness.

Walking into a strange Hold was dangerous, she knew, particularly from the direction she had. But she was not about to hang back and let them find her cowering in a niche. Better to meet them head on. If some of the good fortune due her came in, the worst that could happen was that they would throw her out onto the surface, just where she wanted to be.

Again, the inability to speak was an obstacle. If she could call out to gain attention it might not appear that she was sneaking up on them from the interior. As an alternative, she made loud noises by clicking the ends of the calidrium torches together.

She wandered the back corridors to the Common. It was empty. Fine grit coated the wooden furnishings. The spare community pot was empty. A calantani rib bone lay beside it. The Hold was abandoned, but the utensils, pots and wares remained. Only the people were absent. The main pot set on the gas flame glowed a dull red and radiated heat. A couple of plates and a bowl lay in the aisle between two upset benches.

Fir'ah started to leave, stubbed her toe and lowered the torch. Kodjelu shells and bones littered the floor beyond the cook pot. She blinked twice, trying to grasp what was there, sat on the edge of a table and put on her sandals. There was something obscene in walking barefoot on carcasses.

The bone trail led to the Hall of Rooms, a hall much like the one in the Ah-te, though many more rooms were, or had been, occupied. The doors were eaten through at the bottoms. Mounds of armor barred the other sides and tried to keep her from opening them.

Once the kodjelu had gotten inside and eaten their fill, the sheer numbers of starving beasties kept them trapped inside, as others fought and killed the killers. There was not a scrap of flesh left over.

Much as she wanted to check the entire Hold on the slim chance someone had escaped, the nausea which had been plaguing her reasserted itself and drove her to find a way out.

She ran down the corridors. Bones and armor bit her feet, reached up and tried to grab her ankles and calves. The night breeze sent salvation and direction. It was cold and chilled her under the perspiration-soaked garb. She continued to run, slowing when she realized the stars were hidden by clouds.

She scrambled out to a secondary ledge, moved over the face of the cliff and pulled up onto a narrow shelf. Between seizures of dry heaves and light-headed perspiration floods, she rested.

Uli had sent the first warnings over the horizon by the time Fir'ah regained her strength. Fog, which rolled in sometime during the night, felt good. It soothed away the stench of ugliness trapped in the Hold.

Slowly, Fir'ah climbed down, knowing she had to return to the Common and select a few light cooking utensils if she was to survive alone.

Beads of moisture wetted her hair. Procrastinating, she decided to see Uli's brilliance once more before returning to the death scene. The ominous feelings emulating from the Hold gushed out in waves. She tried to rationalize the necessity of a return with the urge to get as far away from the place as possible. In the end, long-term practicality won. She turned into the Hold.

In a wide place thirty meters inside were half a dozen barrow carts. Fir'ah checked all of them, then selected the one in best condition. Four coils of rope taken from pegs on the wall were the first items into the barrow.

There were enough torches still burning to make out the direction to the Common without having to light more. The barrow thumped over carnage Fir'ah refused to acknowledge. She gazed straight ahead.

Once in the Common, she quickly sorted through utensils, choosing only the most necessary and sturdy: forks, stirrers, spoons, two small pots with lids and a caldron not much larger. Next she went through the linen supply, grabbing anything which might be needed.

The barrow was nearly filled.

Knives were next. She sorted them, picking two long, sharp ones, a short one and somebody's Hold knife, sharpened for hunting. The first three went into the barrow. The Hold knife slipped into her belt.

Last, to be packed on top, was water.

"I hope you brought enough for two."

Startled, Fir'ah turned, openmouthed, heart thudding in her temples.

T'lar leaned against the arch, robed down to his feet. The hood covering his head hid everything but his eyes.

A new smell wound through the Common. Fir'ah could not place it, but knew it was more pungent than the raw horror she felt seeping through her dilated pores.

Chapter 20

"GET UP. HURRY! SOMETHING'S COMING."
J'erik shook Lor'ee, pulled his knees under him and
groped in the heavy mist to find his weapons and belt.
Chamblis! Diearka! Subtle tremors in the ground took on
a distinct rumble.

Lor'ee swung her pack on and helped J'erik center
his, grabbed the blankets and stuffed them in while he
fastened it. "What is that noise?"

"I don't know." He rolled the stripe, fastened the loops
and placed it on the pack. Lor'ee whipped the calantani
rope around and knotted it.

The rumble became a quaking roar. Mist flew around
them as the two calantani settled to the ground, the
sounds of their great wings lost in the dawn.

A sheet of water slapped Lor'ee along the left side.
More water shot over the rocks where the Tor-ad-ih once
existed. The torrent surged higher and higher, its true
menace obscured by fog.

Lunging, J'erik grabbed the edge of a boulder and
threw his right arm out to catch Lor'ee. He felt her slide
off his fingertips.

"Lor'ee! Lor'ee! Find something to hold onto."

Squeals from advancing kodjelu punctured the oscil-
lating roar. It became impossible for him to move against
the water. He used both hands to keep from being
washed away. The ground turned to mud and eroded

under his weight. Boulders, once removed by the zanstyrs, shifted, slipped and rolled with the water's power.

Chamblis. Diearka. Find her. Get her out before the kodjelu or the water . . . The statement could not be finished, even nonverbally.

The land pitched and rolled. Water erupted out of the hold faster and harder. One instant it was so cold it numbed his arms up to the shoulders and his legs up to the hips. The next, it was warmer than the swirling pool at the Techi. Then, hot and flesh-burning. He held on, feeling the losing battle his muscles waged, shouting to Lor'ee.

The rock slid. He lost the left grip, struggled, bashed his knuckles and turned the water red. Something hard and bulky slammed into his chest. He glanced down. Lor'ee's name curdled in his throat.

Two bulging black eyes stared up at him, open mouth swollen and filled by a whitish tongue. The corpse dragged the head away. It was C'nuba, refusing to stay in the grave the zanstyrs put him in before moving north.

Cassilee trembled and shuddered. The rock moved again. J'erik worked in the mud, grappling for a firm hold.

Water exploded into the air and fell to the ground with a force so tremendous that it cleared the source area.

J'erik frantically pushed away from the boulder and entered the main flux out to the plains, rolling and banging against the rubble on the path. He tried to protect his head, but the momentum slammed him into rocks which seemed to know where he was vulnerable. The bludgeoning action encompassed his body, filling the world with muddy water. It turned him, pulling him down where there was no air to breathe, bounced him along the bottom and vomited him over the sinkhole lip.

The jarring bumps no longer hurt when he snagged against the rocks. The semidarkness spreading across his mind shielded the pain.

I have Lor'ee, Lord J'erik. I have her.

Who was that? Was it Fir'ah calling? No . . . Fir'ah's gone for all of time. Lady Ladida? Chamblis . . .

The violent surge mellowed. He tried to lift his head. Tongues of pain lapped his body. He rolled, feeling his hand drag on the ground, knowing he should stand up.

The water carried him gently onto the plains. Squealing kodjelu flailed in the murk, unable to swim, trying to stand on the dead and dying to reach him. The blackness left his vision. Hundreds of red eyes rushed through the gray fog to greet him.

Diearka. Come and get me. Come and get me. His head pounded. The red eyes disappeared. The squeals reached a crescendo.

The kodjelu formed a jetty over their dead as the water brought the Betweener closer to the edge of their high spot.

A feeling of weightlessness encompassed J'erik. The security of the orange one's tail against his back and wound around his legs seemed a blissful illusion. He opened his eyes. A night without stars? So dark. Tiny circles danced in the black, playing at light warfare behind his eyeballs.

The air lost its thickness. Uli was clear and bright in the east. Her brilliance registered and hurt his head more. He turned, paying a stiff price for the trade. Through a narrow gap where Diearka's clawed feet held his shoulders on the tail and the tail itself, he saw a fountain of water rising above the fog line and into the blue morning.

He wanted to smile at the irony. Cassilee, he thought groggily, too much or too little. Will you ever balance?

"You ran out on me, Fir'ah. That made me very unhappy." T'lar shuffled across the Common.

Fir'ah's heart sank. She retreated, careful to keep at least a table between her and T'lar.

He changed directions. Awkwardly, he shoved benches, chairs and tables aside. The black eyes burned with a fire not wholly produced by the torch reflections.

The distance to the outside door was half the width of the room. T'lar kept the main exit blocked.

"You did not expect to see me again, Fir'ah? We were meant to be together." He pulled the facecloth down and threw back the hood. Angry wounds, swollen and red-purple, oozed yellow through his stubbly beard. Gouges spaced the width of kodjelu claws extruded in front of his left ear and hid under the robe. Their seepage stained the collar.

Silence could not hide Fir'ah's revulsion. The fire in

his eyes was more than an obsession: it was sickness, mental and physical. The fever produced a foul dampness to his garb that vexed her sense of smell.

"The kodjelu almost had me back there." A slight head motion indicated the subterranean passages. "I had to try four tunnels before I found this." He staggered, recovered and shoved a bench aside. "There were so many bodies in one of the pits, stragglers were able to climb over them.

"I need you to take care of me, Fir'ah. Just once, will you give me something of yourself without my having to force you?"

She looked desperately for an escape and came up empty. While transfixed upon the grotesqueness of T'lar, she had retreated into one of the few areas without a door.

"I need you, Fir'ah." He climbed onto a table and waited to see which way she moved before crossing to the next one.

Fir'ah faked left, turned right and ran toward the arch, skirting the red-hot caldron.

T'lar jumped down, caught himself and circled, going around the cooking area and closing the gap. Using his forearms, he rammed a table and pushed. It grated along the floor, plowed into a second one and drove it against the wall. As though caught by the momentum, he rolled on top of it.

"Looks like I'll have to lead you by a rope, Fir'ah. You refuse to come willingly. And I refuse to leave here without you." Panting, his voice changed to the whine of a frightened child. "We do have to leave, don't we? But the surface is more dangerous now than ever, even for my pretty Betweener."

Fir'ah yanked the straps of her pack and let it fall.

"Think you can outmaneuver me?" he bellowed.

She watched his waist. Eyes were deceiving, but motion usually betrayed itself at the waist level. Except that he did not seem to have any balance, trembling and weaving as he was. When he jumped, she leaped to the side, almost avoiding him. The impact threw her against the table behind her.

He laughed wildly as she fought to get free, pulling

her closer until she was pinned. Abruptly, he shouted, "Enough!"

Fir'ah spat in his face.

T'lar backhanded her, clubbed with his palm and backhanded again.

She tried to block with her arms. Her head banged the table as it snapped from side to side under more blows.

"Hey! What's going on here?"

T'lar did not stop. His knee came up between her breasts and held her against the wood.

Fir'ah went limp, not hopeful about the voice she thought she had heard. Desperate, she whipped the hunting knife from her belt, brought her right arm out and slammed the blade into T'lar's ribs.

His mouth opened, though not a sound escaped.

She pulled it free and slammed it in again.

He stopped hitting her and arched his back.

There was noise in the Common; things breaking, shouts, running.

T'lar slumped toward her. She scooted sideways, leaving cloth and skin on the table edge. He fell face down and moaned into pooling blood, garbling her name. Fir'ah punched his shoulder with both fists, knife down. He slid, hit the bench and landed face up on the floor.

She lifted the knife high into the air. One jump put her on top of him. He reached out and tangled the last two remaining fingers of his right hand into her tunic. She stabbed at his shoulder, burying the knife to the hilt, freeing it, and plunging it in again, and again, with every bit of strength she could muster. Blood splattered into her face, coating her arms and body.

T'lar's expression never changed; staring, grinning, baring the red shards that were his teeth. Chips of white mingled with cartilage splitting his nostrils.

For a fragment of stationary time, something grabbed Fir'ah's hand and pried out the knife. She went back to stabbing, empty-handed, beating the open flesh, splashing in the torn muscles gushing red, until exhaustion vanquished the demon inside her.

T'lar gasped, mouth twisting as he wheezed out a couple of words. "You . . . should be the one . . . I'm free of . . ." The last reserve of air exhaled from caving lungs.

The smile lingered. The death stare focused on Fancher, though Fir'ah did not notice. T'lar's gnarled fingers held the material of her tunic as though not letting go even in death.

Fancher gaped at the carnage, not quite grasping what he had witnessed. His hopes for finding anyone alive among the skeletons had nearly died before he heard the noises in the big room. Then to find one killing the other—it was a nightmare he would wake up from any minute, and not a second too soon. While still trying to make some sense out of it, he heard the woman begin retching. He reached down and took her hand.

A seizure of dry heaves made her a tug-of-war line between Fancher and the dead man pulling down. Instantly, she had his sympathy and undivided attention.

He shoved the knife into his utility belt and used both hands to get the tunic off her, extricating her from the corpse. It fell over T'lar's face and soaked up blood.

Fir'ah's arms folded to support her aching stomach muscles. She kept looking at T'lar, waiting for remorse, knowing the day would never come when she was sorry.

Her legs moved. The force guiding her away maintained a firm but gentle hold. The retching subsided for another wave of light-headedness to move into the cycle she knew would run the gamut.

Fancher kept an eye on the woman, figuring her as hardly more than a girl, while retrieving the pack on the floor. It belonged to her, if by no other reason than default. She was alive.

The barrow looked interesting. He took stock of the contents and tried to watch her at the same time. It was a difficult feat. The Hold artifacts were intriguing, but so was the half-naked woman, bloody and sick or not.

He opened the pack, rummaged through and found a short robe which was neither a shirt nor a tunic. It would cover. Judging by his body reactions, the sooner the better. He returned, holding the robe so that it blotted out all but her head. As he started to put it around her, he noticed the ugly scrapes bleeding into the waistband of her breeches.

Gooseflesh crawled over her back.

Fancher decided to check her wounds later, after he

found the water source for this place. He glanced around, sure a habitat this size had one somewhere.

To her, "Can you stand?"

The last of the chills dwindled into warmth. Fir'ah raised her eyes. Openmouthed, she sized up the stranger in his bright outfit totally foreign to anything Dwellers were accustomed to. He was tall, possibly even as tall as J'erik, dark-haired and bronze-skinned. The incongruity made her blink several times, just to be sure.

His appearance stayed the same. His eyes were neither light nor dark. The exact color was obscured in the flickering light. There was something else about him that awed her and conjured a respectful fright all its own. She could not place it.

She wanted to speak, trying, moving her mouth. The words stayed frozen, though closer than ever.

"Please. Put this on." Grasping her shoulders, he helped her stand.

Fir'ah watched his face change. When this man looked at her body the sick expression crowding his face was not like T'lar's. He indicated the bruises and healing fingernail lacerations, then pointed at T'lar. "Did he do that to you?"

It took a moment to analyze the heavily accented words. His language bore the emphasis of the ancient. Unsure, she nodded, wondering what kind of Hold he had come from.

"Is that why you killed him?" Fancher held the sleeves low to her hands.

The hard set of her jaw accompanied a second nod. The expression promised an equal reward should he decide to resume T'lar's role.

"Father's son of a codpiece sniffer," he mumbled, closing the robe and looping the ties. Out loud, "I hope you can understand. You're safe. Will you speak to me? Say something? Anything? Please? It's been an eternity since I've heard a human voice."

Expectant, he waited, fairly sure that she understood sufficiently to reply.

"You going to just look at me with those big eyes?"

Nodding slowly, she sidestepped toward the pack, watching, reaching nervously until she had possession.

"Hey, don't put that thing on. Your back's all ripped

up. I'll carry it. Is there any water around here?" He pantomimed drinking.

She held the pack, but did not sling it over her shoulder. Fir'ah crossed the Common, checking once to be sure a safe distance was maintained, and lifted a heavy slab of ironwood from a bubbling trough. The water at the top slipped over the back side into blackness. She scooped a pot full, emptied it on the floor, filled it again and pointed to the wall.

A dozen waterskins Fancher would never have recognized as such hung on pegs above the source. He moved beside her and began to fill them, surprised by how much they held.

Fir'ah chose a spot across the room where she washed her sores, then her body, as best she could. Twice the stranger discreetly brought more pots of water and linens from the cache near the caldron. She heard him lash down the barrow contents for the trek. The scrape along her back was the most difficult to clean, but she managed. When finished and robed, she returned to the water bin and looked a question at Fancher.

Shoulder raised to his tilted head, "I'm done with it."

Always the necessity to conserve every drop of pure water had been paramount to the Ah-te. The need was gone. Who was left to use it? Impulsively, she bent to it, took the hard soap bar off the inner ledge and lathered her hair. By the time she had finished, gadid aroma filled the hollow and she felt cleaner than at any other time since T'lar's first assault.

Hair dripping down her back, Fir'ah was ready to leave and greet Uli clean and new. She picked up the barrow handles and shoved it forward.

Fancher's hands wrapped around hers. A sudden look at him close up brought back the fear.

"You just take you, Princess. I'll be the brawn." He removed her hands and turned them palms up. There were no fingernails above the quick. Raw spots along the tops were thickening with calluses to match the palms. "I'm not going to take anything that is yours. I'd like to share the water. I'm short on it. You're perfectly safe with me. Understand?"

Her expression did not change.

Fancher took her knife off his utility belt and offered it, prepared to counter if she attacked. "Take it."

Her left eyebrow rose, but she took the weapon.

Fancher grinned. "You're very beautiful, Princess, but I'd never touch you without you wanting me to." Taking the barrow handles, "Besides, you're three thousand percent more than I'd ever hoped to find on this battleground."

Fir'ah watched him cross the Common and stayed close enough to be sure he practiced the spoken words. Curiosity poked holes through her misgivings. She listened intently to her inner self. When nothing urged her to run, she neared, and finally walked beside him into the light of Uli.

Chapter 21

Chapter 21

DIEARKA PARALLELED CHAMBLIS OVER THE lowlands. Updrafts enhanced their soaring abilities. Their sharp eyes searched for the zanstyr feeding ground. During the initial third of the morning's journey, water leaked and shot out of the ground below, playing with the shadows cast by their great wings.

Uli had begun her decline by the time a green and purple fuzz appeared on the land far below.

Where are we, Diearka? Jerik rolled his head from side to side, working on the stiffness that was worse than the bruises. *How is Lor'ee?*

We are almost to the zanstyr feeding grounds. The Lady is fine. She asks of you often.

J'erik picked up the secondary thought "too often" and smiled.

I have informed her of your well-being. She is delighted. She thinks often of the Choosing Ritual. You have changed one another. The equivalent of a sigh rippled his thoughts. *There is nothing quite like mating.*

J'erik did not respond. Silently, he agreed, wondering why the Chosen in the Ah-te had spent so much time performing extraneous activities when that time could have been spent so much more enjoyably. The night spent by the Tor-ad-ih had nearly cost them their lives. Yet given the same circumstances, he would have spent

185

the time in exactly the same way, only slept less and left earlier.

Diearka settled on the ground. Zanstyrs moved in close to the Master.

J'erik screened the bombardment of questions and news from the zanstyrs. Stoically, he sat up, then tried to stand. Lor'ee ran to his side.

Chacon moved through the gathering, and a silence befell the pasture. *Master, there is much news. Lorff has left the horde and goes the Path of the Living Death, from which he may never return. Our Life Code does not permit it, nor contact, even should he wish to come back.*

J'erik grimaced, limped slightly and demanded, *When?*

After he dispatched the blues to you, Master.

Was he fit to travel? Looking across the purple expanse, *No, he couldn't have been. He'll die out there, Chacon.*

It is his choice. He was not Leader without reason, Master. And it is difficult to say, since it is Lorff.

I understand. Which way did he go?

North by northwest.

What else?

The remainder can keep until you have rested, Master, if that is what you would like.

I don't like any of this. What is it? He sat on the grassy land and rubbed the purple bruise on his ankle.

Water, Master. There is water pouring out of the surface for as far as the scouts can see. Calantani have come and are flying westward to look for more land. They will return by starlight.

J'erik looked up, then at Chamblis. *Lady Ladida?*

Chamblis scoured the heights, tail flicking in excitement.

Absolutely disgusting, Diearka interjected. *He's the most lustful Lord we've ever had.*

Lor'ee giggled, reached out and slapped the orange one's foot.

"Eavesdropping?"

Grinning, she nodded. "Don't let Diearka fool you. He is the worst of the bunch. Wait until the green female Fannia arrives."

"It figures. Are they up to scouting the northlands for Lorff?"

"I think so. It will fill the time until the rest return at night."

The zanstyrs were sent to graze and the calantani into the air. Chacon stayed.

Master, the calantani Lady reported to me that her scouts flew for two days in the extreme northlands. The thing called 'ice' is melting into rivers so vast they could not comprehend it. She asked me to relay that information to the Mistress when she learned of the Choosing.

Ashen, Lor'ee took a few steps and stared north, trying to see beyond the horizon.

"Lor'ee? What does it mean?"

"In the north, there is a land that is not land, at least not at the bottom. It is frozen and creeps along the ground for more distance than a calantani can fly. None have been able to cross it. It is too cold. The winds freeze them. I have been there, J'erik.

"There are mountains which rise into the stars. If they were to be warmed, there would be so much water . . .

"Where they melt, at the warming lines, the water disappears into the ground. That is where I presumed the springs and the Hold supplies came from. I do not know for certain.

"When the ice becomes water, there is fog. Sometimes Uli takes many turns trying to touch the land." Turning to him, "The fog. That is why it comes so often.

"J'erik, we must go north, not to the ice lands, but north, where the mountains are high off the plains. We must get the zanstyrs up there to the highlands. The calantani can fly, but the zanstyrs—"

'What about the Techi?"

"I don't know if they are high enough. And I don't know what they'll do for food even if they are." Shoulders drooping, she returned to kneel on the grass. "You have to go back and take them out with the calantani."

"We," he corrected softly.

Head shaking, "I'll go north, to a place the calantani know, and get it ready." Taking his face in her hands, "There isn't time enough to go together. Look what happened this morning.

"The calantani can take them to the nearest safe land. From there, zanstyrs, waiting at the spot, can bring them the rest of the way."

Scowling, "How long?"

"The journey will take anywhere from thirty to fifty revolutions, depending on the zanstyrs and how much they carry. The calantani cannot take more than three per trip—that's provided the water stays where the lowlands are." Her thumb ran over the edge of his frown. "Don't look like that."

"I want you to go with me. We can work it out as it comes."

"No, we don't have that kind of time. The ice is melting. I don't want to be away from you, J'erik, even for a partial revolution, but if we are to preserve the Techi and survive the Demons, we must move quickly."

Lor'ee relaxed onto her heels and dropped her hands. "They will not come easily. I must be ready for those who survive the ordeal. Besides, my presence at the Techi would complicate matters, since I am banished."

He hated the idea. Worse, he hated the fact that her logic was flawless. It would be an arduous journey. They would lose some of the Dwellers to Uli, and the blind might outnumber the sighted at the end. Lor'ee had to be prepared to help them care for each other. But she would be alone if the Star Demons returned.

As though reading his misgivings, "I have taken care of myself for a time since I was a small child. I will take Chamblis as a constant companion."

Glancing at her, then the clouding sky, J'erik resigned himself to the inevitable. "Do you think there is a hand against the sun's time for us, before you send me away?"

Eyes narrowed in mock cynicism, "It depends on how close to your face you place your hand. There might be time for two."

Fancher lowered a second barrow from the Hold. The concept was an improvement over carrying everything. He checked eastward. The land gently sloped up to the north. The gray-brown hues changed gradually as reddish hemotite made its presence known. The painted-on splashes of richer land gave the scene in front of the

Hold the appearance of a magnificent pseudogram, like those in the travel agencies.

Dead iron trees were gargoyles in the sand. Dunes shifted against pyramid-shaped rock piles. Coalescing taluses softened the hard lines of thrusting cliffs that marched west, each one higher than the eastern counterpart.

To the north stood a wall of columnar jointed rock, reaching up to the gathering clouds. Broken spires lay in a scrap heap at the base as an example of Cassilee's brutality through the ages. Gray clouds, trying to cluster into a solid mass, moved shadows over the land, cooling the terrain for brief intervals.

Leaning away from the ledge, Fancher could not see farther. He climbed down to where Fir'ah was coiling rope into the new cart. She wore the pack, heedless of his protests. When finished, she walked the final distance through fallen slabs of cliff, disappeared behind their mass and emerged on the smooth land where her barrow waited.

Fancher wormed the cart through a narrow passage eked out over the centuries and joined the woman. At the small collection of belongings, she had unlashed the full cart and was unloading waterskins.

Half of them were set aside. Rope whipped through the side holes. In minutes Fir'ah's cart was ready to travel. Ignoring Fancher, she walked a dozen meters out onto sandy ground. One by one, she faced eight directions, trying to feel out the best one.

Fancher made the most of the time by packing the second cart and trying to lash it in the same fashion as the first one. He saw that she knew what she was doing when it came to packing securely. Not one of her rope crosses was slack. He could wiggle a forefinger one joint under the rope and no farther.

When she returned he was almost finished. "Do you have any idea where you're going?"

The question merited a half-shrug.

Sure now that she understood, "How about traveling with me until you're certain? Then maybe I'll want to travel with you for a little ways."

She looked north.

"Yeah. I'm headed north, too. Gotta see a man about

a job." He grinned, thinking of Satow. The memory of Mikel soured the levity. "Maybe I'll get lucky and see an old friend, too." Mumbling, "Doubt he'll thank me for destroying his future, but he's still a friend." He quieted, realizing that the references were directed at a couple of men who knowingly or unknowingly were responsible for the killing of a countless many like her.

Fir'ah led. Fancher delved into his thoughts and the significance of the dead Hold he found her in. How many places like that had been demolished by the initial phase of restructuring over half a century ago? And how many prelims before that? Four? Five? Phase two, twenty-seven years earlier? Phase three, only a decade ago? Now? Let alone the ecological imbalance and the starving hordes of little beasties. The great winged creatures no longer flew the night skies. Perhaps they too were starving to death. And the gentle creatures in moody colors who had traveled with him?

If they weren't starving now, they soon would be. His own food supply began to worry him.

Days had lapsed since he had seen a living piece of vegetation. Granted, the seeds dropped into and around the intended water basins would provide a substantial amount of edible foodstuff in a relatively short time. The survival manual had tactfully omitted how long it took to starve to death.

Fancher quickened his stride. "Sorry, Princess, but we're going to have to really move it. The only chance we've got for not becoming beastie fodder is to reach the green belt and pray it's intact. No guarantees, though. It could be stripped as bare as this place." He found that he could not look her in the eye when she searched for an explanation. Thunder rumbled in the dark clouds churning overhead. They personified his growing anger at New Life Enterprises.

Fir'ah watched the skies, stumbling occasionally. The growling and the streaks of light were new. Hard as she tried, she could not sense the menace of the Star Demons beyond the turmoil.

The wind grew stronger, the gusts blasting their exposed skin with sand. Fir'ah wanted to travel in an old arroyo. Fancher yelled over the growling storm and climbed to a ridge. Hunched against the wind, he waited for her.

Rain shot out of the sky in a solid sheet. Fir'ah sank to her knees, bowing to the end of Cassilee and her hopes. Water from the sky was surely a sign that the end was soon. On hands and knees, she wondered what she had done as a Betweener to bring about this catastrophe. Rain beat onto her scalp. Her forehead sank to the wet sand. She did not want to see the Star Demons with no aura when they came to kill. The face of death would not be looked upon. It would smile unrecognized and strike unseen.

"What in three shades of hell is the matter with you, woman? Haven't you got enough sense to find shelter from the rain? Water's gonna shoot down this alley in a few minutes!" Irate at many things in general, Fir'ah in particular, Fancher yanked her up and shoved her toward the rise. Cursing, he dug out the wheel and got the cart moving.

"Keep going! Get over to those cliffs and find a dry place to camp. I'm right behind you."

Fir'ah did not move fast, but she did as he said, as though in a trance guided by his shouts. Fancher grunted and groaned. The fine dust and sand absorbed the water to form a glue over the hard-packed earth, which also lapped water into the cracks and spat it out. Climbing was strenuous. Rocks slipped and crumbled under the cartwheel.

Fir'ah helped to get the barrow into a shallow cave which was dry in the rear. She barely noted his absence when he departed for his belongings. Instead, she watched the rain, listened to the thunder and was enthralled by the streaks of lightning. The smells and sounds excited her out of her doomsday fears and lured her into a fascination. She became so thoroughly engrossed that Fancher's return, huffing and puffing, went unnoticed.

It was so strange, this bath from the clouds washing the dust off Cassilee's ancient innards thrust up to Uli in offering. Yet, the essence of Cassilee seemed angered by what was happening to the land and her few creatures.

"You'd better get dried off and change your clothes, Princess." Fancher closed up his old flight suit, turned on the beacon to a dim setting and started toward Fir'ah with one of the treasures rescued before the journey. "Here. I found this in a pack near the river. You may as well . . . "

Fir'ah saw the glittering silver suit. The day she went looking for J'erik flashed back in its entirety. The Star Demon egg with eyes all around it . . . the crack where the vermin had spilled seed onto the land . . . the slanted place where the path led to the brush. The red-blotched silver thing which sparkled under Uli . . . the touch!

A Star Demon. Loose upon the land. Ready to devour everything and everyone.

The robe extended to her hung midway between them. She recognized her embroidery and no longer allowed a doubt. Somehow she must rid Cassilee of the Demon disguised as a man. Somehow he had to be eliminated. She snatched the robe and hugged it to her breast, beseeching Cassilee for a method to obliterate this monster who could pull water from the sky.

Chapter 22

THE RAIN STOPPED IN THE MIDDLE OF THE night. Starlight teased through trailing clouds. Inside the shallow cave, a dull light glowed in a no-man's-land. On one side, Fir'ah sat against the wall hugging her robe and occasionally nibbled at a strip of dried calantani. The silence she had practiced for so long was no longer mandatory. The words, sought so many times, were available, but there was nothing to say.

On the other side, Fancher tried to rest. Sleep refused to rescue him from the confusion he thought he should be able to clear up. Hours earlier attempts to talk with, to, or at the woman had been abandoned. He was frustrated and miserable. The nagging threat that she would go her own way in the morning and leave him utterly alone made him wish that he had never laid eyes on her. The idea of her wandering over the planet, where water could rupture the dry ground at any time, the little beasties swarmed in giant hordes, and there were no certain food sources, pressed him to find a solution. If not a solution, at least an inkling of why she had changed so abruptly or the possible significance of the robe.

Life seemed like a three-dimensional puzzle, the ones with ten thousand pieces that six experts assembled in only four weeks. He thought he knew how the lost piece felt.

A gagging noise forced his attention across the void.

Her hand fumbled for the knife. Knees tucked under her chin, Fir'ah attempted to watch the Demon and control the heaves which turned her stomach inside out. When he rose and started to near, she clutched the weapon tighter.

Fancher crouched down, grabbed her hand and massaged her wrist until the knife dropped. "Look, woman, you're sick. I want to help you. Will you let me do that? Will you?"

Perspiration flowed down her face as though she had just come in from the rain. Had she not known he was a Demon, she knew she would believe him. But a Star Demon could only bring destruction.

Helpless, Fancher watched her shiver without answering. "Okay! That does it!"

With a hard, unexpected tug, he pulled the robe away, blocking the flailing hands trying to strike. He put his hand out, signaling a halt. When she complied, he put the robe over her.

Fir'ah glared for a moment, then rested against the wall, eyes closed and waiting for the Demon to end her life.

He tucked the robe under her chin, wondering how the man she killed ever got close enough to her to . . . "Holy prophet in a bawdy house," he whispered, running his hand over his dry mouth.

She did not move.

He touched her cheek. It was flushed, but cool and damp. "Are you pregnant?"

Hands, feet and teeth struck out from under the robe, fighting the Demon and the truth she could no longer deny. She clutched the invader around the neck and held, toppling them onto his back. Head down, she attempted to ram his face. She was stronger than Fancher anticipated. The best he could do was cushion the blow with one hand and absorb the shock with his ear. His head rang for the effort.

Her thumbs worked at a nodule she thought to be his larynx; instead, it was the control for the suit seal. It tightened around his neck, steadily choking off the air supply to his lungs.

Fancher threw his left arm over his head and tried to pry her hands loose with his right hand. Body rocking, he could not easily unseat her. The choice of whether or not to punch her was quickly evaporating.

Suddenly he grabbed her shoulders and lifted and flung her to the floor, rolling to set himself on top. Scrambling, he straddled her stomach and pinned her arms to her sides with his knees. A quick pull unfastened the suit down to his waist.

Rasping air filled his lungs. He rubbed the sore spot near his larynx, looking at her, perplexed more than ever by her behavior.

"Finish it," she hissed, staring back and holding perfectly still.

"You can speak. Why . . . now there's a question!"

"Finish it."

"Finish what?"

"Your killing rampage."

"I haven't killed anyone." Hands running through his hair, "You really expect me to kill you? Why would I want to do that? You're young, pretty, strong—a slight pause—"and pregnant. Aren't you?"

"Because I know. That's why."

"What do you know?"

"You are a Star Demon. Not a man. You murder Cassilee and her people. You destroyed the Ah-te. The Tor-ad-ih. How many others? How many? The Techi?"

"Sorry to disappoint you, but I am a man, quite mortal, very fallible and extremely confused." Absently, he reached inside his suit and scratched the scar tissue twinging across his right shoulder and breast. "I haven't the faintest idea what you're talking about. What's an Ah-te?"

Squinting, she hissed, "The place I lived near where the Demon egg hatched you."

Click. Another piece fell into place. The first level took shape. He chuckled, shaking his head at the simplicity of it all. "Well, Princess, I think we have some talking to do. You're the reason I'm here. At least, I think you're part of it. See, when I first spotted you, and there was another reading a little ways away, and you were human readouts—my plug got pulled." Head lifted to the ceiling, "They think I'm dead. They did their level best to make sure I was."

Fancher gently moved her arms, folding them across

her breasts. A hand signal warned her to keep still. She responded with a belligerent nod.

"You were the one I touched after I crawled out of the ship? Blazes, I thought you were a dream."

"You stole my words."

"Huh?"

"You stole my words so I could not speak. Why do you give them back now?"

"Tell me what happened. Why were you there?"

She considered for a moment, then said, "I will tell you, but then I want answers before you kill me, Demon. If you are a man, I will know when you speak. I will feel you."

Every time she opened her mouth Fancher found two dozen more questions.

"It is simple. I went to the surface to find J'erik, my brother. I could not. You had changed the land and eaten the long butte. Instead, I found you. When I reached the Ah-te, T'lar was waiting in the outer cavern." She looked away for a few seconds. "J'erik willed me to live and took away the Choosing fear, but he could not give back the words you stole."

Level three moved together around the perimeter of the puzzle. The superstition, the power, the life-changing force of the terraformers as viewed by the inhabitants of Cassilee, coupled with what had met her at home could certainly be traumatic enough, Fancher surmised.

"Princess, if I stole your words, believe me, it was unintentional. Please accept my apologies for any part I had in causing you to be silent. I have no wish to hurt you, or bring harm your way. What you call Star Demons are ships. Inside them are people—men and women. Most of them are good people who would resign from the service of New Life if they knew what was taking place here. But there are others who do know."

Emotion worked through her face in tiny spasms. "I do not want to believe you."

Silent, Fancher did not react when she took the front edge of his suit into her thumb and forefinger, pulled it aside and peeked in.

"I still do not want to believe you, but I can feel truth. And I know you are a man and nothing else. I can feel you very easily. You do not even have the Gift."

196

Rejecting the disgust in her tone, "What do you mean, 'feel me'?"

"Inside, where you think and know, there is a peace when the truth is spoken. It is something which tells when the words match."

"You can read my mind?" He did not realize he was squirming until his body reacted independently.

"Not specifically. I know when you lie and when you don't."

"And if I tell you you are safe with me until I ask you to go, will you believe me?"

She paused, fighting internally. "I think so, but there is a part of you that is like T'lar."

A faint blush spread over Fancher. "You mean that I want to have sex with you?"

No answer came out of her mouth.

"I do. If the time comes when I don't think it's a controllable urge, I'll let you know. Then you can leave or take care of it. The choice is yours. Rape isn't my operational mode. Okay?"

Brow wrinkled in disbelief, "You want me to Choose you?"

"Did I say something wrong?"

"You would want to be father to the child I carry?"

"I did say something wrong. Maybe I'd better rephrase it. I said that you could make a choice."

"And that is what you mean?"

"Yes."

"You? A Star Demon?" Giggling, "Chosen by a Be-tweener with a Dweller's babe?" Fir'ah laughed for the first time since the Ah-te. It came out long and hard, shaking her convulsively.

"I think my next career will be in the entertainment business," Fancher mumbled, climbing off.

By the time Fir'ah stopped laughing she was on her side of the cave and looking at Fancher through watery eyes. "I wonder if Betweeners go mad when they receive shock after shock. All I seem to have left is an acceptance for what I cannot change. There is no real understanding, no forthcoming explanations. I wanted to kill you, Star Demon, for what you have done to Cassilee and her people. But you are another victim in a way I

197

do not begin to understand. You look like a Betweener. Are you?"

"How should I know?" He took a swig from the water-skin and offered it to her.

"Can you walk in the light of Uli bare-skinned and not go blind?"

Even before asking, "What's an Uli?" he knew he had a lot to learn about Cassilee and the sandy-haired woman wiggling in and out of his mind.

In the Techi equivalent of a Common, J'erik addressed the gathering, summed up the situation as he knew it and turned to J'osh-uah.

He took full advantage of the unnatural silence J'erik had created. "I would like to say that we are safe from any force which threatens Cassilee. Mostly, we are. The Techi is impregnable to all known enemies. Water is an unknown.

"It is still rising and has reached the cliff base." Nodding to the Seeress of the Tor-ad-ih, "The thing both histories refer to as rain continues to fall. How long this will go on we have no way of knowing."

Hands clasped behind his back, he moved closer to the listeners. Crow's-feet deepened around his eyes. Tight indentations beset the frown he wore. "It is with deep regret that I advise you to leave and journey north on beasts of prey. Even the Betweener has not been to where we are going. We have been offered sanctuary by one who had lost favor with the Techi."

Straightening, "However, it seems a wiser choice than staying. Water surrounds us on all sides. I personally have gone with J'erik of the Ah-te on one of the calantani to see this. Even in the first strains of Uli, there was no land visible. We are isolated. Our food supply from the land no longer exists. The time to act is now, before it is too late."

He turned back to J'erik. "Uli will leave the sky shortly. Those who wish to go in the first wave, speak now."

"I'll go!" Star-ii jumped off the seat between Cor-ii and Kali-te. The old woman struggled to her feet and followed. J'erik swept the child up and exchanged hugs. "You are the bravest of the lot, Star-ii."

198

Whispers and murmurs buzzed over the gathering. Quick looks filled with fear were taken at the Betweener.

"Will Lorff be there? I can't wait to see Lorff again. He's a good friend. Does he feel better? I hope so, 'cause I love him." Star-ii wound her arms tightly around J'erik's neck. "This is gonna be fun."

"Star-ii, Lorff has left the herd."

She leaned back, not understanding.

"He felt that Fir'ah's destiny was his doing and thought that he had not served me well."

"But where did he go?"

"I don't know. Chacon is waiting for you, though."

N'oblic led six Dwellers. "We will go in whatever group you feel is best." Looking over his shoulder at the Techi vehemently conversing in circles, "Perhaps it is easier when you are already dispossessed."

J'erik set Star-ii down and addressed the gathering. "There are nine Dwellers ready to go. I want a minimum of twenty-seven from the Techi. You are going to have to rely on the Dwellers for directions in daylight. They will be heavily wrapped, whereas you may dress comfortably, but I want your eyes bound so Uli cannot find them."

The Techi quieted, but none moved.

"Is it not better to go with the voice of someone who can see whispering into your ear than in black silence?"

As though keyed by an invisible force, the Techi began to move into new groups. These, in turn, formed divisions. Less than half remained at the back of the room. J'osh-uah morosely approached to persuade them to leave.

J'erik set to work assigning a balanced number to the first wave. Already too much talk had been expended convincing the upper echelons at the Techi, J'osh-uah being the most difficult.

"I cannot save you from your fears any more than you can save yourself from the rising water. I've lost too much time here." J'erik turned to his group. "Come, I will get you started. Take only what you must. Kali-te will show those in N'oblic's group how to protect against Uli."

"I too could be of service," Cor-ii said quietly from the middle of the room. "Please, J'erik Betweener of the

Ah-te, search your heart and see if there is a shred of forgiveness in it for me."

The soft touch on his arm was a plea from Kali-te. He turned to her, "You suffered greatly because of Cor-ii's actions. Do you extend forgiveness?"

"You righted my misfortunes, and, perhaps, changed more than my life, J'erik. I did not raise you to be unyielding."

"You did not raise a fool, either. She goes with me, then, so I can watch her." He stepped away from the group and faced Cor-ii. "I will not leave you here to die, but I do not trust you, either. That you will have to earn by deeds. You stay with me. Do not leave my side, and you may not carry a Hold weapon. Is that agreed?"

Head bowed, "It is far more than I deserve and more than fair. I will not fail this chance you have given me, J'erik."

When she looked up to meet his gaze, he wished again for Lor'ee. She could divine the truth as the words were spoken. The reluctance to practice what he did not understand, and therefore could not accept, left him dependent. He did not want to see the totality of this woman. And wishing he could be different in that one respect did not help to make him so.

Chapter 23

FOR THREE DAYS FANCHER AND THE BETWE-
ener conversed, climbed and moved north. Fir'ah talked
incessantly. A voice against the wind was an exhilarating
sensation. It made her feel whole. Fancher asked hundreds
of questions, many of which she tried not to laugh at. In
turn, she learned about Star Demons as people; Betweeners spread across the stars on a hundred worlds.

The nights grew colder, the fog heavier and the rain
daily. After seven days the two travelers had settled into
a routine. Fancher was able to ascertain the beginnings
of Fir'ah's illness cycles. During those times he managed both carts, one pushed, the other pulled on a chest
harness, until she became insistent on pushing her own.

On the tenth day, they spotted the first big patch of
reddish blue in the distance. It stood as a bastion, growing east and west to the horizons, in front of lofty mountains, gray with distance. It took a full day of hard travel
over the foothills to reach it.

Shortly before dusk, Fir'ah cut gadid berry clusters,
eating while she filled a caldron to the brim. The mountains forced secondary glances out of her. Arêtes jabbed
into thin, still clouds basking in Uli's dregs.

Fancher could not help grinning as she flitted across
the giant bushes, unable to reach the tops or the inner
ripe clusters. He unloaded the barrow packed with night
camp supplies and spread extra clothing and blankets

201

into two piles. Already the night chill had influenced him to slip the top of the flight suit on.

"Bring another pot," Fir'ah called.

Obliging, he gathered up two spares and took them to her. "Can you make wine out of these?"

"Wine . . ." She thought for a minute, then grinned and shoved two large berries into his mouth. "Wine, a drink which lightens the senses?"

"Um-hum."

"Um-hum," she imitated, "but it is very strong." Pointing to a heavy stalk out of her reach, "Can you get that one?"

He tried and fell short. "I'll hold you up." Bent-kneed, he sat her on his left shoulder. "Ready?"

He stood, arms wrapped around her legs in case her balance faltered. The knife whipped through the woody stalk. She grabbed the berries before they dropped. "Almost ready." After the knife went into her belt, she patted his head to be released.

Unexpectedly, she twisted, bouncing, and slid down the front, laughing and holding the berries off to the side.

Fancher's stomach jumped into his mouth, changing his mood. He did not let go of her, nor did she pull away. "Fir'ah!"

One glimpse of him turned the laugh into a fading giggle.

"Fir'ah." He cleared his throat in order to speak. "We're doing a lot of traveling. You're having to exert yourself more every day. You can't take chances like that. What if I had dropped you? There's more to think about than just you. You're pregnant! You're going to have to change the way you live for a while."

"Want a berry?" Her voice was light, but the smile changed into a grimace of contrition.

"No. I want you to take care of yourself." Holding tighter, he pressed her head against his chest and kissed her hair. "I don't want anything ever to happen to you. You really scared me, Princess."

"Fancher?"

"Humh?"

"Is it Choice time?"

Stiffened, then relaxing, "No. You'll probably know

202

before I do. It's funny. I've been all over the Port System and never came close to finding someone I could chuck it all for and settle down. Plenty of women, most of whom I cared for in one way or another. Then I get dumped on this wasteland . . ." He laughed when she looked up, ready to take exception at his description of Cassilee. "Even Cassilee is beginning to look and actually feel good to me."

"Fancher? Would it be all right if I asked you to kiss me the way a, a . . . " Lost for words, she did not finish.

"As a man who loves a woman would kiss her?"

He cupped her face, turned his head slightly, bent down and touched her lips. Gently, he teased her mouth open, settled his lips on hers and reveled in the response. What began with restraint culminated in a lingering, passionate kiss, wherein he explored the curves of her back for as far as he could reach. Her arms tightened around his neck, bringing her body tightly against his.

In a flicker of sanity, he pulled away, realizing that she was just as engrossed in what was happening as he. "I . . . ah . . ." He paused, breathing as he did after a difficult climb. "Fir'ah, I don't think that was a particularly good idea." The words rushed out. He swallowed twice. "It makes it pretty hard on me."

Fir'ah slid one arm from around his neck and into his suit, then rested against him. Her cold goosebumps helped him calm down. "I should not have run from you on the plateau, Fancher. I know that now. I also know that I cannot Choose you because it would not be fair. Cassilee is not your home. The Demons will come. You will go."

She looked up again. "But you have made me think that there could be great joy in what T'lar made ugly. I would have you show me without the burden of Choosing."

Fancher laughed, head back, shoulders heaving. The irony of his fate settled in. What he refused to think about had become a certainty that he never had to think over. "Princess, I want you to Choose me. You've got me now. I won't let go."

"The babe?"

"Mine, just as the next one and the one after would be. He'll have a Betweener mother and a Star Demon father." He chuckled at the sound. "No. You've told me about Choosing. We'll work by those rules. Think about it."

"I'm cold."

The berry find lost its glamour. At Fancher's insistence, Fir'ah ate the last of the dried-meat strips along with the fruit. In near darkness, he rigged a drying platform for the berries and set out crude kodjelu traps. When finished, he crawled into the mound of bedding beside Fir'ah.

"I'm turning the field up tonight, so don't move around without waking me first. Okay?" After he felt her nod, "Where there's food, there might be kodjelu."

"All right. I'll think about that, too. Meantime, you think about me."

He reached over and set the field on maximum protection, then rolled onto his back to watch the stars. Would that he could not think about her, so near, so warm, so frustratingly willing. The decision which had evolved in the back of his mind amazed him. The lack of doubt did not blend into his usual decision-making process.

Tiny splatters of color, radiant in the starlight, moved in single file in the east. He watched, wondering if they were the same panavers he had traveled with or a different group. Their slow motion ate into the night. They disappeared into the gadid barrier, solving the problem of a trail to the mountains.

Fir'ah's reasons for not Choosing him bounced around in his mind like rocks in a drum. Strange, he thought, I never considered going back. To what? New Life Enterprises? Satow? Palama? There's always the Port System —new planets, old colonies. But no Fir'ah. No panavers, no Fir'ah. He felt his innards dissolve and acid spray his brain. Good, bad, hot, cold, temperamental or guileless, Cassilee *was* home.

Fir'ah sat up, startling him. "Are you going to go to sleep?"

"Nope. I don't think so."

"Why not?"

"I'm too wound up trying not to compromise my morals." He grinned and pointed at the sky. "We'll go calantani hunting tomorrow."

204

"Fancher, will you kiss me again?"

"No."

Blankets fluffed in the air. They followed as she moved on top of him, giggling.

"Get off, Fir'ah." The hair curtain tickled his nose. Inexperienced or not, he felt his determination waver under her presence.

Between small kisses around his mouth, "What's a moral?"

"Something I'm wondering if I have any of." She countered his move to depose her by locking her arms around his neck.

"Will I catch it?"

"I hope not." He met her mouth, eager yet restrained, hands exploring all they could reach, probing for the warm flesh under her clothes and finding reward after reward.

Raised on one elbow, she went for the suit fastener. He took her hand, put her fingers to his lips and said, "Choose me, Fir'ah. I won't leave you."

"I will Choose you for tonight and free you in the morning. What difference does it make now? I love you." She smiled, mystified. "I do not know why, but I do love you, Star Demon." A flick and two snaps released the grippers.

Fancher had little trouble removing Fir'ah's garb. Most of it was already unfastened. Under different circumstances, he would not have found being second-guessed amusing, but this time it was beneficial.

Before Uli brightened the east, Fir'ah Chose with a promise not to rescind. They slept a quarter of the day before waking to make love again.

"Everything is ready and loaded," Cor-ii said to J'erik. She struggled up the face of a yellow striper shared with the Betweener and supplies.

He nodded, hearing only the words, brooding over the fifty-two who remained in the Techi. Depression set in keenly when the clouds over the endless murky stretch rolled their way, spitting light and grumbling in the night. Methodically, J'erik mounted the yellow and sent out the signal to move north.

The calantani not dispatched to advanced groups as

scouts stayed behind for rest and feeding. Diearka bellowed a few low notes to his comrades and took to the air as the Master's scout. The rest would catch up in a day or two, then spread out among the other six caravans, each a day apart. A pale-green female, Fannia, yodeled at the orange one, flapped her great wings and lifted to join him.

J'erik watched, impervious to the mating dance the two performed, soaring, diving, climbing vertically, the green wings folded against the orange. Fifty-two stayed, electing to die a horrible death instead of facing the lifegiving change. He tried for consolation by admitting that the success factor was greater than J'osh-uah had predicted. Eighty percent was a good number.

"Why would they stay to die?" he mumbled.

Cor-ii cleared her throat and spoke timidly, as though expecting to be struck silent for daring the words. "They are so afraid of another way of life and the differences involved, their decision was the only one they could make."

He turned sharply, halting her words. "Go on."

"You really do not realize the power your difference wields, J'erik Betweener. Look at yourself. You do not share our weaknesses to Uli. Were it only the physical, it would still be sufficient to cause some to reach the same decision. You are more than that. And they do not possess the Gift to see.

"How would you feel if someone tried to tell you everything you believed in was in error, that you must abandon the only way you know how to live, and that someone was vastly superior to you?

"I am weak and afraid easily, but I'm too stubborn to throw my life away." Chuckling sadly, "And I have known you all of your life. They have not. Watching you these last days has told me that in my worst hour, there is only one who has exceeded the fear I hold for you."

They rode in silence for a hand against the stars before J'erik asked, "Who is it that fears what you see of my difference more than you?"

"It is you, J'erik."

The first day passed smoothly.
Late afternoon on the second turned into a nightmare

for the sighted. Gigantic carcasses, all bones and broken parts of spindly legs, the barbs torn and scattered, lay across the trail. Smaller bones, human ones, mingled with the teeth, fangs and molars belonging to the dead zanstyrs. Not a piece of cloth or clump of hair remained. Kodjelu shells were strewn along the ground for as far as the eye could see, all of them eaten out.

J'erik summoned the resting calantani and ordered them to scout and decoy any nearby hordes.

That evening, cliff calantani began to circle. The scrawny band numbered around twenty-five. Diearka and his mate took to the air, chirping and calling over the collected gray screeches. Fannia circled low and began to attack the leader at the center. Diearka's sibilant bass vibrated the night. She backed off, diving, then climbing back to him.

The zanstyrs bellowed in unison, tongues snapping like whips at the sky, bodies contracting, barbs glistening in the starlight as their legs flexed.

The gray calantani retreated cautiously and flew south toward the nebula. Fannia sang a high note which changed to a whine as she carved a half circle in the night and settled among the zanstyrs. A high-pitched lament accompanied her rocking. J'erik ran to her, speaking quietly, trying to find the right words to ease her grief. He had listened to Diearka persuade the calantani that easier prey traveled south in the form of a kodjelu horde. He had also heard of the fate suffered by the scouts belonging to the caravan ravaged by the kodjelu. The continual boasting of the grays sent Fannia into an emotional frenzy.

Diearka settled beside Fannia. *I do not know if they will return.*

J'erik left the calantani to mourn in privacy. He checked rope harnesses securing people and food upon the zanstyrs' backs. The episode had loosened the Techi's collective tongue. Their objections and demands for an explanation of the afternoon were met by a desensationalized account of the carnage fifty kilometers back. Respect for the Dwellers riding with them drew from a deeper well. It could not have been easy for them to be silent when they saw the caravan's fate. And those who could not see would conjure a horrifying image of their own without an accurate description.

They moved straight west through the night. The zanstyrs picked a speed and held it, covering better than the hundred kilometers J'erik hoped to average in a day. He watched the sky constantly for Star Demons and calantani. The same land which allowed speed and distance was void of shelter, food and fresh water. Only wind and dark earth were companions.

By the fourth day, plateaus in the eastern distance that had followed them for a day and a half began to close in and offer shelter. They entered the land of the spires and were turned north.

Kodjelu shells crunched beneath the zanstyrs' feet. The land was a dull-reddish color and alive with whispers uttered by the wind against the stone. J'erik waited for a scouting report from Diearka. The final result was that they would have to go over the ridge sitting on the land as a barrier. Loaded as the zanstyrs were, the operation was carried out in two stages, halving the burdens.

The beasts expended most of the energy. A Techi man panicked and tore the wrappings away. A straight-on glimpse of Uli cost him a partial loss of sight.

They moved into a valley where buttes and mesas guarded the sky. Night settled with a violent wind. It blotted out the stars and bit through their robes. At the height of the fury, Diearka summoned his Lord.

The cliff calantani were back.

Diearka and Fannia flew above the maelstrom, their battle songs lost in the wind and sand eroding the land. Talons bared, lips curled back to expose their sharp teeth, they circled the straggling nine driven to do battle by hunger.

The zanstyrs moved through the sandstorm. One warrior stayed back to protect the people huddled in a shallow cave away from the wind. He was unhappy with his role, but bowed respectfully to the Master's wish.

Fannia struck at the left flank of the loosely formed aggressors. Her great wings folded, plummeting her entire mass onto the back of the much smaller gray. A shriek pricked the wind. The bone snap was lost. The gray fell, wings spread and unnaturally pointed at the head.

On the ground, zanstyrs galloped to assure the kill.

Diearka flew head on at the two charging him. At the last second, the pair split, one over, one under. He pirouetted in the wind, his much larger size not a hindrance. Upper wings folded, his slight drop put his tail into striking range. It snapped around the lower calantani's neck and wrapped, jerking the beast over backward. Diearka flapped his upper wings, tugged, and released, concentrating on the beast diving at him from overhead.

The lower calantani beat his wings futilely, caught by the downdraft in the sandy wind. The zanstyrs relieved him of his agony.

The smaller beast turned, flicking his tail at Diearka's head. A swath of orange ringlets flittered into the roar. Diearka's claws on his finger protrusions flayed the end of the tail. Two hard pumps against the wind, and his right talons struck the gray across the left haunch and the connecting membrane of the great wing.

Fannia called. The remaining six closed in, limiting her effectiveness at any one of them.

Diearka dove into the storm and came out of it just under the battle. The element of surprise allowed him to down one calantani with his tail for the zanstyrs to finish and bite into a second at the outer base of the tail. Using talons and tail, he sent the screaming beast into the storm.

Fannia shrieked, her tail wrapped around a gray, a second one digging into her back, his teeth buried under the ringlets.

Tail whipping the air, Diearka bellowed and charged. The tip sliced across a gray's eyes as it tried to close in on the orange's blind side. Screeching, it flew in circles, bleeding a trail.

Diearka threaded his tail neatly between Fannia and the gray, brought it around the gray's neck and squeezed.

The last gray charged the underbelly of the green, flipped to put his clawed feet up, and ripped her open before Diearka could free his tail from the corpse on her back. The last effort of the green was rewarded when her talons snared the gray's right great wing and trapped him as she fell out of the sky.

As though stunned, Cassilee's wind stopped.

Diearka flew in circles, looking for an object to vent his grief upon. The low, melodious notes became a dirge

moaning to the stars. Below, the zanstyrs feasted on
grays, skirting the green lump twisted by red-splattered
gray shapes. Fannia's innards were strewn over the sand
for ten meters, slowly being buried by the last dregs
settling out of the air.

The orange one flew the entire night. His moans, cries
and songs kept the land awake.

In the last hours before light, the Techi and Dwellers
butchered the cliff calantani and prepared the meat for drying. A blue zanstyr burrowed into the earth and carved
a tomb which the others lined with rock.

At the first strains of Uli in the heavily clouded east,
the zanstyrs retreated to the cluster of watching people,
anxious to be gone from this place.

J'erik remained at the gravesite.

Diearka answered the summons of his Lord and
slowly, defying gravity, settled beside Fannia. Yellow
tears, most dried, some still wet, stained the orange and
bled across his upper wings. His moves were mechanical,
his eyes not focusing upon the green-and-red mass stif-
fening on the ground. The formidable tail, capable of
instant killing, moved of its own accord to collect the
remains of his mate. The tomb was too narrow for him
to carry her down. He used the tail to lower her, turning
her head toward the surface where her glazed yellow
eyes could watch for him in the skies.

The blue zanstyr lumbered closer. Diearka's tail
flashed a warning. The blue halted.

J'erik took out his knife, climbed on Diearka's left
haunch and cut a handful of hair off the side of the
orange head lowered into his reach. Heavy-hearted,
throat constricted, J'erik climbed into the tomb and
wound the ringlets through Fannia's stiff fingers and
over partially extended claws.

Standing again beside Diearka, J'erik watched the blue
lay rock slabs over the tomb and replace tons of sand
which blended into the desert. The zanstyrs rocked back
and forth in unison, the joyous death song subdued by
a calantani sorrow they did not comprehend, yet respected.

A Dweller baritone filled the dawn with the ritual dirge.
His voice was clear and strong. A second, then a third,
finally Cor-ii's beautiful alto chimed in. They sang with
emotion, bringing a hum of the melody out from the

Techi. The song was for Fannia, for the life they no longer had, for the unborn children and for the dead loved ones given to the mercy of Cassilee.

Diearka took to the air, an orange creature of sorrow trying to find appeasement in the growing light of Uli.

A quiet day and a half later they came upon a field of gadid where caravans before them had stopped to replenish food supplies and rest. The signs indicated that the previous groups had chosen to go around the gargantuan mountains rising in the north-northeast. It was a good decision which he knew the calantani and zanstyrs had made together.

He looked at the magnificent peaks, yearning to take a straight-line approach, and would have, if alone. The toll on those in the caravan was too great to justify it.

While they rested, he rode Diearka into the mountains. At least he could explore from the air. They crossed the first ridgeline and saw a dozen more. The new sights and changes on Cassilee were magnificent. Deep valleys plunged between the peaks, some filled by vegetation, others rock deposed from the heights.

They flew until dusk, each free in the open air to shed the depression and loneliness the caravan seemed to magnify. Just before reaching the final ridge on their return, Diearka circled low over the lush valley. An iron tree heavy with amilglibs and gadid vines shook unnaturally.

Diearka tightened his pattern and flew closer.

Out at the edge of the tight gadid mess fuming into the air came a chartreuse stripe. Lorff moved onto the rock and climbed. The dead flesh he dragged swept anything fragile or light to the side.

Lorff. Lorff. Come back with me. We need you. Be my adviser again.

The huge head swung to the sky. *I am dead.* He returned to the drudgery of climbing.

J'erik pleaded, using every scrap of logic he could muster. It was a fruitless effort.

Heavy-hearted, yet relieved that Lorff was alive, he returned to the camp, where night always brought memories of Fir'ah and a yearning for Lor'ee.

Chapter 24

"DID YOU SEE THAT?"

Fir'ah joined Fancher on the lip of a rock shelter they were to spend the night in. "No. What was it?"

"The big orange calantani. I've seen him before, or one like him, near where I crashed. He circled the riverbed as though he was looking for something." He put an arm around her and shook his head. "It's been a long day. I could have sworn somebody was riding on it."

"H-how sure?"

The trembling against him drew concern. She stared off into the distance. "Hey. What's the matter?"

"How sure are you that somebody was riding the calantani and that it was orange?" Each word was pronounced utilizing his accent.

"I'm sure it was orange. It was pretty far away. Now, tell me what's wrong." Fancher did not expect the smile that lit her face.

"J'erik. J'erik!"

Fancher turned back to the darkening sky, deflated. "We should have gone around. He could have helped make this trip easier on you. At least you would have seen him."

"No. This is the best way. He does not know that I live, nor that T'lar does not. But it is good to know that he is well."

"I can't be positive that I saw a man on the orange," he said, musing out loud.

"Shhhh." Her fingertips touched his mouth. "Let me believe it. I need to."

Fancher took her hand and kissed it. "In that case, I saw a Betweener on the orange. He was a little taller than I, but not quite as good-looking. His face lacked the character mine has."

Giggling, "I don't know about that, but you're more fun to sleep with than he was."

"If you didn't work me to death, I'd sweep you off your feet and show you how much fun. You'll have to walk, though." Pointing to the deepest part of the shelter, "Go. Prepare thyself, Betweener Princess, whilst I set up the field to ensure our privacy."

He placed small metal bits around the opening and focused the field. "I am going to build you a house, Fir'ah. When we get to where we're going, it will be the capital of Cassilee. When it's done, we'll have a little berry wine and you can christen it. How does Cassilee Castle sound?"

"What's a castle?"

"Whatever I build and call one." Loading the empty waterskins into the bottom of the cart, "Your relatives are welcome anytime. But we're not sleeping with your brother. I don't care how good-lookin' he is, or how tall." He held up the better of the two flight suits and motioned for her to come over. "Try this on. I'll mark it and to-morrow, before we leave, I'll use the Destro on it. Better that than dulling the knives."

"Tomorrow." The echo was a whisper. She sat facing the rock, legs crossed, stark naked with her hands on her knees. "Can you feel the Presence here?"

Fancher checked the field and looked around. Only two strong urges stood out. Fir'ah would take care of one before sleep eased the other. He dropped the suit into the cart and undressed.

"I have felt this Presence before, in the tunnels. It saved me from death." She held out her hand for him as he settled. "It knows my name."

It tingled where her hand touched. He let go. The sensation ended. Her skin was cool. Before further exploration of the phenomenon, he threw the Ah-te robe over her.

Trying to understand the reason for her beatific smile, he stilled and took her hand. Fatigue melted away from his aching muscles. A total serenity wiped away concern and worry. In the flicker of an instant, he thought about the panavers. The dull sand-colored rocks took on colors and changed shapes. The movement was inside of him as well as in front, billowing soft waves, sparkling points of translucence in the air. It seemed that there should be fear associated with the uncontrollable thing inundating him. When he searched for it, it was not there. Only peace and contentment filled his emotional capacity until it seemed to overflow into the gentle hues.

Fir'ah's hand closed and squeezed several times. He did not know if he responded, though he thought that he did. Her skin had turned warm and continued to tingle where it touched.

A bit of regret crept into the euphoria when the colors diminished and faded into the rock and the Presence withdrew.

Fancher blinked several times, not sure of where the light was coming from now. He glanced at Fir'ah. She was watching, folding her robe and wearing a smile. Openmouthed, he gazed at the entrance.

It was morning.

He dressed and fitted the suit, then chopped off the extra length at the arms and legs. Both were silent as they ate and loaded the carts.

After shutting down the field and removing the spreaders, he went to the cart. The light disappeared. Abruptly, he turned. A monstrous head filled the entrance. Thin black daggers around nervous eyes looked as though they would be ejected at them any second. A snake tongue flicked at the air from between a zoo of teeth. Heart thudding, Fancher grappled at his utility belt for the Destro-Lase II.

"Lorff! Lorff!"

Before he could stop her, Fir'ah ran toward the creature, arms extended.

"Get out of there, Fir'ah!" He ran, weapon ready. He'd fight the beast barehanded, and win, if it so much as touched her—or die trying. He caught her several meters from the head and tried to pull her back into the depths.

"Don't hurt him, Fancher. Please! Don't hurt him. He's a friend."

Both hands came down on the weapon and held it pointed at the ground. "Fancher . . . *Please*. Let me talk to him."

A heavy sigh filled the shelter. "Fir'ahhh." He could not watch her implore with her eyes and refuse. "You'd better let him know that if he so much as flicks that tongue in your direction, he's dead. Right then!"

She nodded, but did not move until the weapon rested. Arms extended, "Lorff, I've missed you. I was afraid you would never get out of the rocks." A few steps took her onto the lip.

"Fir'ah! That's far enough. Talk louder. Yell, if you have too, but don't get any closer." Fancher ran his fingers over his thumb and up his palm, itching to draw the Destro-Lase II, hoping he was quicker than the beast's tongue.

Fir'ah concentrated, freeing her mind of extraneous concerns, trying to find the vein J'erik used to communicate with Lorff. The link was sketchy at best, furnished by Lorff. The time consumed during the search-and-probe ordeal failed to do anything to ease Fancher's worries. Fir'ah pieced together enough to learn part of what had happened since the Tor-ad-ih.

A sad smile marred Fir'ah's mood when she turned back to Fancher. "We have transportation north. Lorff is no longer in my brother's service. Nor will he rest until he has returned me to his old Master."

The sharp blade of urgency dissipated with a realization that this was one of the zanstyrs Fir'ah had praised. The size didn't quite register until he had seen one eye to tongue. "All right. Tell me what to do and I'll get it done. You're still the brains of this outfit. He can be the brawn from now on."

Amid the clamor of rocks Lorff descended to a gentle slope and waited. Fancher lowered a rope and tied Fir'ah off. She rappelled most of the way and untied the hitch from her waist.

A few minutes later the first barrow bumped down to the slope. Lowering the second one, Fancher could not believe he was going to actually ride that shaggy monster dragging part of his own decaying body.

He threw the rope clear and descended the face. Fir'ah was already lashing ropes around the zanstyr, patting the beast as she moved to the head. The tongue curled around both carts and hurled them into the air, snapped around and lifted Fir'ah up beside them. She went on working, not missing a beat.

After the initial shock, Fancher laughed. "I've traveled a lot of places, seen a lot of things, but now I know I've hit the big time. Is he cave-broken?"

The mirth changed to a surprised yelp when the tongue lifted him through the air and ungracefully deposited him on the chartreuse head stripe. Fir'ah walked along Lorff's back carrying two coils of rope. Fluid motions and the tight lines of concentration bespoke the information swap taking place.

Secured, Lorff began climbing, going straight up when the northerly destination was best served that way.

One day passed much the same as another. The land never ceased changing. For a while, the complaints were frequent. Those too halted as a total resignation filtered through the group. There was no turning back, only endless hot kilometers going north and west by day and the frozen wind at night.

Rains fell. Strange patches of grassy and woody vegetation sprouted beside eroding water paths. Olca bushes grew higher than the zanstyrs. Azaix plants with tubers gigantic enough to feed four people flourished near dry streambeds waiting for the next downpour. The iron trees, few when the vegetation appeared, grew more plentiful the farther north they traveled.

The food crisis eased. When half a morning passed in gathering panor nuts, gadid berries, tubers and amilglibs, the time was compensated for by night traveling.

Fifteen days out they caught up to the fifth group. J'erik's brief account to J'osh-uah concerning the fate of the sixth caravan was the only one given.

For another fifteen days they traveled across rugged mountains which they could not go around. Calantani survey teams plotted the easiest courses and urged the zanstyrs on with a promise that the end was near.

Cooler daytime temperatures helped the zanstyrs. Simultaneously, the air became thicker and difficult to adjust to.

On the forty-third day, Chamblis flew out of the clouds with Lor'ee. It was dusk when he spiraled down, calling, flaunting his beauty, and settled beside a yellow-striped zanstyr J'erik was unloading.

Techi and Dwellers crowded around Lor'ee, each with a dozen questions. Even J'osh-uah failed to contain his excitement and relief that the end was finally near. The age lines mapping his face had deepened and filled with embedded grit from the day's journey. They softened ever so slightly as he pushed to the front.

J'erik released the zanstyr to graze and listened to the melee. A smile started that would not fade.

Lor'ee managed to silence them and promised a few announcements. A flurry of voices cheered by some of the first genuine laughter since the trek had begun died away.

"First," Lor'ee said, a bit nervous, "by this time tomorrow, you will have arrived in the valley. Everything is as ready as it can be."

A cheer roared. The zanstyrs picked it up, then the scouting calantani.

She caught J'erik watching from beyond the crowd. The silence had resumed for several seconds before someone asked her to continue.

"Oh." She focused on the listeners. "The casualties have been moderate in the last four caravans. On the brighter side, Kal-id of the Tor-ad-ih has given birth to a healthy boy."

A birth was something to celebrate. Techi and Dwellers alike lost their personal distances and swung into merriment. Dwellers brought reed instruments out of nowhere and spun music while the others danced.

The hard times were near an end. The lone campfire was fed until flames leaped high into the dark sky and rivaled the stars for power. Even without gadid wine, the travelers achieved a state of inebriation.

Through the maze of gyrating dancers, Lor'ee found J'erik. They walked, unspeaking. Away from the sweaty bodies, riders and carriers, and the blazing fire, the air was cold. Fog crept over the ground, dampening ankle-high grass so it clung.

218

J'erik glanced back to the camp, thinking how much they needed a night free of worry and filled with hope and merriment. The rolling mist swallowed much of the noise. The fire glowed, fuzzy bright.

Lor'ee lifted the brown striper mat off his shoulders, untied the fasteners and spread it over the ground.

It took four days of Fir'ah's communications with Lorff to yield a certainty that the putrid flesh he dragged was dead. After another two, Fancher severed it with the Destro-Lase. Up until that time, Lorff had merely tolerated the Star Demon. The new freedom, brought by the reluctant man, won the beast over completely.

They traveled at a very leisurely pace, no one in a hurry to get anywhere. Lorff wandered around thickly foliated mountain valleys for days at a time while the pair rested and experienced the Presence which had guided the zanstyr to them.

Three massive mountain chains bled into one another in the south. Fancher stood in waist-deep water, holding Fir'ah around the hips and stomach. She pushed away and tried to swim the crawl stroke. Stubbornness forced her to learn. Fine coordination made the effort pay after the skepticism wore thin.

A rope snagged on a line of sticks ten meters from shore defined the shallow boundaries. Fir'ah swam under Fancher's scrutiny until tired. Shivering, she climbed out and put on a robe.

A frog kick broke the water. Fancher lay back and enjoyed the vision beside the rocks. The curves where her waistline had been the night she Chose him were shallow above the hips and nonexistent in front. The growing fullness of her breasts distorted the fine scars left by T'lar.

"What's the matter?" she asked.

"Nothing." He grabbed the rope, stomped out of the water, dried a bit and dressed. Next he found the wrist computer and began running measurements through. Muttering, he put it away and whistled for Lorff. The zanstyr roared back, on the way.

"We're closer than I thought. Let's pack it up and go home. I've got a lot of work to do before Fancher Junior makes his debut."

Dressing, trying to hide a grin, "What if it's a Fir'ah?"

Appalled, Fancher looked over for a moment, then answered, "In that case, I guess it'll be a girl."

Lorff crashed through the brush and drank heavily from the pool while Fancher gathered belongings.

A quiet laugh bubbled out of the bent-over figure securing the last rope on a padded bundle. Fancher threw his head back and laughed harder.

Lorff hoisted the burdens for the Betweener to tie into place.

"I never considered the possibility you might be carrying a girl."

Fir'ah shook her head, smiling, listening to him address Lorff in his own peculiar fashion. "Okay, old buddy, vacation time is over. We're going to go until we get there. Can you handle that?"

Lorff's right feeler shot out from under his eye and spun.

"Yeah, I hope so too." He dragged over the rope harness. "You'll get one day off, then you and I are going to build a castle for the Princess here."

Moments later they were secure atop Lorff. Fancher wound his arms around Fir'ah and sang at the top of his lungs into the onrushing breeze. Often he adapted songs which were not suitable for Fir'ah's ears with nonsensical words to make her laugh. And today was a good day for laughing. He was going to push them and the zanstyr hard until the journey's end.

Chapter 25

FOR THREE DAYS, REUNION FESTIVITIES ECH-
oed through the valley carved by an ancient glacier.
It had been deepened by a mighty river shooting out of
the northern rock. Far above the pale-green torrent, peaks
spent days in the clouds. Below the source, lush vegetation
competed for space. Pink citrus, oblong and fatter than
two doubled fists, grew on gangly bushes. Variations of
iron trees supported tons of equally varied forms of
gadid. Fat kodjelu skittered through the shadows of the
ilankor vines during the day and hid at night.

The zanstyrs wandered away for much-needed solitude.
Only four calantani stayed close to the new Hold settled
into the edge of a cavernous granite mountain. Natural
gas leaking through a minute fissure made it the best
place to settle. It sat above a gradual slope that fanned
out onto open flatland. More foreign plants grew near the
riverbanks. The calantani fetched samples which had
proved to be edible.

At night, the mountains groaned. Those from the first
caravan were used to the shifting when earth all around
them moved. And whether it could be attributed to the
experience of the journey or sheer stupid bravery, many
of the Dwellers worked outside during the day. The colder
climate made the required wrappings less troublesome,
but seldom did the hands stay covered. A few of the

Techi also joined when Uli slipped behind the south-western side of the valley.

Cor-ii assumed the role of Common cook and did a remarkable job of organizing the women into units and shifts. The Hold was a hundred and thirty-seven strong, all busy with tasks that ranged from taking care of the sick and injured to harvesting wood and rock slabs for furniture.

At J'erik's insistence, storerooms were designated and immediately stocked in the event that Star Demons laid waste to the Hold. N'oblic spent most of his time carving out a new caldron from an iron tree the calantani felled. He longed for a smelting area and forge, but those had to come later in the Hold's development priorities. The pot needed to be cured before it was ready for the test of fire. Kali-te gathered herbs, shaking her head from time to time about the dubious varieties.

They were busy days which followed the reunion. Exhausted men and women gathered in the Common to eat before finding a place to sleep. The high points came when Star-ii was the serving girl. She did more entertaining than serving and never ran low on either words or energy. Kal-id brought the baby out on a regular basis during the commotion. When he cried, the sound was as delightful as Star-ii's laughter and stories.

It was during one of these lighthearted times, twenty days after J'erik had arrived, that he was summoned by Diearka. He left quietly for the outside.

Lor'ee, on Chamblis, was already taking to the air. When he was ready, Diearka followed. Uli warmed them from overhead. J'erik looked around as the calantani climbed. Surely this was the most beautiful and peaceful spot on all of Cassilee, a place to stand. The flatland would grow more varieties of food than any dreamed existed.

Where does the Mistress wish to go? J'erik asked Diearka.

We go straight up the valley. A zanstyr, Lorff, is coming.

Lorff? Lorff is coming home? J'erik strained his eyes for the chartreuse stripe in the foliage.

He is not alone, Master. He carries two riders, a man and a woman. He refuses communication with any but

222

you. His riders are dressed not of Cassilee, but they feel as though they are more of her than those in the Hold. It is part of the Presence I spoke of before. Do you remember?

Yes, Diearka, I remember. He saw the zanstyr wading through high green barriers as though they were not there. The sun caught on the brilliant garb worn by the riders. *I am here, Lorff. I hope you have come home to stay. You are always a welcome friend to me.*

I have come, but with a new Mistress and Master.

Diearka dove to the ground, lifted his head and skimmed to the tops of the brush before halting in front of the zanstyr.

"J'erik! J'erik!"

J'erik rubbed his eyes, not quite believing what he was seeing, let alone hearing. Diearka's tail helped him onto the trampled ground beside Chamblis and Lorff. "Fir'ah?" he whispered. Dumbfounded, he gaped at the two struggling on Lorff's head.

"Fir'ah, so help me, if you aren't more careful, I am gonna truss you with rope and dump you into a cart." Fancher grabbed her a second time before she fell off the zanstyr. "Come on, Lorff. Get her down. Safely."

Lorff's tongue snapped into the air as Fancher said, "Thanks." He curled it around Fir'ah and set her in front of her brother. Arms already stretched, she lunged, wrapping his neck.

J'erik was slow to respond. When he did, it was with a yell for joy.

"I never expected to see you again."

"I can swim now."

"The Tor-ad-ih and the Techi are gone."

"Fancher's gonna build me a castle."

"There are only a hundred and thirty-seven of us—with you, thirty-nine."

"Lorff's healthier than ever and wants to see Star-ii."

Fancher climbed down and approached Lor'ee, hand extended. "Hi. I'm Fancher Bann, castle builder. I can make a deal on two if you furnish the labor."

The Betweener mumbled her name and stared at the outstretched hand, not sure why it was there or what to do with it.

"Are you family?" He put the naked hand to use by

poking a thumb at the duo running scattered pieces of conversation at each other.

"Yes, I think so. I am the Chooser of J'erik."

"According to Fir'ah, you made an excellent Choice." He moved past her to the familiar orange one. The magnificence of the beast at this close range astonished him. The intricate patterns of hair, fur and scales around the leathery skin were more than he had anticipated from the distance at the river. He marveled when Diearka flashed finger claws, folded his limbs over the leather-skinned chest and bent down to inspect him. Diearka uttered a low note that silenced the valley and exposed his teeth.

Two hard blinks allowed Fancher to speak again. "Does he bite?"

Fir'ah answered, "Only once," and giggled.

J'erik managed to collect his bearings and introduced the two women. Lor'ee looked perplexed by the entire situation. He fingered the strange fabric Fir'ah wore. "What is this? Where did you get it?"

Fir'ah's smile dimmed. She settled against Fancher when he came up behind.

Fancher cleared his throat and looked J'erik in the eye. "Before we go any further, let me introduce myself. I'm Explorer First Class Fancher Bann, formerly of terraformer *Minaho*."

Head shaking, J'erik said, "I have not heard of that place. Where is it?"

He glanced down at Fir'ah, then back to J'erik. "It's gone now."

"I fear they are all gone, except the one in the valley."

"No. You don't understand. It's not a Hold on Cassilee. It's up there." He pointed at the sky, then dropped his hand with a slap against his thigh. "There's no easy way to say it," he told Fir'ah. "I'm a Star Demon." It was like confessing to murder.

The idea was inconceivable. Where was the metal skin? The light? Sound? Death? Could the hideous demons change into the forms of men? Would he blacken the valley and flood the Hold?

Fir'ah came to his rescue. "It is not as you think, J'erik. He is a Betweener of another kind. I love him and I do not care how any other than myself sees him. I have Chosen. And we have sat in the Presence of Cassilee."

She sighed heavily. "There is much we have to speak about, J'erik. Very much."

J'erik reached for Lor'ee. When she did not respond, he took a frightened look to see the reason. The expression she wore was the same one that changed her face when she was trying to divine the truth. The Star Demon had her complete attention.

"Look," Fancher said, "I realize I'm a slur on the neighborhood, but I can be of help. Fir'ah and I talked about the problems we're going to face here. And we've been revising since the orange one there buzzed Lorff.

"I am what and who I am. I suppose I could pass as a Betweener, but that's not my style.

"There are other things I'm more worried about. Seen any big Star Demons lately?"

A slight headshake was the only change in J'erik's hostile presence.

"You won't, either. There's a time schedule. I'd like to try to do something to beat them at their own game. It'd be easier if I had some help. I'm looking for friends, not enemies. I've got too many of those already.

"There's something I will ask of you, as Fir'ah's brother. Two things, I should say." Looking at Fir'ah, "When her time comes, will you find someone willing to help me deliver the baby? Secondly, when they,"—a glance at the sky—"come back, take her and the kid for a while."

"Oh, no!" Fir'ah interrupted. "I stay with you."

For the first time, J'erik noticed his sister's exploding waistline. "T'lar?" The seething word dripped hatred.

"He's no longer among the living," Fancher answered. "The kid's mine."

J'erik's left eyebrow lowered. "Because you want it to be, or because it is?"

Evenly, "Because it's mine."

In a brief silence, J'erik struggled with his emotions and seemed to arrest a conclusion. "We need time." He kissed his sister's forehead, as he always did when they parted. "Spend the night with us and visit with Star-ii and Kali-te. They will be happy to see you."'

Fir'ah nodded and walked to the orange one with him. Lor'ee took a few timid steps toward Fancher, stuttered a bit, then said, "You are strange. But I see truth in you,

Star Demon. Truth and beauty." She held out her hand in the same manner as he had done earlier, openly curious.

"Thank you." He took her hand and shook it.

One arm around Fir'ah, the other resting on Lorff, Fancher watched the calantani depart. Idly, he scratched Lorff. The gap of difference had closed easily with Fir'ah. But J'erik—the gap was so wide it seemed that it would take light-years to cross it.

The first edges of depression bit sharply. If half of what Fir'ah had said about J'erik was objective, there was little hope for a warm reception at the Hold. The Dwellers and the Techi had trouble tolerating one another, and they suspected Betweeners. He hoped that attitude had mellowed with the migration. Even so, it did not seem likely that he and Fir'ah would be able to stay there more than a night. A Star Demon in a Hold?

"Fir'ah . . ."

"I go with you. It is settled."

"J'erik will take care of you. Just until I build some shelter, maybe get a couple of rooms going with a roof."

"No." She turned, forcing a smile. "I must make sure you do it right."

Surprised, "You've never even seen a house. How will you know I'm building it right?"

"I will be—what is it? Boss. Boss and cook."

The depression retreated. He gave her a playful shove toward Lorff. "I know six places that would hire you on the spot with those logical qualifications. Hey, Lorff! Take her up."

A few minutes later they were underway. No loud songs filled the air around the travelers. Fancher was busy checking his compass. The Hold was close, too close, to where the first ground crews from New Life Enterprises were going to establish a base. At first, it seemed freak coincidence. Straining, he remembered the orb model in the planning room on the *Minaho*. No coincidence, he mused. This is the best spot on the entire planet. He shrugged. It would be the safest one for a few years, too, until the water receded into carved-out ocean basins and the rains fell in regular cycles.

He thought about the hundreds of kilometers he had walked over parched land. It would be as lush and green-purple as that around him by the time the babe was Fir'ah's age. More than ever the determination to undermine the hierarchy at New Life Enterprises and save Cassilee for her own obsessed him. He wished for the Presence to give him peace. And he hoped to be there when the child walked as a man—or woman—across the land.

He pulled Fir'ah close and began to hum a slow lullaby from childhood. It often soothed him.

As if understanding this would be the last quiet time the three of them shared for a while, Lorff moved exceptionally slowly down the valley toward the Hold.

Lor'ee waited at the entrance. Fancher took up the offer of assistance for unloading Lorff. The process he had down to a science was slowed in order for her to be helpful. Nervously, she informed them that J'erik was still talking to those in the Hold about him and Fir'ah. Her apprehensiveness imparted more information than the words.

"I told him that you would not hide the fact you are a Star Demon. Instead, you would say so," Lor'ee said, meeting Fancher's gaze. As he nodded, "He thought it best to prepare them. I have assured him that you are a man and nothing more."

Fancher lugged their possessions inside the cave mouth and set them where a sudden rain would not drench them. Fir'ah brought one of the carts, and Lor'ee followed with the second.

He returned to Lorff. Stroking the shaggy chartreuse around the lower edge and pulling out stray greenery, "Stick around, Lorff. We might not be here long."

The left feeler shot out and spun a lazy circle.

He adjusted Fir'ah's old pack squarely on his back and started into the Hold. The few treasures of technology he possessed were inside. If someone wanted to inspect their belongings, they would have to go through him to see these.

A bleak silence hung over the Common when the trio entered. The uneven rhythm of their feet sounded loud. J'erik stood alone in a clear spot several meters from the steaming caldron Cor-ii worked. The paddle faltered in the vapor, Cor-ii looking wide-eyed at the Star Demon flanked by Betweeners. J'osh-uah fidgeted beside Kali-te and Star-ii. The latter two beamed at Fir'ah. Kal-id's babe whimpered until she pressed him tighter to her breast. He puckered and nursed vigorously.

Few of the Techi mingled with the Dwellers. The segregation was obvious at the group's fringes. Rough benches and tables, in the process of being smoothed, were clustered around the open space.

Unexpectedly, N'oblic stood and spoke. "Welcome, Fir'ah Betweener, last survivor of the Tor-ad-ih. A few of us have been told, and shown, that difference is not always a bad thing." He glanced at J'erik, then to Fancher. "Rather, it is something to be respected and judged individually." He looked around to those who had been among the last to leave the Tor-ad-ih after C'nuba's death. One by one, they rose, until there were ten, counting the babe, who fussed at the disturbance created by his shifting mother.

N'oblic continued. "I myself fear you, Star Demon. Perhaps a time will come when I can trade this feeling for understanding." He smiled at the gaping dark faces on the left. "There is much I would like to understand. It is difficult to walk in the shadow of fear all the time. That is not the way of this Hold." To Fancher, "But we are also a cautious people. Many of us have lost nearly all there is to lose. There will be a time when we will want to know why this is. Not tonight. But soon. That is all the Tor-ad-ih and I have to say." N'oblic sat, openly pleased to see that all the Dwellers and five Techi had stood to be counted with him in the statement.

Star-ii remained standing, wiggling, anxious to be near Fir'ah.

J'erik felt proud of N'oblic. Perhaps it was easier for him than the Techi, who did not truly know the extent of difference J'erik possessed. It was easier every day to deny its existence.

J'osh-uah glared at the Star Demon his daughter had chosen. He rose and led his council from the Common. At first, only a few of the Techi followed, then all but four clambered to their feet and left.

N'oblic nodded to J'erik and went through his people to organize work parties. They departed in groups, a few staying to work on the tables and benches with pumice.

Kali-te embraced Fir'ah. The tears in the old woman's

228

eyes were for joy. Any words would have been superfluous between the two. However, the reunion was short-lived. Star-ii wormed in for a hug and the answer to a thousand questions.

She was pacified when Fancher told her Lorff was just outside and waiting to see her. A look of awe that a Star Demon had spoken to her, personally, turned to delight when Lor'ee said it was dark enough for her to play outside.

J'erik took two steaming bowls from Cor-ii and set them on a nearby table. "Be comfortable. Eat. Then we will talk of many things."

Fancher squeezed Fir'ah's shoulder. "I've got a few questions of my own. For starters, how did you keep them from mutiny when you told them a Star Demon was dropping by?"

J'erik sat across the table and folded his hands. "I asked them not to insult my sister's Chosen one. It would have been an insult to me if any had. As you saw, silence was preferred."

Lifting the bowl, "I expected them to try lynching me, to be honest."

"That was our father who led the Techi out?" Fir'ah asked. His nod brought a frown. "Instead, he chose to insult me. I am dead to him."

Fancher set the bowl down and swallowed the mouthful. "Princess, from all you've told me, I'm not sure you were ever alive to him." Glancing at J'erik, "Sorry. My alien family attitudes are showing. In the backwater place I come from, a man may leave his woman, or the other way around, but if something happens to the one with the children, the other will break his or her neck to get those children and raise them.

"Palama is only about a century ahead of Cassilee in terraformed redevelopment. On the young worlds, life, children in particular, is the greatest asset. Unfortunately, that view is not universally shared."

The idea disturbed J'erik. He said so and asked, "What if both parents fail to survive?"

"It happens. You take care of each other. I was twelve when mine were killed during an unscheduled earthquake. My sister and her husband took me in. They already had four, so one more was easy. Before I signed on with New Life, I helped deliver three more of their kids, all boys. Several years later, they, ah, became statistics on the probability curve for the fix I've ended up in."

"I do not understand." J'erik listened intently, hands pressed together, trying to see the Star Demon as a man, not too unlike himself.

"There was an underground river which wasn't plotted. It should have been. The settlement was erected directly over it." Fancher took off his pack and secured it between him and Fir'ah. "It takes a long time to terraform a planet completely. Some seem to have an intelligence of their own and totally defy all accepted patterns, laws and concepts. Cassilee is that way.

"Anyhow, the river surfaced. The people died. That's it. I got curious. While I was waiting for reassignment, I pulled the survey plans on Palama. Not an easy thing to do, by the way. It cost me three years' pay. They had never done a complete survey over all the contingencies.

"Cassilee was my next assignment. Since I was already there, I pulled the plans on her. I thought Palama was bad, but this . . . this was awful. No deep life scans, not even a mantle stability survey. Discreetly, I sent inquiries to the Federation Trade and Development Bureau. That's probably why I was pegged for the recon mission down here. New Life found out.

"Of course, when I sent life readings back to the *Minaho* . . ." Grinning, "They'll sweat trying to erase them, too. But it can be done.

"At any rate, the long-term objective for Cassilee is to make it a recreation port. It's strategically located to the existing trade routes and the freshly prosperous worlds looking for a place to blow their wealth."

Slowly, J'erik grasped bits of what Fancher was trying to put delicately, and was, for Fancher. "You mean they would kill all of Cassilee's inhabitants to take the land? For what?"

Fancher sighed. "A playground. One big fun-time playground."

"Lor'ee? This is truth in his mind? It is real? I cannot understand."

"It is what he knows, what he believes where there are

no lies. He has not spoken falsely, J'erik. He must talk and we must listen until we do understand."

Fancher continued talking, explaining, simplifying. The Betweeners listened, not missing a word.

Hold members entered, ate, and talked in whispers, then left throughout the night. Fancher continued long after Fir'ah left to sleep with Star-ii and Kali-te.

Chapter 26

THE SEASONS CHANGED AS FANCHER HAD said they would. When the weather turned cold, Fir'ah was confined to their three-room sod house. Before the first hard frost, she bore a girl child, named Kreista after Fancher's deceased sister.

Fancher was gone much of the time before the first snows. Kali-te, Lor'ee, and sometimes Star-ii came to stay with Fir'ah during his absence. The half a day's distance by zanstyr, less by calantani, from the Hold kept them far enough out of range from those who vehemently objected to what Fancher termed his "effect on the caliber of the neighborhood."

The modest soddy was expanded in the spring. Two new rooms were added and had reinforced iron-tree cellars with a cache of food and water. Woven reed mats covered the dirt floors. The house took on the aura of a well-lived-in home.

By summer, J'erik was spending as much time with Fancher, Lorff and the four volunteer calantani as he was with Lor'ee, who had all but moved in with Fir'ah and Kreista.

Gradually, after a brief explanation from the Star Demon, J'erik and Lor'ee accustomed themselves to the fact that J'erik's exposure to the terraformers' light might rob their future of children. The night they asked Fancher if the effects were temporary, and J'erik detailed his illness, was a bleak one. The sad truth evoked a violent scene. J'erik lashed out at the Star Demon and all he represented, beating, flailing and pelting him with his fists and anything he could grab. Fancher did not strike back.

The following morning, Fancher, bandaged and colorful, went to J'erik and asked for help at the site. The incident was never mentioned.

Evenings, Fancher kept a log on kaloer parchment, furnished by Kali-te along with a sharp reed filled with dye. J'erik maintained his own account of all the things he could remember since first exploring the territory around the Ah-te.

One late summer morning, N'oblic appeared at the two soddy houses. The robes he wore did not cover his arms or lower legs. It was a test of one of Fancher's prophecies. The refortification of the ozone layer around Cassilee better protected the inhabitants against Uli's harsher rays, made the sky less blue and the air slick. In spite of Fancher's attempts to explain, not all could be attributed to the invisible layer.

"Some of us would like to live on the land, as you do," N'oblic told Fir'ah.

"And we would be glad to have you join us."

Six more soddies went up before fall. When the sixteen, ten Dwellers and six Techi, moved out of the Hold, tensions between J'osh-uah and his followers heightened. The young faces that brightened the mealtimes after weary hours of work were gone. Kali-te and Star-ii shared a temporary home with J'erik and Lor'ee. Since N'oblic had been Chosen by Kal-id, no toddler wandered in and out of the tables in the Common.

Cor-ii stayed on at the Hold, visiting her daughter often, talking with J'erik for long periods. Mostly, she was a class unto herself, hearing all and saying little at the Hold. The remaining Dwellers became a closely knit group, not ready to leave, not wanting to stay.

The zanstyrs migrated in and out of the grassland marked by enormous tree stands. Creeks froze over with the advent of winter. Two warm springs bubbled out of a granite rock cluster half a kilometer from the semicleared soddy compound. The women carved out trenches, lined them with stones and diverted the flow through the compound's center.

This second winter, a new strain of vegetation popped through the ice crusts. A vibrant red fruit grew on fragile, leafless stems over the white snow. It flourished along the water steaming into the cold, crisp winter.

Fir'ah and Fancher were the first to try them. The Presence, strong in the locale they picked to build on, had sanctioned the fruit as good. The new source of protein compensated for times when kodjelu were scarce.

In midwinter, another variety of purple-leafed pink fruit sprouted through the snow. It grew in one place only —around Fir'ah's home. She tried to explain the gift from the Presence, which was Kreista's favorite. Few understood.

By late winter, it was clear that Fir'ah was pregnant again. The small community celebrated with prized stashes of gadid wine. The festivities were well underway when a banging at the door froze the dancers and killed the shrill notes inside reed flutes.

Half a dozen Techi stood in the snow, shivering, holding all they could carry.

Warmed by the fire and the smell of celebration, they pleaded for lodging until they could erect a place of their own in the compound area.

Skeptical about J'osh-uah and his Great Plan, J'erik's hopes took an upward swing as two of the women took offers from three men sharing the farthest soddy.

Fancher approached him with an extra cup of wine. "The old boy sent us a few ringers, eh?" He handed off the wine. "Well, however it goes, it will make spring come quickly for the con-er and the con-ee. At least he had the devious foresight to send a couple of guys for our women.

"It's going to thaw tomorrow. How about Diearka and Chamblis taking us out to see how the project fared?"

Smiling, head shaking, "You always know the weather. How is that?"

"I used to have a five-minute spot on hallucivision with a crystal prism that spelled out the forecast in dot lights." He glanced over his cup to Fir'ah.

"And you always have answers which give me more questions." J'erik pulled lightly on the wine. "I am learning, though."

Serious, "There are a few things I've been meaning to talk to you about, J'erik. So, I'll start with an answer. I know the weather because of the Presence here which speaks to Fir'ah and me. It has for a long time. She calls herself Cassilee and tells us things, warns us of storms, says how the rest of the planet is doing, geologically speaking.

"Come on. Listen to me this time." He placed himself to corner J'erik between two tables angled behind them. "First, it was just sort of a feeling, an emotion which absorbed and absolved all the negative things.

"After a while, it began speaking words. I listened, sure I was losing my nuts and bolts. But Fir'ah heard, too. Kreista babbles at it all the time." Head tilting toward Lor'ee juggling an armful in the form of Kreista, "Lor'ee hears her. Not in the same way, but Cassilee knows her, and she knows you, J'erik. There is some kind of barrier in you which cannot be penetrated. I suspect you not only don't want to believe, you don't want to hear her, either." He set down the wine and reached for Kreista.

"Come here, daddy's girl."

J'erik felt lonely for the first time in nearly two years. Young as Kreista was, she had her mother's coloring and T'lar's features. He wondered how Fancher was able to accept the child as his own. He was also sure that no one had remarked upon the similarity or questioned the paternity. There had been no reports of a beating or death.

"Because she is part of me," Fir'ah said quietly.

Shaken, he glanced around, realizing only now that he was standing alone with his sister.

"You have always wanted to understand things so you could accept them. Even as we grew up, you were like that. J'erik, sometimes you have to accept what is before you can understand. Usually it grows less important and the meaning becomes clear when you least expect it. Fancher and I, we know about the things you can do with your mind, but you do not tap those resources unless you're compelled too.

"You pretend the gift you have isn't there. How can you ever hope to accept, or understand, when you are hiding from yourself?" On tiptoes, she kissed his cheek. "Love yourself more freely, J'erik, as we love you. Leave

236

judgment to Cassilee. It will come soon enough for all of us."

The following morning a warm breeze started the spring thaw. Fancher left the house with Kreista while Fir'ah slept. He held a branch down for her to pluck a delight for breakfast. They picked a few extra and walked to the closest soddy.

Lor'ee was brewing tea when they entered. She poured a second bowl for Fancher and gestured to the opposite bench. He sat with Kreista on his left leg. She swung her feet and munched on breakfast.

"He left on Diearka before sunrise," Lor'ee said. "He did not sleep last night." She rubbed her eyes. They were bloodshot and puffy. Faint circles under her lower lids extended down to her cheekbones. "He is disturbed over something. I tried to find out with both words and thoughts what it was."

"And?"

Head shaking, "I hit the wall." The sudden smile disappeared almost immediately. "That makes sense?"

Nodding, Fancher smiled back.

"He would not let me in. That is so strange for J'erik. He does not change his barriers. He does not use them. . . ." Shrugging, "He asked that I be patient. So, I will have to be patient."

"Where did he go? The project?"

"I think so."

"I'm going out there on Chamblis. Why don't you get some rest?"

She reached for Kreista. "When he comes home. I'll take care of daddy's girl here. You go. Chamblis is coming." A sticky hand wound into her hair as the child hugged her. "Fancher? Be careful."

Startled, he laughed. "Careful? We're talking about J'erik, right?"

"That's right. J'erik. I have not seen him like this before. Be careful."

Heavy-hearted and more than a little frightened, Fancher left, stopped home long enough to pick up his utility belt and found Chamblis waiting.

He reached the dig site at noon. The Presence was strong, stronger than at any other place or any other time.

He looked around for signs of Diearka and J'erik. There were none. Across the open clearing blanketed in white, he noticed panavers. The leader watched him, right hoof lifted and poised.

A glob of slush fell from an iron tree onto the ice crust. Fancher jumped, his stomach a fist in his throat. Exhaling relief, he chided himself. There was nothing to fear on the land. Nothing.

A couple of hundred meters brought him around the trees and to a black hole in the snow. A rope, strung from the nearest tree, disappeared into the ground. Fumbling, he removed the light from his utility belt and climbed down to the first ledge.

The tunnel supports, cut by the calantani and installed by Lorff in a domino fashion, creaked and groaned over the sounds of water dripping all around him. The Presence continued to strengthen, yet did not seem to acknowledge him.

"J'erik?"

"I am here." The voice was distant, and so calm that the normal resonant echo did not exist. Fancher shuddered, feeling as though parasites had invaded his backbone and were playing tag in his discs.

"Where?"

"I am everywhere, Fancher."

A forced laugh fell short. "You from the Vice Commission?"

"Stay to your left. That is ad-vice."

If Fir'ah had made an attempt to play on his words with the identical comment, it would have been amusing. But J'erik did not usually respond, nor did he utilize a comeback when he did. It was not funny. It was scary. Nothing fit. Least of all him. The Presence filled every cranny of the project, but there was no appeasement or solace in her. She seemed to ignore him, as though she had found a new lover. The warmth of the ground added to the eeriness sweeping through the tunnel he had practically lived in every day it was not snowing.

He shone the light along the far wall on his right, then down to the floor. A two-meter-wide ledge clung to the wall. Below, the light became lost in velvet darkness. He intensified the beam. The chasm swallowed it without yielding a thing.

238

"What's happened here?" How could it have happened? Why didn't the Presence inform him?

Confused, he moved along the ledge.

"I am learning the secrets of life here."

"Secrets of life?" Fancher's hollow whisper died in the dripping snow melt.

"Yes, Fancher."

He heard J'erik walking in the darkness. The walls shimmered until nothing was stationary. Warm rock moved under his touch and denied stability.

"I am learning acceptance, change and understanding."

"You're . . ." Fancher stopped short of saying "kidding."

J'erik broached the light sphere. The beatific smile he wore illuminated his face. The bronze skin glistened as though coated with a thousand tiny stars. Eyes, which had always looked upon Fancher with suspicious friendliness, were clear and glowing, seemingly able to look through to what lay deep inside. "It is so simple, yet so difficult. I sought to find a way to destroy the Star Demons, and could not. I looked to you for our salvation, rather than seek it. Because I could not understand the Demons, I was willing to abdicate my role for Cassilee to you and hope your bluff worked. You gave it your all, while I actually contributed nothing."

"It's not a complete bluff. Not with the tunnel. We can make it work." Suddenly, he doubted that the hierarchy of New Life or the Federation Trade reps would believe the planet was rejecting them. They lacked the sensitivity it required. It seemed like wasted effort on a stupid plan. It probably would not even buy them a year, let alone a generation.

"Let me finish. I gathered the remnants of Cassilee and brought them to a safer place. But I could not unite them. Even the sanctuary was Lor'ee's. I did not know it existed, until she told me.

"Cassilee was being changed. I did not understand why, nor could I accept what was happening without that understanding." His hands lifted, shining light against the flimsy curtains of rock. "It was like being captured in the wind of events. So long as the wind blew, and continued to move me along, I moved. I tried to outrun them, but there was no place to go.

"Fancher, until today, I did not realize how brave you

239

are, nor how unselfish you are in your love for Cassilee and those around you."

The pause left Fancher without anything to say.

"Your plan for confronting the Star Demons is still the best there is—under other circumstances. But there is an alternative now."

"I'm listening."

"We will do all that we planned, all of it. The alternative is me. You have them open the door, if you like, just as you planned. Then I will walk in. It's so easy now, Fancher. And there is no uncertainty. It will be, because we never were alone in our desire to be rid of the Demons."

Chapter 27

THEY CAME IN LATE SPRING WHILE ULI struggled to warm the land. Winds off the snow-capped mountains ebbed to chilly breezes across the low elevations. A myriad of color and new vegetation flourished in random patterns for as far as the eye could see.

Fancher and the three Betweeners watched the giant metal beasts descend. A heavy sigh escaped from Fancher when the last of the seven ships landed within the circle he had calculated. J'erik grinned and slapped Fancher's knee.

"Why is it that the more confident you get, the more nervous I become?"

J'erik shrugged, still grinning, and led them around the rocks. They retreated a couple hundred meters to the tunnel. Lorff, Chacon, six more zanstyrs and twice as many calantani stood in the trees, waiting.

Fancher took the Destro-Lase off his belt and held it in Fir'ah's hands. "Promise me something?"

She nodded.

"No matter what happens, don't fire this at any of them. If things don't work out, you get out of here, get Kreista and the others and find some kind of safety. Don't let them find you, Fir'ah." Suddenly there were a thousand things he wanted to say to her and a million words jumbled in his head.

241

"I understand." A tender kiss reached his lips. "I understand, Fancher."

Lorff moved stealthily from the trees.

J'erik touched Fancher's arm. "You do not have to do this. We can turn them over to the mercy of Cassilee."

"Yes, I do, J'erik. Cassilee would justifiably swallow the ships, but they would be back. They're not all like Satow. Somebody who believes us has to take the message back. And I have to do this for me." He ran his hand through Lor'ee's hair and gestured to Lorff.

Once on the stripe, the field was activated. It spread to encompass the zanstyr. "Okay, old buddy, let's go. We don't want them unpacking."

Lorff skirted the trees around the circle, until directed to approach the ships. Five of the seven were cruisers, four redesigned to double as freighters to accommodate heavy equipment and supplies. Fancher tried to imagine the insides. Stacks of bunks—even the mess hall was likely to have them dangling from the ceiling over the tables. One trip like that in a lifetime was one too many.

The sixth ship was not too different from his Star III Recon Prober, though much larger in all dimensions. He stared at it as Lorff moved, knowing Satow was just inside, watching, waiting, wondering.

He grinned, knowing the pandemonium he was creating with Lorff.

The last ship was approximately the same size as Satow's. It bore the insignia of New Life Enterprises on its rounded hull. The sides flared, inflexible wings. The heat in the circle rose around the ship and tried to invade the wind.

"That's far enough," came a booming voice from the last ship.

"Paydirt, Lorff," he whispered. Loudly, "I am unarmed."

The voice trembled when it spoke again. "We can see that."

"I'd like to address a delegation from New Life Enterprises and the members from the Federal Trade and Development Bureau assigned to Cassilee."

There was a long silence before the voice came again, the pitch half an octave higher. "Identify yourself, please."

242

"Explorer First Class Fancher Bann, formerly of Palama, now of Cassilee. Deceased."

"I beg your pardon. Did you say 'deceased'?"

"Yes, sir. You'll have to check the back memory for my file. Commander Satow has declared me dead." He could not help grinning. It was dangerous to play games with Satow, since there was no way of knowing how the bureau representatives stacked up. Very dangerous. Still, it felt good to flaunt Satow's mistake.

He waited almost a hand against the sun before the speaker responded. "There is a delegation prepared to speak with you. Please send that thing you're riding away for their safety."

Fancher shook his head. Spar one. "As I'm sure you know, the zanstyr, Lorff, here"—patting the chartreuse—"is encased in a field. Now, since I'm not armed, you surely don't expect me to disengage the only thing which prohibits your records from becoming accurate. Do you?"

As a delayed answer, the hull split and a platform stretched to the ground. Six men and a woman filed out. One face was very familiar: Mikel.

Fancher tied the field-control unit into Loriff's stripe. The zanstyr's tongue flicked around and set him on the ground.

There was a moment's hesitation on the ramp, broken by a quiet chuckle.

"You one of the big boys with New Life now, Mik?"

Still chuckling, "No. I've been an Investigator for years. The bureau assigned me to Satow when we received your inquiry. Palama is closed, if that's any satisfaction. Satow thought you were the investigator." Mikel regained his formal attitude and nodded to the woman. "This is my boss, Inspector Hensy."

"You look familiar, Inspector."

"I should. I served on the *Minaho* as orders dispatcher."

Seeing Mikel, now her, a final understanding of why it was he who had received the orders dawned. And it had nothing to do with him personally. All errors—theirs, Satow's, his. Browsing over the rest of the somber delegation, he thought of J'erik, Lor'ee, Fir'ah and Kreista. "As it turned out, you did me a favor."

A graying man almost as wide as he was tall stepped forward. He introduced himself as the project overseer.

His name, Blythe Hamrut, fit. Squinting at Fancher, he cleared his throat with a noise that came from inside his well-oiled boots. "Just what is the purpose of all of this— the possible problem of Commander Satow aside? Or is that it?"

"No, sir. That is far from being *it*." He scratched the side of Lorff's face. The signal went out. "I represent the remaining people of Cassilee. The charges against the corporation known as New Life Enterprises, Commander Satow in particular, and the Federation Trade and Development Bureau, are listed here." Fancher opened the front utility pouch and withdrew a scroll of kaloer paper.

"They range from trespassing to the almost successful genocide of three known human races and an additional, equivalent number of intelligent species.

"In the ambition to steal Cassilee from her people, you have destroyed thousands of years of culture, taken countless lives, disrupted the geological and ecological balances and incurred the wrath of Cassilee herself."

"This is preposterous!" The handsome speaker wore a New Life uniform. "There are no people here! There never were. Wrath of Cassilee? Ptah! You've been in the sun too long."

"Have I? Show me your in-depth survey reports. Show me your life scans. Show me how you missed anything as large as Lorff here. Show me how you overlooked the readings I sent: two humans and three calantani. What's a calantani? you must be asking yourselves. That is a calantani!" He pointed up, where Diearka and J'erik led a formation through the sky, right on cue.

"In case you don't recognize the strange growths on the orange and white ones, those are people. They live here." Fancher checked his sarcasm and felt the Presence work on the rising anger.

Zanstyrs moved to the other side of the invisible circle. Panavers converged from the forests. Once they had stopped, Fir'ah fired the Destro-Lase into the hole. Low rumbling and shaking ground pulled the surface into the bowels of Cassilee. Clouds of black dust rose into the wind.

The calantani put on a flashy show, circling opposite ways, alternating on the updrafts, always maintaining a flank formation. They settled beside Fancher. Lorff turned off the field long enough for Fancher to join the Betweeners.

One by one, the delegates recovered and came to gaze expectantly at the bronze-skinned Betweeners. Mikel and Hensy started toward them, openmouthed. Hensy paused, took a quick glance at the interior of the ship and called, "Are you sending all of this, Palor?"

"Yes, Inspector," came the voice over the speaker.

The Commander's ship opened for a foursome to stand on the ramp and watch. Even at the distance Satow kept, his shoulders drooped as though recognizing defeat.

The handsome man in the New Life uniform opened his mouth to protest. Nothing came out. He shut it.

"Apparently there has been some misunderstanding here," Blythe Hamrut said. His composure and diplomatic tones seemed as though they had never been shaken. "I'm sure we can work out a solution. A great deal of time and monetary investment have been spent on the development of this place. You, the present inhabitants, are benefiting from the work we've done here and will continue to do."

Irate by what he knew would follow, Fancher turned away and clamped his mouth shut. It was J'erik's show now. The door was open and the bugs were crawlin' out.

"I am J'erik, Betweener, Calantani Lord and Master of the Zanstyrs. The Presence of Cassilee, which is all there ever was, all there is and will be, has designated me as her spokesman."

Diearka snapped his tail. Fancher darted, whirling, and grabbed Lor'ee, taking her down. A burst of heat exploded the air over them. Diearka screeched, tail whipping madly, thudding the ground. A curl of smoke ascended out of a smoldering hole in his right haunch. The stench mingled with the blood dribbling to the lower part of his foot.

J'erik calmly turned toward the Commander's ship, stretched his arm, diverted his thoughts and levitated the perpetrator from the ramp and out to open ground. He dropped the man from a meter up. The thud muffled a terrified scream.

J'erik pointed at the man's right thigh.

The assailant rolled into a ball, holding his leg where an ugly wound smoked.

Lor'ee soothed Diearka, stroking his belly for as far as she could reach.

Leaning down, J'erik helped Fancher up. Shaking, the Star Demon began to realize why neither of the Betweeners had shared his nervous trepidations. Cassilee had been accepted by her Chosen.

J'erik faced the horrified delegation transfixed upon the writhing man. "The next one dies. I promise that each of you will feel his death agony. It will be a slow death, similar to that suffered by those trapped in Holds when you leveled the escape routes and filled the cracks with water.

"Do not push me to seek vengeance of my own. It would be very easy."

Two of the converted freighters started their pre-ignition cycles.

J'erik looked serenely at Fancher, smiled apologetically. The communication link materialized. For Fancher, it felt as though his brain cells were being scrubbed with soap and water.

A half nod and J'erik watched the ships with a new interest.

The engines whined and died.

Frantic accounts poured out of the open ships. The insides of the cruisers' engines were melted to scrap.

"As I was saying," J'erik continued, "we are trying to be a peaceful people. Our only wish is to be left alone. You cannot bring back our dead, nor can you compensate for their loss." To Blythe Hamrut, "There is no price, no negotiation, no compromise. You leave and do not come back. Whatever you touch here will die in your presence. The water you drink will turn to acid in your mouth. The land will open up and eat your ships, as your ships have eaten the land. And the cries of the thousands dead will ring in your ears. Uli will blind you, as she once did the Techi. She will flay your exposed hides down to the bone, as was once the fate of the Dweller.

"There will be no escape, no reprieve, no remorse."

"There is doubt," Lor'ee said.

"Yes, I know. I am finite. The man Hamrut counts on that." Smiling, "But it is not me who issues the ultimatum. It is Cassilee. She will never tolerate you, any of you, at any time. You have raped her in the most insidious manner there is. Now, she protects and does not forgive."

Lorff ambled to the perimeter. A roar precipitated J'erik's leisurely glance and gesture which allowed him to cross to the other side, the means of support unseen.

Ladida, Diearka and Chamblis received riders. The delegation stumbled back into the ship, Mikel last. He stood at the top of the ramp. From atop the Lady, Fancher tossed the scroll to him.

"Not coming back, huh?"

Fancher shook his head. "I'm a family man now. And I'm happy here. Besides, I'm dead. Right?" The thought still amused him. He grinned broadly.

Mikel tucked the scroll under his arm and saluted, looking around at the new life his friend found peace in. In one unbelievable instant, he saw Satow. Before the warning scream cleared his throat a burst of light swathed the day and pierced Fancher's head.

Fancher's neck snapped back, open hands spread as they rose up the contorting trunk of his body. The Lady flinched at the feel of death upon her. Leg muscles relaxed. He fell, bouncing off her left haunch and flopping to the ground, eyes opened to Uli through the blood splattered across his face.

The panavers turned vibrant crimson and stared in unison, eyes exposed from under the slit flaps, at the delegation ship. Mikel was thrust inside and the ship hurled away from Cassilee.

And Cassilee looked upon Satow through J'erik's blazing eyes.

Fir'ah heard the agonies of the Star Demons as they suffered with Satow. The death cries of the Techi and Dwellers rose out of the ground and into the black clouds rushing in from the four corners. The panavers began to radiate violent color changes which controlled the cataclysm.

The child inside of her moved. She clutched at the tiny babe, blessed by the Presence and spawn of a Star Demon.

She remembered the first storm when she discovered Fancher's identity as a Star Demon and the death she had waited for in the rain. It rained now, hard. "Fancher," she whispered, sobbing inside, eyes dry as they watched the maelstrom descending upon the Star Demons. "There has to be a time for us. Oh, Fancher . . . we were just beginning . . ."

The wrath of Cassilee had only begun to afflict the Star Demons in the circle.

Epilogue

KREISTA AND HER BROTHER, FANCHER STOOD
at the freshly covered grave of their mother. Fir'ah
had seemed to wait until her children were nearly grown
before joining her Star Demon. The emptiness created
by her passing was vast, but it was not marked with sorrow.

Earlier in the day, Lorff had taken J'erik and Lor'ee
into the mountains to celebrate the death ritual with the
zanstyrs.

Uli slipped behind the western mountains in the silence
of the evening. Kreista and Fancher waited, watching
the eastern sky. The stars winked on one by one in the
waning glow.

A second light illuminated the distant crags. It radiated out to the stars as it rose, an orange moon, climbing
over the ridge and into a clear sky.

"You were right, Fancher. Ever since I can remember
it has always been half a circle. Incomplete, just as they
were without each other. Now, it is whole and they are
whole. The Presence is at peace."

"And so are they, Kreista," Fancher said in a low voice
that carried through the mountains. He raised an open

hand to the sky. Clouds scurried from the distant heights and ran together until they hid the Star Demon moon. "Let's give them this night alone." The last cloud raced in to blot out the light.

Kreista smiled, nodding, and took her brother's offered hand. "It's not as though they're gone."